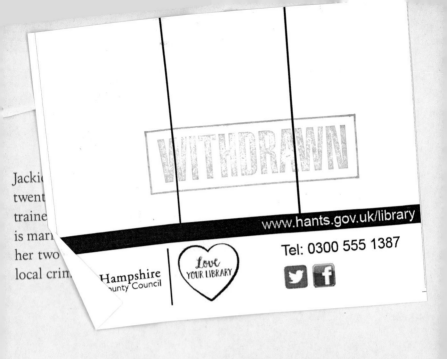

Jacki
twent
traine
is mar
her two
local crim

Also by Jackie Baldwin

Dead Man's Prayer
Perfect Dead

Avenge the Dead

Jackie Baldwin

OneMoreChapter

One More Chapter
a division of HarperCollins*Publishers* Ltd
1 London Bridge Street
London SE1 9GF

www.harpercollins.co.uk

This paperback edition 2020

First published in Great Britain in ebook format by
HarperCollins*Publishers* 2020

A catalogue record for this book
is available from the British Library

ISBN: 978-0-00-838391-6

Set in Birka by Palimpsest Book Production Ltd, Falkirk
Stirlingshire

Printed and bound in Great Britain by
CPI Group (UK) Ltd, Croydon CR0 4YY

In memory of Maureen and Denis Thomson

Prologue

15th May 2005

Colette flopped back on the pillows, the enormity of what she had just done creeping in around the edges of her intoxication. She could hear them laughing and joking, stumbling around the tiny cottage on drunken legs, as they gathered up their stuff before making their way back to the guest house. There was a light tap on the door.

'Come in!' she yelled, pulling up a sheet to cover herself.

He stood framed in the doorway, looking at her with a concerned and slightly worried expression.

'Are you sure you're OK? I can stay if you want, keep you company?'

Her expression softened. As the effects of the alcohol started to wear off she suddenly felt a rush of blood to her head. What on earth had she been thinking? How would she face them all in court tomorrow? Her breath caught in her throat. She needed to be on her own. She heard his name being called. If she didn't get rid of him the others would come clattering in and that was the last thing she wanted.

'Honestly, I'm fine. Best if you head back with the others. I need to get some sleep. We've got court in the morning.'

'If you're sure.'

He crossed the room on unsteady legs and leaned over to peck her cheek, swaying from side to side.

'You'd better hurry,' she said with a weak smile. 'They'll not wait for long.'

The sound of slurred voices gradually receded down the country lane leaving her alone with her thoughts. Trying to pre-empt her inevitable hangover she padded down to the kitchen, knocked back some paracetamol and filled a pint glass with water. Now that the effects of the alcohol and ecstasy were wearing off her teeth began to chatter. Fortunately, the log fire lit without protest. She went back up for the duvet from her bed and dragged it down to the couch, huddling beneath it for warmth.

It had been a long boring two weeks in Jedburgh with each of them acting for one accused from a drunken brawl that had resulted in multiple charges. The evidence had been so convoluted that the sheriff had decided to rule on it the next morning.

Denied the freedom they had hoped for and with the trial effectively finished they had all decided to blow off steam. She had joined in with gusto taking them all by surprise, but already the night's events were starting to disperse from her memory like wisps of smoke. She had been quite the free spirit before she moved to Dumfries and took up with Peter Swift, the fiscal depute. Realizing how conventional he was she had succeeded in subduing her wilder impulses. Until now. What if they talked and word got back to him? She shuddered. Too late for regrets. It was done. She'd been feeling more and more stifled by the relationship anyway. Maybe it was time to draw a line under it.

The doorbell rang. She rolled her eyes. What now? Making her way to the door she flung it wide expecting to see her friends.

Her eyes widened in horror as she was grabbed by the throat and pushed back into the house by the masked intruder. Terrified, she realized that he was holding a hunting knife. The tip pressed into her neck and she could feel the heat of it as it pierced her skin. Still, he said nothing.

The knife pressed deeper. She felt an itch as the warm blood trickled down her neck. Adrenalin flooded her system as she weighed her options. He'd backed her into the lounge, still at knifepoint. His silence was, if anything, more unnerving than the knife pressed to her throat. He backed her up to the couch which was piled high with blankets and throws.

Suddenly, the mound shifted.

'Colette?' a voice slurred. 'What's going on?' The blankets slid off to reveal one of her friends, still drunk and with an expression of confusion and burgeoning fear on his face. He lurched to his feet.

Colette sagged in relief. Thank God, everything would be all right now. There were two of them.

'Phone!' hissed the man. 'Or I'll slit her throat and then yours. Leave now and keep your mouth shut or die here.'

Colette saw her friend frown, swaying from side to side.

3

She held her breath. All he had to do was lunge at her attacker, dial 999, anything! What was he waiting for? No! What was he doing?

Hot tears wet her cheeks as she watched him throw down his phone.

'Tell anyone and I'll hunt you down and kill you,' her attacker snarled.

Unable to look her in the eye, the man she had called a friend ran past her. She heard the door slam.

Maybe he's gone to get help? she thought, her mind reeling at his betrayal. But Jedburgh was two miles away.

It was down to her now. With a surge of rage she twisted and kneed her attacker in the groin. His grip loosened for a second, but then he roughly threw her on to the couch, pinning her down. All she could see were his pitiless blue eyes boring into her. Screaming obscenities, she clawed at the rough wool balaclava, determined to see his face. His fist connected with the side of her head, but she managed to pull the balaclava half off. She froze in shock.

'You stupid bitch,' he snarled. 'Now, you have to die.' The next punch he landed knocked her unconscious.

She awoke confused and disoriented. All around her flames leapt and the acrid smell of smoke burned her lungs. The house was on fire! She had to get out! Throwing off the already smouldering duvet she crawled to the front door. The way to the kitchen was blocked by the advancing flames. As she stood up and fumbled with the handle she realized to her horror it was locked and there was no sign of the keys.

She ran to the window and swung a nearby vase at it. The vase broke but the window didn't.

She knew then that she was doomed to die here in this fiery coffin. She remained at the window, her hands outstretched, peering into the night, not wanting to observe the march of the fire as it started to crawl up her body. Hope flared. There was someone out there. She could see a shadowy form silhouetted against the moonlight. She thumped her fist against the glass and screamed for help. Her friend must have come back. He could save her! He could break down the door, get her out. She beat harder, her hand aching, the heat almost unbearable now. What was wrong with him? Why wasn't he moving? Could it be her attacker? She banged furiously, screaming in agony and terror as the flames curled up her body, releasing the meaty aroma of charred flesh.

The shadowy shape melted silently back into the trees.

The cottage continued to burn.

Chapter 1

15th May 2015

Mhairi tapped lightly on DCI Buchanan's open door in Dalgarnock police station. Over the last two years she had gradually acclimatized to living in Glasgow. She liked her new boss and had acquired more pairs of shoes than she knew what to do with.

'Come in, DS McLeod. Sit yourself down.'

DC Thomson was already there and she flashed him a warm smile. It looked like her boss was assembling a team for an investigation and she felt a fizz of excitement in her belly.

Lorraine Buchanan was so tall and willowy that she made Mhairi feel like a garden gnome. Her hair was scraped back in a tight bun as usual and her make-up minimal. She had a forceful personality and could be intimidating but at least she was consistent. You always knew where you stood with her.

'I asked DI Farrell to meet with us here,' the DCI said with a frown. 'Has either of you seen him?'

Mhairi and DC Thomson glanced at each other. Mhairi could feel a telltale blush stain her cheeks. Dammit, she had been covering for Frank more and more recently. At this rate he was going to drag her down with him.

'I'm sure he's on his way,' she said.

DC Thomson nodded enthusiastically to back her up.

'I see,' said the DCI, tight-lipped. 'Well, we can't wait any longer. I trust you can bring DI Farrell up to speed, Sergeant?'

'Yes, ma'am.'

'Right, let's get on with it. There's been a murder in Dumfries. A woman in her early thirties, Gina Campbell, stabbed to death in her home.'

Mhairi's heart sank.

'They've requested a Major Inquiry Team and I'm sending the three of you down. People are always criticizing the MIT teams for their lack of local knowledge. Given that the three of you hale from the area you're an obvious choice.'

Dave Thomson looked as gutted as she was.

'Her husband discovered the body this morning.'

'Sounds pretty straightforward. Can't they handle it them-selves?' asked Mhairi.

'The husband was covered in blood and his prints are on the knife ... but he has an alibi,' the DCI replied. 'I take it I can rely on you to locate DI Farrell and get down there inside three hours?'

'Yes, ma'am,' said Mhairi.

'That will be all, DC Thomson. I have another matter I need to discuss with Sergeant McLeod.'

'Yes, ma'am.' DC Thomson left the room.

Mhairi stiffened and her mouth went dry. She had a fair idea what was coming.

'Off the record, I need to know how Frank is. You're a sergeant now and that means you have a responsibility, not just to your boss but to the police and the wider community as well.'

'He's been better,' Mhairi said carefully. 'He might be a touch erratic at times, but he's still up to the job and I have every confidence in him.'

'I know that he's been through a lot. You all have. But that was nearly two years ago now. He needs to put it behind him and move forward. I take it there has been no change in DCI Lind's condition?'

'No, ma'am.'

'That's unfortunate. A fine officer, by all accounts. Nonetheless, you've been covering for your boss for some time now and it can't continue. I hope that in sending you back to Dumfries, DI Farrell can start to better come to terms with things. If he can't ... well you get my drift.'

'Yes, ma'am.'

'That's all for now. Keep me in the loop,' DCI Buchanan said as Mhairi rose to leave.

'Will do, ma'am.'

DC Thomson was waiting along the corridor.

'Can you sort us out a couple of nights' accommodation in Dumfries till we see how the land lies?' Mhairi asked. 'Farrell will stay with his mother. Try Ronnie Stirling. He runs a B&B with Vera now he's retired from the force. Wherever it is, it'll need to take pets as Frank and I will be bringing our cats.'

'Blimey, you don't exactly travel light, do you?'

'I didn't know when I got Oscar that with Police Scotland I'd have to hare all over the bloody country,' she said, as she continued on her way.

She tried Frank's mobile but it went straight to voicemail. What the bloody hell was he playing at? Was he wanting to get the sack? It's not as though he could even fall back on the priesthood. He hadn't exactly been a model for clean, sober living, of late. They had to get down to Dumfries pronto. Suddenly, she knew with utter certainty where he'd be. Swearing under her breath, she took the stairs two at a time and left the building.

Chapter 2

Frank Farrell sat motionless beside his closest friend and former boss. John Lind lay unheeding and unresponsive in the hospital bed where he had lain since being injured in the line of duty. Not quite dead but not quite alive either. He had progressed from the initial coma to a minimally conscious state, but Farrell had long given up praying for him to sit up and talk. He could no more forgive himself for allowing this to happen than he could God. If he'd only managed to put the pieces of their last case together quicker, his friend wouldn't have fallen foul of a depraved killer. Lind's eyes either stared off into the distance or roamed haphazardly around the room, blank and unfeeling, as though no one was home. Farrell glanced up and noticed that the drawings the children had done for their dad in the first few months were now peeling and torn at the edges. There were no flowers and no cards. Laura hadn't been to visit for months and had slammed the phone down on him the last time he had remonstrated with her. Even if John did by some miracle wake up again, what would he be coming back to? He suspected Laura had moved on and found another man. Why else would she have abandoned him? Like he always did, he enfolded his friend's hand in his and squeezed gently, hoping against hope he would feel an answering pressure. Some sign of higher activity in his friend's once acute brain. He never did.

He looked round as the door behind him opened and a very irate Mhairi McLeod stalked in. Shit, he'd missed the meeting. He'd lost all sense of time sitting here ruminating on the past.

'Mhairi, I'm sorry—'

'Save it, Frank. I covered for you. Again.'

He felt shame burn through him. Had he even showered this morning? It had certainly been a few days since he'd shaved. He couldn't seem to motivate himself lately. Ever since he'd come to realize his friend really might never wake up.

'There's been a murder. In Dumfries,' she said.

He felt himself freeze. He couldn't go back there. It was too much.

'Frank,' hissed Mhairi. 'We need to get going. They're expecting us by one o'clock.'

'I can't ...' he faltered.

'You bloody have to. DCI Buchanan is going to fire your ass if you can't pull it together. It's my career on the line too, you know.'

'How long will we be away?'

'How the hell should I know? But I do know this: the quicker we get down there and solve this murder the quicker we'll be back.'

She grabbed his jacket and thrust it at him.

Reluctantly he rose to his feet.

Mhairi leaned over the bed and muttered something in Lind's ear. She then squeezed his hand and straightened up.

'Right, let's get this show on the road.' She turned on her heel and marched out.

Farrell followed her with a last lingering look at his supine friend.

Chapter 3

Mhairi drove in tight-lipped silence back to the apartment block near the Velodrome where they both lived.

'Meet you in the garage in an hour,' she said as they left the car. 'Time enough for you to have a shower and shave.' She wrinkled her pert nose in case he hadn't got the message, then continued past him on to the second floor.

Farrell let himself in to his cheerless flat and fought the urge to slump onto the sofa. He collected up and binned the remains of last night's takeaway. His head still throbbed from whisky. He knew he was sliding towards a drinking problem, but couldn't resist the urge to seek oblivion these days. Alcohol had filled up the space left by the departure of God.

He couldn't let the Dumfries station witness the wreck he had become since they saw him last. He winced as he turned on the lights in the small bathroom. There were dark shadows like bruises under his bloodshot and bleary eyes. The beard that he had allowed to colonize his face suddenly reminded him of his brother, Michael. He shuddered. That hadn't struck him before. Determinedly he lathered up. It had to go.

That done he stripped off his stale clothes and stepped

into the shower. Setting the heat to all but scalding he soaped vigorously before turning the water as cold as it would go. Every day he looked for new ways to punish himself, but it was never enough. He knew the whip he kept in the wooden box had become addictive. The welds it raised upon his back a self-indulgence that was now frowned upon by the Church.

Ten minutes later he opened out a blue shirt from its cellophane and threw three other packs into his open holdall. He also tossed a bundle of new underwear and socks into the bag and a selection of ties then looked at his suits. All of them, bar one, were spotted with food stains and stinking of nicotine. He threw them in a black bag. Nothing the dry cleaners in Dumfries couldn't sort out. He pulled off the price tags of a navy suit that he'd had the self-preservation to keep untouched. Looking in the full-length mirror he reckoned he could just about pass muster as the version of himself they would all remember.

Glancing round the shabby impersonal living space, he felt he would either return from Dumfries ready to make a fresh start or he would give up on himself entirely. Right now he couldn't call which way the chips were going to fall. He left the most important thing to last. Henry was glowering at him from the top of the wardrobe. Farrell retrieved his carrier and slung his cat's considerable accoutrements in another bag.

'Right, Henry, I know you're hacked off, but there's no point making this even worse,' he murmured as he pulled him down into his arms. The large black and white cat twitched his tale but purred in spite of himself. Farrell gently shoed him into the carrier, picked up the bags and locked the door behind him.

He met Mhairi outside in the car park. She was carrying an identical carrier with an equally frosty cat inside. When she turned and looked at him her eyes welled up. It stung him that she still cared. He had to do better.

'Time to get this menagerie on the road,' he said, deflecting her tears with a grin. 'We can drop the moggs off at my mother's then head straight to the scene from there.'

She nodded, as if not trusting herself to speak. He squeezed her arm as he passed and got into his dumpy Citroen. She opened her own car door and followed him out into the morning city traffic.

DC Thomson had loaded up all the necessary equipment into a police van and should be well ahead. Henry's plaintive meowing grated on Frank's ears. It had been nearly two years since they had last set foot in Dumfries and none of them wanted to return.

Although it was well into May rain lashed against the windscreen and fog rolled in from the hills as he drove down the motorway towards Dumfries and Galloway. A wave of depression swept over him. Not for the first time he found himself sizing up the trees he passed along the way for the potential to deliver a death blow should he ram his car into them. The world would still keep turning if he was no longer in it. He was dragging everyone down into the abyss with him. An angry miaow startled him from his reverie, as if Henry had read his mind. He switched on the radio, trying to lose himself in cheesy music that reminded him of happier times, but turned it off after a couple of minutes.

Ninety minutes later he pulled up outside Yvonne Farrell's neat bungalow, with Mhairi's red Fiesta tucked in neatly behind him. The rain had eased off but the humidity stuck his shirt to his back. Farrell rang the doorbell, guilt twisting his guts that he hadn't been back to visit his mother before now. He expected her to look frailer but the woman who threw open the door was positively glowing. Her jaw dropped in dismay when she saw him, though.

'Frank. What's happened to you? Are you ill?'

Never one to mince her words.

'I'm fine. We're down for a case. Can we drop off the cats? We need to get to the scene right away.'

'Of course. That'll be the murder that was on the news, Gina Campbell. Solicitor's wife. Lived in one of those posh houses on the Edinburgh Road. Left two wee kiddies. Mind you by all accounts it was the nanny raised them not her. She spent half her life in that fancy beauty parlour in town.'

'They said all this on the news?' said Farrell.

'No dear, of course not. One of the ladies at my bowling club lives beside them. I bumped into her in town this morning.'

'Did she find the body?'

'No, that was the husband. You might have come across him. Local criminal defence lawyer, Fergus Campbell? His parents are County types. They attend St Margaret's. I gather they've rather washed their hands of him.'

'Doesn't ring a bell. Anyway, thanks for stashing our stuff.

18

Mhairi's staying with Ronnie and Vera. She'll collect Oscar later.'

He gave her a quick hug then ran to the Citroen.

The address given for the Campbells was a detached sandstone house set well back from the road.

'Not short of a bob or two then,' muttered Mhairi as they walked up the curving driveway.

'He must have family money behind him,' said Farrell.

The SOCO van was still there. PC Rosie Green was manning the outer cordon and brightened when she saw them approach.

'I was hoping they'd send you down, sir.'

DS Byers popped his head out of the front door and motioned them over.

'Long time no see,' he greeted them. 'Miss me?' he said to Mhairi, nudging her with his elbow.

She glowered at him.

'Like a plague of boils,' she said.

Byers too looked well, fit and happy. Had they really all been able to put what had happened to Lind behind them so easily?

Janet White and Philip Tait were still processing the scene. Farrell and Mhairi suited up and walked along the spacious hall towards the kitchen. Everything they encountered spoke of muted good taste. The place was stuffed to the brim with valuable antiques. They stood at the threshold and looked in. The metallic stench of blood hung in the air. A toxic cloud mixed with undertones of waste and decay. Farrell looked at the corpse and felt unusually detached as if he was viewing a scene from a film.

Even in death, Gina Campbell was beautiful. Spread out on the oak flooring like a collapsed mannequin, her long brunette hair fanned out behind her. She was wearing an emerald green silk dress with a full skirt and one black stiletto, the other not far from an outstretched leg. A large carving knife lay on the floor a couple of feet away. An exotic bloom that didn't belong in this subdued house filled as it was with relics from a past she couldn't share.

'The stab wound appears to have sliced through an artery, judging by the volume and distribution of blood. If so, she would have bled out quickly,' said Janet White.

'Was she already dead when the husband found her?' asked Farrell.

'Allegedly,' said DS Byers. 'I spoke to him here just minutes after he called it in.'

'Could he have stabbed her himself?' asked Mhairi.

'Not if his alibi checks out. He claims he was with friends all night, playing poker.'

'Are his friends lawyers too?' asked Farrell. 'Odd thing for them to do on a Monday night.'

Byers consulted his notebook.

'Yes, two of them are criminal defence lawyers but from different firms. Max Delaney and Jack Kerr. One of them is a prosecutor, from the local fiscal's office: Peter Swift. Delaney and Kerr both contacted the station after hearing about the murder this morning, to vouch for Fergus Campbell, the husband.'

'Bit odd, wouldn't you say?' said Mhairi.

'Almost as if they'd been primed in advance,' said Farrell.

'That's one way of looking at it,' said Byers. 'However, given their occupation they're bound to think we'd be looking at the husband, so it's only natural they'd jump straight in there if the alibi is genuine.'

'What about Peter Swift, the fiscal?' asked Farrell, rising to his feet after examining the body. 'He's nominally on our side at least.'

'He was apparently there until around midnight,' said Byers. 'He went home because he didn't want to leave his fiancée on her own.'

'She confirmed that?'

'Yes, a Beth Roberts. She was still up watching TV when he returned, and they went to bed not long after,' said Byers.

'If you want to speak to the alibi witnesses, Kerr and Delaney, today, it might be worth your while popping down to the court. They should be getting clear in about half an hour. The husband and his two kids are at the nanny's house until we're done here. He said he'll make himself available at the station when you want him.'

'Were the kids in the house at the time?' asked Mhairi. 'What age are they?'

'They're one and three. Fortunately they were staying the night with the nanny.'

'Bit strange for the nanny to keep them at her house, isn't it?' asked Mhairi. 'A place this size you'd have thought she would stay with them here so as not to disrupt their routine. Unless the wife wanted them out the way for a particular

21

reason?' she said, nodding towards two red wine glasses on a low coffee table beside the settee. There were a few bowls of snacks set out that appeared to be untouched.

'Who have you appointed as Family Liaison Officer?' asked Farrell.

'That would be PC Rosie Green, if you've no objection,' said Byers, a sudden undercurrent of hostility hardening his gaze.

'Excellent choice,' said Farrell. Although it had been nearly two years since Police Scotland had come into being, it was the first time he had been sent down here with a Major Inquiry Team to lend expertise. Their reception had varied across different stations. For the most part, as long as they didn't throw their weight around, they were welcomed with open arms.

'Is Dave Thomson not along for the ride?' asked Byers.

'He came down in the van with the equipment,' said Farrell. 'He'll have arrived at the station and be setting up the MCA room by now.'

'That's us done here,' announced Phil Tait, the other SOCO, packing away their gear. 'You can call the bus to pick up the body.'

Farrell thanked him and glanced at his watch.

'Mhairi and I had better head off to the court then,' he said to Byers. 'I'd prefer to speak to the alibi witnesses as soon as possible. We'll keep it informal for the time being. It'll give us a chance to observe them before they know who we are.'

Chapter 4

The court was located in Buccleuch Street. As they approached the weathered sandstone building they could see a small throng gathered outside. The usual assortment of mates and girlfriends with the odd scrappy mother in their midst. They wore their sense of grievance and outrage with pride. Alliances were forged and relationships severed in scenes like this across all the courts in Scotland. Farrell stopped suddenly causing Mhairi to run into the back of him. She swore under her breath, but when he paused and took out a packet of fags and offered her one, she immediately twigged and played along, searching her jacket pockets for matches.

'Got a light?' she asked a young guy with a pockmarked face and the obligatory baseball cap.

He paused mid-flow and extracted a lighter from his jeans pocket.

'Cheers, mate,' she said, passing it to Farrell who lit up and handed it back. 'They're taking their time in there. I thought my sister's trial would be finished ages ago. We've got better things to do than hang around this dump all day.'

'I was meant to go to trial but my brief didn't turn up.' The

23

guy pocketed his lighter. 'Turns out some wanker offed his wife.'

'No kidding,' said Farrell, inhaling deeply.

'I was in the dock waiting for the sheriff and heard some of them talking. She was running around on him.'

'They said this in front of you?' said Mhairi.

'They weren't exactly shouting it from the rooftops, but they were at the table right in front of me and I was quiet like.'

'I bet they didn't have the balls to say who it was?' said Farrell.

'No. I reckon a couple of them know though. I could tell by the way they looked at each other.'

Farrell stubbed out his cigarette and handed over the packet to his unwitting informant.

'Here mate, keep the packet. I'm trying to quit. We'd best go and see what's what.'

'Cheers, man,' he said, sounding as if he couldn't believe his luck.

The court clientele had thinned out considerably by this time, so they were able to walk straight up to the court officer's desk. Farrell thought the tall angular man looked vaguely familiar and rumbled about in the recesses of his mind for a name. It had been a while. As usual, he was saved by Mhairi.

'Bob, how are you?'

'DC Mhairi McLeod,' he exclaimed, his face splitting in a smile. 'You're a sight for sore eyes.'

'It's Sergeant now,' she said with an answering grin. 'You'll remember my boss, DI Farrell?'

'Aye, of course,' he said, looking as blank as Farrell felt.

'Can you tell us the name of that guy out there, the one with the blue hoodie?' asked Farrell, opening his notebook. 'He was meant to be up today but the case was put off. His solicitor's Fergus Campbell.'

Bob leaned over the desk and squinted down the hall.

'That would be Barry McLeish, one of our frequent fliers,' he said.

'Got an address and date of birth?' asked Farrell.

The court officer rifled through a pile of complaints before pulling one out.

'DOB 13/3/95,' he read, 'address is 29 Polton Avenue, Lochside.'

'Thanks. We're here to speak to two of your criminal defence lawyers,' said Farrell. 'Max Delaney and Jack Kerr?'

'Yip, both still here,' he said consulting his list. 'You'll find them in Sheriff Robert Granger's court right at the bottom of the corridor. I suppose you're here about Fergus Campbell's wife? A terrible business.'

'Did you know her?' asked Mhairi.

'I came across her a few times.' He leaned in closer. 'Gorgeous to look at but hard as nails. I wasn't a fan, to be honest.'

'How so?' asked Farrell.

'Well she was one of those who could flick the charm on and off like a switch. If you were of no use to her, she was barely civil.'

They took their leave and walked down the corridor. Entering the court, they paused while a solicitor was on his feet addressing the sheriff and then slipped in to the first row of spectators when he was done. Despite their consideration, they still attracted an ugly look from Sheriff Robert Granger as they sat down.

'What's his problem?' whispered Mhairi.

'Silence in the court,' the sheriff thundered. 'If I have to speak to you again, young lady, you will be removed.'

Mhairi flushed but said nothing. Her hand clenched into a fist in her lap.

A spotty youth was brought up to the dock.

A woman at the oval table stood. She looked to be in her late twenties and she was visibly trembling underneath her black gown.

'Miss Roberts, your client's fate hangs in the balance,' the sheriff said, peering at her with ice-cold eyes. 'As you know, I am considering a custodial sentence.'

She haltingly embarked on a plea in mitigation, putting forward reasons for leniency which he interrupted and ridiculed at every turn. Farrell and Mhairi glanced at each other. It was painful to watch. The other solicitors at the table were clearly uncomfortable too.

The sheriff gave him six months.

'Useless bitch,' the man could be heard shouting as the door closed behind him. The young woman gathered up her things and rushed to the door.

The sheriff's voice stopped her in her tracks just as she reached the exit.

'Haven't you forgotten something?'

'Sorry, my Lord,' she muttered and bowed her head.

The look of triumph on the man's face was unmistakable.

Chapter 5

The remaining half hour was uneventful. The fiscal was concise and rattled through the cases efficiently. They soon identified the two men they were looking for. Jack Kerr's accent had an abrasive Glasgow twang and he was tall and lean, the skin pulled back taut over his cheekbones. He had the restless energy of a habitual drug user, a cheap, shiny suit and dandruff on his collar. Max Delaney was plump and plush, the cut of his suit expensive and his demeanour confident and calm. The snarky sheriff failed to get a rise out of them. After he had gone off the Bench Frank and Mhairi approached the table as Delaney and Kerr were gathering up their papers.

The fiscal made them as coppers straight away and came forward with a smile and an outstretched hand.

'Peter Swift, Fiscal. Can I help you with something?'

'DI Farrell and DS McLeod,' said Farrell. 'Thank you, but it's these gentlemen we've come to see.'

Quick on the uptake the man nodded and picked up his files.

'I'll leave you to it, then,' he said.

27

They turned to the two men who were stuffing their files into worn briefcases as the last straggler from the public benches left the court.

'We'd like to ask you a few questions in relation to the murder of Gina Campbell. Thought we would save you a trip down to the station.'

Kerr looked like he was going to protest, but Delaney smoothly interrupted him.

'We appreciate that, Inspector. Happy to help. There's some interview rooms just around the corner.'

'Excellent! We'll start with Mr Kerr, if you don't mind?' said Farrell.

A momentary look of panic flashed across Kerr's face as he glanced across at his colleague.

By the time they settled in the interview room, Jack Kerr was waxy white.

'Are you feeling all right, sir?' asked Mhairi. 'Would you like some water?'

'I'm fine,' he replied. 'Like we said on the phone, last night was poker night. Had a dodgy curry and a couple of beers too many.' He attempted to smile.

'You told the police that Fergus Campbell was with you at Max Delaney's last night. Can you indicate when he arrived and when he left?' asked Farrell.

'He arrived around seven and stayed all night. Max has a big house. We often crash at his if we've had a few beers.'

'Did you all sleep in the same room?' asked Mhairi.

His mouth opened then closed again.

'It's not a hard question,' said Farrell leaning forward.

'Yes, we did. Sorry, things are a bit hazy, the demon drink, I guess. We just fell asleep on the couches in the lounge. We didn't make it upstairs.'

'What time did you wake up?'

'We'd set an alarm for six. Fergus and I had to get across town to shower and change. I'd just got out the shower at home when Fergus phoned, said what had happened.' His mouth twisted. 'I still can't believe it.'

'How well did Fergus and his wife get along?' asked Mhairi.

He paused for a beat then frowned. 'Is that really relevant?'

'You're the defence lawyer, you know it is,' she said.

He sighed. 'They got along fine as far as I'm concerned. I didn't really know her that well.'

'Any chance she was cheating on him?'

His face flushed and he averted his eyes. His friends must have cleaned up at poker last night, thought Farrell.

'Go on, you might as well tell us. It could have some bearing on her murder,' he said.

Kerr pulled out a pen and fidgeted with it for a moment. 'There'd been talk. Fergus hasn't a clue, though, and I didn't like to interfere.'

'Who was it?' asked Mhairi.

'Another lawyer, apparently, but that's all I know. Whoever it was they kept it quiet.'

'How long have you known Fergus?'

'About eleven years. We started down here within weeks of

each other.' He glanced at his watch. 'Is there anything else, officers? I do have somewhere I'm meant to be.'

'Thank you, you've been most helpful,' said Farrell.

Mhairi showed him out.

Max Delaney came in next and took a seat. Plump and smooth, his face bore a faint etching of broken capillaries that spoke to a fondness for hard liquor. He had the kind of hair that was styled rather than cut by a barber and the type of clothing that shrieked legal aid abuse.

'Take me through the events of last night,' said Farrell. 'Is it still your position that the three of you were together the entire night?'

'Yes, of course. It wasn't a one-off. We often play poker, have a few drinks and whatnot.'

'Was there anyone else there?'

Delaney looked wary.

'My wife and child.'

'Names?'

'My wife is Chloe and my daughter is Mia, but she's only three.'

'Presumably you didn't stay up the whole night when you had work today?' said Mhairi.

'It was fairly late. We were still up at two a.m., I recall. Given we were all there when the alarm went off at six, there wasn't much scope for someone to have sneaked out, committed a murder and crept back in,' said Delaney, with a hint of a smirk which he quickly extinguished.

'Where did you all sleep?' Farrell asked.

Again, a fleeting look of panic. They clearly hadn't rehearsed that aspect of their story. He could see the cogs turning fast in the canny solicitor's brain.

'All together in the lounge. After a few too many beers we decided not to stumble upstairs and risk waking the family.'

'What do you know about the deceased, Gina Campbell?' asked Mhairi. 'Did she ever cheat on Fergus Campbell?'

His face clouded.

'There were some rumours a while ago but nothing concrete. A small Bar like this is a hotbed of gossip. I don't think Fergus ever knew. It certainly wasn't my place to interfere. All marriages have their ups and downs.'

'Did she have any enemies?'

'Not as far as I know.'

'Has there been anything worrying Fergus Campbell?' asked Farrell.

Max looked startled.

'Not a thing. Unless you count having to appear in front of that jackass of a sheriff every day.'

'He looked a right charmer,' said Mhairi. 'A bit power crazed?'

'He got drummed out of Glasgow by the Glasgow Bar Association. Some poor kid hanged himself as a result of his bullying. Plus, he's a total misogynist. They've palmed him off on us, unfortunately.'

Farrell and Mhairi thanked him and escorted him out. As he walked away they could see him already talking into his phone.

'That sheriff was a nasty piece of work.' said Mhairi.

'A bully through and through,' Farrell agreed. 'That lass

will have to develop a thicker skin if she's to survive in her line of work.'

'Do you think they're on the level?'

'Possibly,' said Farrell. 'Although, it would please me enormously to split their alibi wide open and shake the dust of this place from my feet within the week.'

'You and me, both,' she said.

As they were leaving, they noticed the fiscal, Peter Swift, walking ahead of them with a red-eyed Miss Roberts. She had her hand tucked in his.

'Must be hard watching that sheriff rip her apart day in day out,' said Mhairi.

'I'd be tempted to punch him on the nose,' said Farrell.

'Now, that I'd pay good money to see,' Mhairi laughed.

'I can't abide bullies. Can you hop over and catch Max Delaney's wife before he has a chance to get to her? Don't let her off the hook about the sleeping arrangements.'

Chapter 6

Farrell entered the station with a heavy heart knowing that Lind wouldn't be there to greet him. A wave of nausea rolled over him and he swallowed hard. He had no idea how he was going to get through this investigation. In all the commotion this morning he had omitted to take his tiny maintenance dose of lithium. Normally he carried it in his suit pocket, but he'd forgotten today. A flash of anxiety ignited within him. He knew he couldn't afford to relax his vigilance or his sanity might start to unravel once more.

He headed for the MCA room which was already a hive of activity. DC Thomson was directing matters with a quiet confidence he had grown into since he had last worked in Dumfries.

Farrell walked to the front of the room and put up his hand for quiet. The room hushed immediately.

'First of all, let me say that it's good to be back' he said, trying to sound like he meant it. 'The three of us are looking forward to working with you guys to nail this killer. He pointed to a photo of the deceased. 'Her body was discovered at 6.25 a.m. by her husband, Fergus Campbell. He claims he was returning home from a night with his friends who, broadly speaking, corroborate his story.'

'You reckon they're being straight with us?' asked DS Byers.

'I'm not entirely convinced,' said Farrell. 'The three of them have been friends for a long time. They're also criminal defence lawyers, so they know all the tricks of the trade. Because of that it would be unwise to accuse Fergus Campbell of anything until we have compelling evidence.'

'DS McLeod will dig into Gina's background. Max Delaney said there was a rumour floating about that she was having an affair. I spoke to a Barry McLeish outside the court. He's a frequent flier but when he was in the dock this morning he allegedly overheard two lawyers talking about our victim running around on her husband. He can't remember or won't say who they were.'

'PC Rosie Green, you've been a Family Liaison Officer before. Given the dual nature of the role you'll need to tread carefully. As the victim's husband is a criminal defence lawyer, he'll be wary of you. It might be an idea to reach out to other members of the family, to get an idea of their marital dynamics.'

'Yes, sir.'

'DS Byers, would you bring us up to speed with the investigation prior to our arrival?'

DS Byers walked forward, a picture of sartorial elegance as usual. However, Farrell felt an unholy twinge of satisfaction to see a slight paunch swelling against the buttons of his expensive shirt. He must be letting his gym routine fall by the wayside. His hair was also starting to recede.

'As you all know,' Byers said, 'the house is set well back

from the road with the golf course at its rear. It would be easy for someone to gain entry that way without approaching from the road. We canvassed the neighbours, but no one saw or heard anything until the police arrived. No one even noticed Fergus Campbell returning to the house in the morning. There's been no previous call outs for a disturbance at that address, and their immediate neighbours had very little to say about them beyond the fact that they are quite aloof and keep themselves to themselves. Nobody noticed any suspicious callers or activity in the area in the weeks leading up to the killing, apart from an elderly woman who lives across the road, who reported a prowler ten days ago. There were footprints and some fag butts beneath the trees, but no one was apprehended at the time. The fag butts were logged as evidence but weren't sent off for DNA analysis as it didn't seem important. Probably nothing to do with the case. More likely to be scoping out the joint with a view to breaking in.'

'When's the post-mortem?' asked Farrell.

'Tomorrow morning,' replied DS Byers. 'On the face of it the cause of death appears straightforward. It'll be interesting to see how tightly he can pin down the time of death.'

'Who was the last person to see Gina Campbell alive?' asked Farrell.

'It was the nanny, Jane Pearson. She picked up the kids at 7 p.m. to take them over to her house. The victim claimed she had a migraine and wanted an early night.'

'Dressed like that?' said Farrell. 'I don't think so.' He pointed to the picture of the deceased. They all stared at her emerald silk dress and stiletto-clad foot.

'Her husband claims he was unaware that she had plans to go out,' said Byers. 'Her password-protected phone has been handed off to the Tech boys. We're arranging to requisition the landline records as well.'

'If there's any truth to the rumours flying around court it could be that her lover killed her or, alternatively, that her husband surprised them together and killed her,' said Farrell.

'You think his pals would risk everything to protect him?' asked Byers. 'That would have to be a friendship forged in steel.'

'I don't know,' said Farrell. 'I don't think we can rule out anything at this stage.'

Chapter 7

Mhairi hadn't eaten since breakfast but despite her grumbling stomach she drove straight to the Delaney place, a gorgeous architect-designed house on the outskirts of town near Terregles. Grudgingly she thought about the one-bedroom flat in Glasgow which she'd scrimped and saved to buy.

The vision of loveliness that answered the door in the shape of Max Delaney's wife didn't make her feel any better. Tall, slender and dressed in a powder-blue shift dress that complemented her tan and tumbling blonde curls, she made Mhairi feel at once short, stubby and travel-stained.

'Mrs Delaney?'

'Yes?'

'DS Mhairi McLeod. I'm here in connection with the death of Gina Campbell.'

Her eyes widened and she ushered Mhairi inside.

'Please, call me Chloe. I was so shocked when I heard.' She gestured to a white leather sofa. A little girl aged about three sprang out from behind it and shouted 'Boo!' Mhairi clutched her chest theatrically and the child bounced on her toes with delight. Her dress was also powder blue and she had long golden curls like her mother. She was carrying a doll dressed the same way. This isn't weird at all, thought Mhairi, struggling not to let her feelings show on her face.

'This is Mia, my mini me.'

'Yes, I can see that,' said Mhairi.

'Mia, why don't you go and play in your room for a few minutes while I talk to this nice police lady? I'll bring you a lollipop when we're done.'

'Promise?'

'I promise, now scoot!'

The little girl skipped off happily.

'She's adorable,' said Mhairi with a smile.

'Thank you. Now, how can I help?'

Mhairi pulled out her notebook and leaned back in her seat. 'How well do you know Fergus Campbell and his late wife?'

'I know Fergus fairly well. He was the best man at our wedding. The three of them, Max, Fergus and Jack, have been friends for a long time.'

'What about Gina?'

'They've only been married four years. To be honest it rather took us by surprise when they got together. Fergus was a confirmed bachelor before then. I always suspected he was gay but he was absolutely besotted with her.'

'It's been suggested that she might have been having an affair. Any clue about that?'

Chloe bit her lip and looked undecided. Mhairi held her breath.

'I shouldn't really say anything.'

'It could be relevant to her murder. We'll be as discreet as we can.'

Chloe swithered. Mhairi resisted the impulse to yell at her. Eventually Chloe sighed and lowered her voice. 'It's been going on for a while. Max worries that Fergus might not even be the father of their youngest child.'

'Who is he?'

'Another criminal lawyer, Gabriel Ferrante, a bit of a rough diamond.' She shuddered.

'He scares you?'

'A little. He's got a scar right down one side of his face. I've nothing to base it on, but he makes me uneasy. You won't say you heard it from me? Max thought it would only make things worse if it got out.'

'Definitely not. Have you any direct knowledge of their affair?'

'I only saw them together once, which was after the Faculty dinner last May. Everyone came back here to keep the party going. I went outside for some air and noticed a glow coming from the shed. I went up to the window and there they both were.' She wrinkled her face in disgust.

'Doing?'

'What do you think?' she shot back.

'And you're sure it wasn't Fergus in there with her?'

'He was inside drinking with Max and Jack. I really don't think he knew.'

'Who did you tell?'

She flushed. 'Only Max. He said it would probably blow over and best to keep it to ourselves.'

'Fergus found her body this morning. Both Max and Jack Kerr claim he was here with them all night until around 6.30 a.m. Can you confirm that?'

'Yes and no.'

Mhairi leaned forward, pen poised over her notebook.

'Max had told me they were coming over for a boy's night at around seven, so I'd got in some beers and snacks. I think that the real reason they were getting together was that it was the tenth anniversary of that poor girl's death. They were all badly affected by it and I think they wanted to mark the occasion in some quiet way together.'

Mhairi stopped writing and looked up. 'What girl? What happened to her?'

'They were all away at Jedburgh in the Borders for a trial. Max and his friends were staying together in a guest house, but Colette, she was staying at a cottage. There was a fire during the night and she burned to death.'

'That's awful,' said Mhairi.

'I think going through all that was what cemented their friendship. Of course it was worse for poor Peter Swift. He was engaged to her at the time. That's why he was there last night too. He doesn't usually come along to poker nights, but I think he appreciated the gesture.'

'The fiscal?'

'Yes. He's engaged to a lovely girl now, but it took him years to get over losing Colette.'

'So, can you walk me through what you know about the evening before the murder?'

'I heard Fergus and Jack arrive about seven. Peter arrived

not long after that. I put Mia to bed at seven thirty and popped in to say hello, then went to relax with a glass of wine upstairs. They were all together in the lounge.'

'How did they seem?'

'A bit subdued but that's to be expected. I didn't see them again as the next thing I knew Max was shaking me awake and telling me what happened.' Her eyes filled with tears.

'It hasn't even sunk in yet and here I am bad-mouthing the poor woman. She maybe had her reasons. I imagine Fergus could be ... difficult ... to live with. He's a bit repressed. A boarding school survivor, you might say. Not exactly a barrel of laughs.'

Chapter 8

Farrell nudged open the door of his old office. It had a stale neglected air and he was immediately assailed by memories from the past, both good and bad. Emptying his few possessions into the drawers on the cheap wooden desk, he stretched his long legs beneath it once more. He'd better introduce himself to the new Super, Crawford Cunningham. He was relieved that DSup Walker had thrown in the towel. The fact that Farrell had been a practising RC priest before he joined the force had proved to be something of a sticking point for his old boss. Hopefully, his replacement would give him a fair crack of the whip. Not that he was planning to be around long enough to get fully acquainted.

There was a light tap on the door and in walked DI Kate Moore. Despite sporadic contact by text, they hadn't seen each other since he had left for Glasgow with Mhairi. He was shocked by her appearance. She had always been slim and elegant, but her clothes now hung on her as though they were struggling to grasp onto something of substance and her skin stretched tight across her protruding cheek bones. Dark shadows ringed her lovely grey eyes.

He got up and gave her a hug. She felt like a pile of bones in his arms.

She gave him a quick squeeze then disengaged herself and stared at him critically, no doubt registering unwelcome changes in him too.

'Kate, you're one of the few things worth coming back for. How's life.'

The strain showed in her smile.

'Pretty good. The new Super, Crawford Cunningham, is fairly decent. It's been a lot quieter, obviously. I can't say I mind that these days. When we caught this case we were all hoping they'd send you guys down.'

'Even Byers?'

'With the possible exception of DS Byers.' She smiled.

'So, how have you been?'

Her eyes slid away. 'Getting there. You?'

'Getting there,' he replied. He missed their easy camaraderie of old. But what did he expect? He'd fled to Glasgow. She'd chosen to stay and tough it out.

'This case,' she said, mask firmly back in place. 'We're dealing with lawyers, specializing in criminal law. We're going to have to do everything by the book.'

'The Criminal Bar is really small in Dumfries. I have a feeling this investigation is going to go off in their midst like a stick of dynamite,' Farrell said.

'As if that wasn't bad enough, I've been doing a bit of digging into the background of our murder victim, Gina Campbell.'

'And?' Farrell asked.

'Her father is Mario Lombardo.'

'The former Glasgow casino owner who's rumoured to have links to the Sicilian Mafia?'

'The very same,' she replied. 'He moved down here, ostensibly to retire, five years ago.'

'If that's true then maybe this whole thing is some vendetta against the father?'

'He's already been on the phone to the Super. I gather it wasn't a pleasant conversation.'

'The last thing we need is someone like him blundering about in the midst of the operation,' said Farrell, feeling the beginnings of a migraine fingering him behind the eyes. His hopes for a swift resolution of the case evaporating like morning mist.

'Have you seen much of Laura Lind?' he asked.

DI Moore dropped her gaze and got to her feet.

'Not much, recently. Anyway, I'd best get on. Lovely to have you back.'

Farrell headed towards the Super's office. As he passed Lind's old room, his stomach clenched. Had it too remained unoccupied? Hesitating, he pushed open the door and peered in. It was occupied by a civilian woman in her fifties, her fingers flying over a keyboard while audiotyping. He muttered an apology and carried on, his heart hammering. Business as normal then.

Running lightly up the next flight of stairs he knocked on the door of DSup Crawford Cunningham.

'Enter', shouted a voice that sounded as if the person it belonged to was speaking from a throne, and not the porcelain variety.

Farrell opened the door and walked towards the tall, clean-shaven man sporting a regal-bearing and aquiline nose.

'Crawford Cunningham,' he said, standing to offer a firm handshake. 'We're very glad to have your team on board for this one.'

'Happy to assist in any way we can, sir,' said Farrell. 'There are already some persons of interest.' He took a seat. 'It appears that the deceased was having an affair with another solicitor. I gather that her father has been in touch with you direct?'

'Yes, Mario Lombardo.'

'I understand that he's rumoured to have Mob connections?'

'Yes, but despite countless investigations, our colleagues in Glasgow have never been able to pin even a parking ticket on him. Right now, he's a victim of crime, a grieving man who has lost his daughter, so tread carefully.'

Chapter 9

Mhairi stuck her head round the door and on seeing Farrell was alone came in and threw herself onto the seat in front of his desk.

'I didn't think you'd end up back in here,' she said, running a critical glance over the neglected room. 'They've cleared a space for me in the Sergeant's Room right next to bloody Byers's desk.'

'Any joy with Max Delaney's wife?'

'Yes, as it happens.'

As Mhairi explained what she had learned, Farrell frowned. 'So the husband is still potentially in the frame then?'

'It would appear so. I also found out the identity of Gina Campbell's lover.'

Farrell leaned forward.

'It's another defence solicitor, name of Gabriel Ferrante. Chloe Delaney saw them together doing the dirty deed last May. It was in the shed at her house during some party.'

'Right under the husband's nose?'

'Must have a death wish,' said Mhairi, then clapped her hand to her mouth.

47

'I get the picture. If Fergus found out she'd been running around behind his back with another solicitor that would provide a strong motive for murder.'

'Equally, if Gabriel Ferrante wanted her to leave her husband and she refused that might have sent *him* over the edge,' said Mhairi.

'We'll take a pop at him tomorrow. See what he has to say for himself. Unless she has more than one lover, she was clearly intending to entertain someone that night.'

'Unless the person who killed her wanted us to think that,' Mhairi sighed.

'We've another possible suspect pool to look into as well,' said Farrell.

Mhairi groaned. 'Tell me you're joking. At this rate we'll be here till I'm old and grey.'

'It turns out that Gina Campbell is Mario Lombardo's daughter.'

'The one who's always getting organized crime hot and bothered?'

'The very same. It could be a vendetta against him. I can't think of a better way to rip a man apart than to murder his daughter.'

The phone rang on Farrell's desk, startling them both. He snatched it up.

'Thank you, we'll be right down.'

'That's Fergus Campbell arrived. He's declined representation.'

'The confidence of an innocent man?' said Mhairi.

'Or the egotism of a cold-blooded murderer,' said Farrell.

48

Chapter 10

Fergus Campbell's face was immobile, as if it was sculpted from marble. His thick black wavy hair had yet to recede and he was immaculately attired in the kind of expensive smart-casual clothes favoured by the landed gentry in these parts. He looked rather too composed for the part of grieving widower, but Farrell knew that he might still be in shock. Settling themselves at the table in the poky interview room, Mhairi switched on the recorder and they identified themselves.

'Can you take us through your movements from 5 p.m. last night?' asked Farrell.

His voice was clipped and emotionless with the kind of upper-class intonation that spoke of a different world from the one they inhabited.

'I came home from work at 5.30. I had a shower and changed.'

'Were your children still there?'

'Yes, my wife ...' his voice faltered for the first time, 'told me Teddy and Amelia were staying the night with our nanny, Jane Pearson. She arrived about half an hour before I left and was getting the children organized.'

49

'Did you see your wife?'

His jaw tightened.

'Yes, she was in bed, with a migraine. I took her a cup of tea. I offered to stay but she said she needed to sleep it off. If I'd known that would be the last time I'd see her ...'

The strain was starting to show. Farrell glanced across at Mhairi.

'We understand that this is painful for you, Mr Campbell,' said Mhairi. 'Would you like to take a short break?'

'No, thank you. Let's just get this over with. It's been a long day.'

'Do you recall what your wife was wearing?' asked Mhairi.

'She was in bed in her dressing gown with the duvet pulled up.'

'Did she mention that she was expecting anyone?' asked Farrell.

'No.' His jaw tensed.

'What time did you leave the house?'

'About quarter to seven.'

'Had you eaten?' asked Mhairi.

'No, we ordered a takeaway about half past eight from the Bombay Palace.'

'Did someone collect it?'

'No, we'd had a couple of beers by then. They delivered.'

'Who answered the door?'

'Max, I guess. It's his house.'

'Did you leave at any time during the night?' asked Farrell.

'No, absolutely not. I had no reason to.' He ran a hand through his hair. 'I didn't kill my wife.'

'Can you tell us what happened after you left Max Delaney's house in the morning?' said Mhairi.

'I got home and let myself in with my key, expecting Gina to be still in bed. I walked through the hall and into the kitchen to make some coffee and then ...'

'Take your time,' said Farrell.

'And then ... I saw her lying there. She was meant to be in bed, but ... the way she was dressed, at that time in the morning, I couldn't take it in. Then I noticed the blood. I looked into her eyes.' His hand gripped the table. 'My brain told me she was gone, but I couldn't help myself trying to shake her back to life. Then I called the police.'

'A knife was found lying next to her. Do you recall whether or not you touched it?'

'I honestly don't remember – I might have done – I was only focused on my wife.'

'It appears that your wife may have had company last night. There were two wine glasses on the coffee table. Was one of them yours?'

'No. Perhaps she had a drink with Jane before she left?'

'Before driving off with your children?'

'No, you're right. Jane wouldn't do that,' he sighed.

'It has been alleged that your wife was having an affair. Was she?'

'Not to my knowledge. The first time I had an inkling was when I found her dressed like that ...'

'You weren't at all suspicious?'

'No, she gave me no reason to be. We were happy. Or I thought we were.'

'What would you have done if you had known?' asked Farrell.

'I wouldn't have killed her, if that's what you're driving at.' He gave Farrell a hard stare. 'You've found out who it is, haven't you?'

'I'm sorry, Mr Campbell,' said Farrell. 'I'm afraid we're not at liberty to say anything about that at the present time.'

'I'll tear the bastard limb from limb,' he muttered.

Farrell decided to change tack.

'Have you spoken to your father-in-law yet?'

A fleeting expression of fear flitted across the man's face. 'No.'

'Someone like Mario Lombardo is bound to have made enemies over the years. Anyone spring to mind?'

Campbell looked startled but more or less immediately shook his head.

'He's never shared much about his business interests with me and I prefer to keep it that way. You'd best ask him that yourselves,' Campbell said. Then after a moment he leaned forward. 'Look, I've told you everything I know. I need to be with my children. They're too young to understand what's happened to their mother.'

'Interview terminated at 18.06,' said Farrell, switching off the machine.

Chapter 11

As they escorted Fergus Campbell out through the reception area, a man in his fifties with close-cropped hair sprang to his feet and approached them. He looked like a heavyweight fighter constrained against his wishes in a suit. Fergus Campbell stopped dead, taking Farrell by surprise. He looked terrified but stood his ground.

'My father-in-law,' he muttered.

'Mario, it wasn't me,' he said, staring straight into his father-in-law's bloodshot eyes.

Mario Lombardo returned his stare for a long moment.

'I'll give you the benefit of the doubt. For now.'

Farrell decided it was time to take control before they both kicked off and stuck out his hand.

'DI Farrell, Senior Investigating Officer,' he said as Lombardo slowly shook the offered hand, his intense gaze subjecting him to forensic scrutiny.

He handed a piece of paper to Farrell. 'I came over to hand in my address and contact details. I expect to be kept appraised of any developments.'

'Of course, sir. I'm very sorry for your loss. DI Moore will be in touch with you tomorrow to arrange a convenient time to take your statement.'

'Thank you, DI Farrell. I hope that you find the person who did this.'

And hopefully before Lombardo finds them, thought Farrell, and exacts his own terrible vengeance.

Mario Lombardo gave Fergus Campbell a last penetrating look, before turning on his heel and exiting the station. Campbell waited a few moments and slipped out after him, turning in the opposite direction.

It was already after eight and Farrell felt a sudden wave of fatigue. Mhairi was looking shattered as well. It had been a long day and they'd done all they could for now.

'What do you think?' asked Mhairi as they walked to the car park after checking in with DC Thomson in the MCA room.

'Hard to say. I would guess that Campbell's been brought up to mask or repress his emotions. In any event, we've still got to break the alibi if we like him for this.'

'Weird that the three of them are so tight,' mused Mhairi. 'They all seem so different and their wives clearly don't get on. Chloe Delaney put it down to them having bonded over the loss of a colleague years ago in tragic circumstances. The girl was Peter Swift's fiancée at the time.'

'We can speak to Jack Kerr's wife tomorrow, see what we can get out of her,' said Farrell, as he reached his car and opened the door.

Exhausted, he sat for a moment trying to rearrange all the

jumbled images from the day into some semblance of order. Something told him that this case was going to be far from straightforward. Pulling out of the car park he drove through the deserted streets of the quiet market town, so different from the hustle and bustle of Glasgow which would still be heaving at this time of night. Driving over Buccleuch Street bridge, he shuddered as he glanced to the left and saw the eerie shape of the convent looking down on the town with a brooding intensity. He still had nightmares about what had happened there that would cause him to jolt awake soaked in sweat and with his heart pounding. He made a conscious effort to drag his thoughts out of this downward spiral.

Pulling up beside his mother's neat bungalow, he got out and let himself in to the house with the key she had given him. Hearing the sound of laughter coming from the kitchen, he went to investigate. To his surprise, his mother was washing up alongside an elderly gentleman. She blushed as he came in, looking as skittish as a woman half her age.

'Frank, this is my good friend, Dermot Reilly. He goes to St Margaret's.'

Farrell stepped forward and looked deep into the man's eyes as he shook his hand warmly. He liked what he saw there.

'Nice to meet you, Dermot.'

'Dermot's an accountant,' said his mother, sounding pleased with herself.

'I'm sure the lad won't hold that against me,' Dermot said with a smile.

There was an awkward silence. Farrell had no script for

this situation. Henry saved the day by springing out from under the kitchen table and wrapping himself round Farrell's legs, demanding a fuss be made.

'Mhairi has already collected Oscar. She's looking well. Such a lovely girl.' She gave him a piercing look. 'Be a catch for some lucky man. Now that you're back, you'll have to pop in on Father Murray. He asks after you all the time.'

Farrell made his excuses and left them to it.

As he lay on the bed in his old room he realized that he'd only been back there five minutes and already he was feeling hemmed in. One of the things he did like about Glasgow was the anonymity. He could wander the streets for days and never meet anyone he knew. In Dumfries, he felt as if every person he met knew his business. He wished he'd had the foresight to grab a bottle of whisky from the supermarket on the way home. No doubt his mother had a bottle tucked away somewhere, but he couldn't face her knowing the extent to which he'd come to rely on alcohol to quieten his demons. The craving gnawed away at his insides and he hated himself for having become so weak. He wasn't physically dependent on alcohol yet, but he used it to numb him. Somehow, he had to try and find a way back to the man he was two years ago. Feeling increasingly agitated as his mind persecuted him with unwanted thoughts, he leapt to his feet and began to pace up and down the room. He had to get out of here. The walls were closing in on him.

He pulled out some old running gear from the mahogany drawers, then grabbed the trainers he had stuck in his bag at the last minute. After limbering up with a few stretches, he slipped out the back door and ran through the town until he reached the river, his stride lengthening as the muscle memory kicked in. It was still light and the air felt fresher than the city fumes. He ran through Dock Park and along the River Nith to Kingholm Quay. The salty tang of the mud was stronger here as the tidal river drew closer to the mouth of the Solway estuary. Exhausted but calmer now, he sank onto a bench to recover. He was finally back in Dumfries, for good or ill. He knew he had to make his peace with what had happened here or it would destroy him.

He pulled out his phone. Before he could change his mind, he called Father Jim Murray.

'Frank? I was hoping you'd call,' said his friend. 'It's been a while.'

'Sorry about that. I had some stuff to figure out.'

'No worries, why don't you pop round? We can have a couple of beers in the garden.'

'You sure it's not too late?'

'Get yourself over here, Frank.'

Half an hour later, Farrell was sitting in the garden behind the priest's house, drinking a bottle of ice-cold lager. His friend hadn't changed in the time he'd been away. He exuded quiet contentment.

'How do you do it?' Frank asked.

'Do what?' asked Father Murray, sipping his beer and swatting ineffectually at the midges.

'Stay so constant, I suppose. Do you never have doubts? About God? Your purpose? Any of it?'

Father Murray laughed.

'Of course, I do. I'm no different to anyone else. My faith waxes and wanes. Some days, I feel filled with the presence of God. Other days, I don't. At times like that I just go through the motions and trust that God will light the way back to Him. There's no guarantees, Frank. You can't lock down faith. It's an elusive creature. All you can do is create the right soil for faith to flourish.'

'I've been so bloody angry. About what happened to John. My rage has been eating me alive. I can't make it stop. Sometimes I feel it's the only thing gluing me together.'

'You'll find your way back to us. I'm sure of it. Now stop stressing and drink your bloody beer.'

'Amen, to that,' said Farrell with a grin as the sun slid below the horizon.

Chapter 12

Mhairi pushed away her empty plate and wished she'd had the sense to wear an elasticated waist. Oscar was lying upside down in his basket, looking like his belly was about to explode.

'Thanks, Vera,' Mhairi said. 'That was to die for. Ronnie's a lucky man.'

'And don't I know it,' he said, sending the indomitable Vera a fond glance.

'You're welcome, love. You can go through to the comfy chairs with Ronnie while I clear up in here.'

'Let me give you a hand,' said Mhairi, getting to her feet.

'Och away with you, I'm fine in here with the radio on.'

Mhairi and Ronnie settled down in the comfortably furnished lounge. Retirement from the force seemed to be agreeing with him. He'd put on a few pounds since they last worked together but looked the picture of health and contentment.

'How's the B&B going?' she asked.

'Keeps me out of mischief.' He grinned.

'You never miss the job?'

'Never. I got out at the right time. How's Frank doing? His mother says she hardly sees him these days.'

Mhairi bit her lip.

'He could be better. I'm hoping being back here will do him some good.'

'How's young Davey adapting to life in the big bad city?'

Mhairi rolled her eyes.

'He's turned into an unreconstructed party animal. A different girl on his arm every week. You'd have to see it to believe it.'

Ronnie laughed.

The next morning she arrived at work in a much better fettle and a tight waistband from Vera's cooked breakfast. She dumped her jacket in the Sergeant's Room then headed off to the 8 a.m. briefing.

As she entered the room she caught a glimpse of DI Moore's skeletal appearance. What on earth had happened to her? Was she ill? Before she had a chance to go over and speak to her she was joined by Dave Thomson who looked so excited he could hardly contain himself. It was like being accosted by a puppy. All he needed was a tail to wag.

Farrell was at the front along with DS Byers. Suddenly, she felt a presence by her side.

'DSup Crawford Cunningham,' the man said.

She glanced up, startled, and stood to shake his hand. 'DS Mhairi McLeod, sir.'

He sat down beside her and Mhairi felt her posture stiffen to the point her muscles ached.

'I've heard good things about you from DCI Buchanan.'

'Thank you, sir.'

Farrell held up his hand for silence and the room quietened. Mhairi frowned as she scrutinized him closely. He too had lost weight. He obviously hadn't had that suit on for a while because it was hanging off his tall frame. No danger of her losing weight through stress. It made her eat like a pig at a trough.

'Hopefully, we'll be able to pinpoint the time of death a bit more accurately after DS McLeod and I attend this morning's post-mortem. Then we'll interview Gabriel Ferrante, the alleged lover of the deceased.'

'Does Fergus Campbell know his identity yet, sir?' asked PC Rosie Green.

'Not as far as we're aware, but I'm sure it won't take him long to find out.'

'For those of you who don't already know, Gina Campbell's father is Mario Lombardo.'

There were one or two low whistles.

'We need to get the nanny, Jane Pearson, in for questioning. She should be able to give us the lowdown on the Campbell household. We also need to speak to Jack Kerr's wife. I'll tackle her with DS McLeod.'

'What about the knife, sir? said DC Thomson. 'Did it come from the house? Were there any prints on it apart from the husband's?'

'It came from the house and the only set of prints on it was the husband's. The killer could have worn gloves, though.'

'As well as being a crime of passion by either the lover or

the husband, there's another angle we need to explore. It's possible that this murder relates to Mario Lombardo's business interests, either legitimate or illegitimate. However, he's also a grieving father so we need to be subtle. That's why I've arranged for DI Moore to interview him.'

Mhairi noticed DS Byers's black expression. Seriously? The man was as subtle as a brick. This job would play to DI Moore's strengths. She was also in the position to call in a few favours from Glasgow after solving their art fraud case two years ago.

'I don't need to tell you that the first few days are crucial. We need to hit this murder case aggressively,' Farrell finished.

As she was making her way to the door amidst a queue of hot cross coppers, Mhairi felt a tap on her shoulder. It was DI Moore.

'Mhairi, it's wonderful to see you.'

'Likewise, ma'am. How are you?'

'I'm great, really great,' she said, her haunted eyes belying her smile. 'Listen, there's a couple of things I need to tell you—'

Farrell materialized and her mouth snapped shut. Mhairi narrowed her eyes. She could smell trouble. Frustrated, she had to follow him out of the door.

Chapter 13

Farrell and Mhairi made the post-mortem by the skin of their teeth. The pathologist, Roland Bartle-White, was a stickler for punctuality. As they approached, he gave them a grim smile.

'I was wondering if they'd send you pair down.'

'Well, here we are,' said Mhairi brightly.

'It's been a while,' said Farrell.

They suited up and followed him into the mortuary suite where the body of Gina Campbell was waiting for them. Cut down in her prime. All they could do for her now was bring her killer to justice.

There was another pathologist standing by the body. He was tall and had warm brown eyes which alighted on Mhairi with evident interest. His name was Sandy Gillespie and they had encountered him a few times in Glasgow.

Cool and professional, she gave him no encouragement as he went on a charm offensive. Ever since she had been so badly let down by her last partner, Mhairi had steered resolutely clear of romantic entanglements.

As Bartle-White began an inspection of the body he frowned and leaned forward.

Farrell glanced at Mhairi and his pulse quickened. What had he found?

'This is rather interesting.' He motioned them closer and pointed at a tattoo on Gina Campbell's left breast. It looked like an eye and Farrell recognized the significance at once.

'It's the Panopticon sign,' he said. Mhairi raised her eyebrows.

'It relates to penal reform. Jeremy Bentham designed a system that made prisoners feel they were always being watched regardless of whether they actually were or not. It allowed one hidden guard to keep control over all the inmates. Simple, yet highly effective.'

'An odd choice for a young woman,' said Mhairi.

'I'm afraid it's rather stranger than that,' said Bartle-White. 'It's not a permanent tattoo but a rather good quality fake.'

'You mean a transfer?' asked Farrell.

'Yes, but that's not the only strange thing.'

Farrell fought against the temptation to tell him to spit it out. Bartle-White was arrogant and did not like to be hurried. 'Oh?' he managed with commendable self-restraint. Mhairi was tapping her foot with impatience and about to blow a gasket.

'It's been recently applied. Whether it was put on before she died or afterwards, it's impossible to say.' Bartle-White straightened up and waited for their reaction.

Farrell glanced at Mhairi and saw the realization mirrored in her eyes that this case was starting to go pear-shaped.

'Can we get any usable DNA off it?' asked Farrell.

'My assistant will take a digital image and I'll excise it for testing,' the pathologist replied.

Glancing across at Mhairi, Farrell noticed she was quite comfortable in such a setting now, unlike the last time they had been in this room. Although he hid it well, the unseemly squelches and smells as the pathologist compelled a body to reveal its secrets still made him queasy.

After what seemed like an eternity of weighing and measuring, the pathologist straightened up with a frown.

'I'm afraid that the deceased wasn't killed with the knife that has been produced from the scene,' he said.

'But it was covered in blood,' said Farrell, confused.

'That, I'm not disputing,' said the pathologist. 'However, that knife did not inflict the stab wound. The width of the blade is wrong. Could the real knife still be at the scene? Could it have been missed?'

'Absolutely not,' said Farrell. 'Our SOCOs would never make such an elementary error. It must have been removed from the scene.'

'Perhaps an attempt to frame the husband?' asked Mhairi.

'Possibly,' replied Farrell.

'I can confirm that she was stabbed once while she was still alive. The wound cut the femoral artery. Exsanguination would have occurred in minutes,' said the pathologist.

'She most likely let her attacker in to the house as there were no signs of forced entry. Are there any defensive wounds?' asked Farrell.

'None.'

'No signs of resistance?'

'Nothing obvious. No ligature marks or fingertip bruises. No wounds at all apart from the obvious one.'

'Could she have been poisoned or injected with something?' asked Farrell.

'We'll need to wait for toxicology to ascertain the former,' said Bartle-White. 'I'm looking for puncture marks now.' After what seemed an eternity he straightened up once more.

'None that I can see.'

'What can you tell us about time of death?' asked Farrell.

'Hard to say with any degree of certainty in the circumstances. Based on the fact that the body had almost reached full rigor when the police surgeon attended the scene at 7.45 a.m. and that she was last seen alive around 7 p.m., I would say you're looking at a window between 7 p.m. and 11 p.m.'

They took their leave, feeling the warmth of the May morning immediately dispel the chill of the mortuary.

'I've a feeling that we're going to be here more than a week,' said Farrell.

Mhairi groaned.

Chapter 14

The nanny, Jane Pearson, lived in a small bungalow at Heathhall on the outskirts of town. Mhairi rang the doorbell. No answer. The lights were on and someone was obviously in, so she rang it again.

A rather harassed-looking young woman with a baby on her hip and a stroppy toddler grabbing on to her leg, answered the door.

'This really isn't a good time,' she began.

Farrell produced his warrant card. 'I can see that you have your hands full, but we really need to speak with you in connection with the murder of Gina Campbell.'

'Er ...' she flustered, glancing nervously behind her.

'May we come in?' said Mhairi, stepping up to the threshold, leaving Pearson no option but to usher her in to the living room.

There, they were surprised to discover Fergus Campbell lounging on the sofa, perfectly at home.

He stood up at once when they entered, looking defensive.

'Is this your little girl, sir?' asked Mhairi, chucking the smiling baby under the chin.

He relaxed a little.

'Yes. Max Delaney did offer but Jane was kind enough to let us stay here last night. We couldn't go home and ... well, I didn't really know what else to do. They're so young and I haven't been massively hands-on up to now.'

He gave a weak smile.

'I'll have to learn, I suppose, but it takes time and when Jane offered ...'

'This must be so difficult for you,' said Mhairi. 'For all of you. Do you have family in the area?'

'Yes, but we're not close, to put it mildly,' he muttered.

'Even so, in such tragic circumstances ...' said Farrell.

'Tragic? They're probably hanging out the bunting. They loathed my wife.'

There was an awkward silence.

'Sorry, I didn't mean ...' he said, running his hands through a mop of dark curls.

'Look, we're sorry to intrude but we do need to talk to Miss Pearson on her own. You know the drill. I don't want to do it at the station if I can do it here,' said Farrell.

Jane Pearson looked on the verge of tears.

Mhairi raised her eyebrows and stared unblinking at Fergus Campbell until he got the message.

'Oh ... er ... right, I'll take Teddy and Amelia out to the park. It's a lovely day for it.'

Farrell noticed how stiff he was around the children. The poor guy really didn't have much of a clue. With the help of the nanny he was soon bundled out the door into the sunshine with the baby, Amelia, and her brother Teddy.

Jane Pearson seemed even tenser when they were gone. She invited them to sit then perched on the edge of an upright chair.

'So how long have you worked for the Campbells?' asked Farrell.

'I started with them three months before Teddy was born, so just over three and a half years.'

'How come?' asked Mhairi. 'Don't most couples have the nanny start after the birth?'

'Yes ... but ...'

'But what?' asked Mhairi.

'Gina wasn't in a good place. The baby was unplanned. She didn't find out in time ... to well ... do anything about it. Fergus needed help. I've been with them ever since.'

'Can you confirm the last time you saw Gina?' said Farrell.

'Yes, it was two nights ago, at around 7 p.m. She'd called me to ask if I could go over and take Teddy and Amelia for the night because she had a pounding migraine.'

'How was she dressed when you arrived?' asked Mhairi.

'She was in her dressing gown. Her cheeks were flushed as if she had a fever. She said she was going to go to bed and try and sleep it off.'

'And Fergus?'

'He was getting ready to go back out. He left the house just before I did.'

'How were things between Gina and him that evening?' asked Farrell. 'Did you witness any exchanges between them?'

'He went in to check on her, took her a cup of tea. That's it as far as I'm aware. They didn't have a row or anything.'

'So you were the last person to see her alive?' said Farrell.

'Apart from the nutter who killed her,' she retorted.

'Was she a good employer?' asked Mhairi.

The nanny coloured and looked away.

'We won't let on to Fergus. We're just trying to get a feel for what she was like as a person, that's all,' coaxed Mhairi.

'I've had better.'

'In what way?'

'I don't want to say. Why does it matter now?'

'Because someone disliked her enough to kill her. Whatever you can tell us about the way she typically behaved might signpost the way to a motive for the killing.'

'If you must know, she was mean and spiteful. She deliberately never paid me on time so I had to go cap in hand to her every month.'

'Why didn't you leave?' asked Farrell.

'How could I? Gina didn't have a maternal bone in her body. Teddy and Amelia needed me. I couldn't abandon them.'

'What about their father?' asked Farrell.

'You saw him. He's pretty clueless. His own parents sent him off to boarding school at the age of seven. He thinks not being shown love and affection is normal.'

'From your time in the household, how would you characterize their relationship?' asked Farrell.

'They were total opposites. He's cool and detached, but she was fiery and had a short fuse. There were times when they thought I couldn't hear them. The things she would say to him were really cruel, enough to cripple someone.'

'And did he retaliate?'

'No, never. I used to wish he would, but he never so much as raised his voice to her. I heard him cry out in pain once. It sounded like she was hitting him. He deserved better,' she said then looked awkward as though she had given too much away.

'You and Fergus,' said Mhairi. 'Have you ever ...?'

'No! Of course not! What do you take me for? He's my boss, end of story.'

'Sorry, but I had to ask.'

'I suppose.' She bit her lip.

'Look, he'll be back with Teddy and Amelia soon. I really have to get on.'

Farrell and Mhairi stood up to leave.

'Thank you for your time. We'll be in touch if there's anything else,' said Farrell.

They walked back to the car in silence.

'I'm starving,' said Mhairi. 'Let's grab a couple of rolls and some coffee from that takeaway on the Whitesands.'

'I'm not really hungry,' countered Farrell.

'Frank, you've got to eat,' she said, more loudly than she had intended.

He grinned at her.

'Someone's getting snappy. All right, if it'll keep you off my back I'll have a sausage, egg and tattie scone roll.'

They parked in front of the river, and Farrell wound down the windows before they baked to death. Mhairi marched over to the takeaway. She came back grasping rolls and coffees and they munched in silence for a few minutes enjoying the view of the water tumbling across the caul.

After a discreet burp, Mhairi scrunched up her paper and shoved it under her seat.

Farrell rolled his eyes. Her mess was like a contagion infecting every surface it came into contact with.

'Kind of a weird set up,' she said.

'He looked mighty cosy on that sofa when we arrived. They could be in it together, I suppose. She certainly carries a torch for him.'

'If the nanny's to be believed it sounds like Gina Campbell was fairly abusive towards her husband,' said Farrell.

'Could he have snapped?'

'It's possible,' he said.

Chapter 15

DI Moore regarded the irate man pacing in front of her desk with some sympathy, despite his coming at her like a bull at a gate. Mario Lombardo might be a gangster with a thin veneer of respectability plastered over the cracks, but right now he was a grieving father and she was prepared to cut him some slack. It had probably cost him dearly to even come in and see her. He'd made no secret of his hatred and distrust of the police.

'Mr Lombardo, I can't even begin to imagine how you are feeling. I want you to know that we'll do everything in our power to catch your daughter's killer. Please, won't you sit down?'

'If it turns out to be that worthless bastard she married, I'll pull him apart with my bare hands,' he snapped, but he did reluctantly sit down. He raised the coffee cup to his mouth, his hand shaking slightly.

'He has an alibi.'

'Pull the other one. Anyone can buy an alibi,' he said.

'There are a number of lines of enquiry. I've been assigned to investigate one in particular.'

He leaned forward, pugnacious jaw at variance with tailored suit.

'Spit it out then.'

'The possibility that your daughter's death might be related to your business dealings.'

Lombardo sat back in his seat and exhaled like a deflating balloon.

'Like I said, we plan to leave no stone unturned. So tell me, anyone you've had a beef with in say the last three years? In any of your businesses.' She paused. 'Both legitimate and illegitimate.'

'All of my businesses are legitimate,' he said with narrowed eyes.

'Our focus isn't your business activities, but whether anything at all might have provided a motive for your daughter's murder.'

Mario Lombardo sighed.

'I operate in a tough world, DI Moore. A number of my associates can be overzealous when they feel they have been wronged. However, most would balk at murdering my only child.'

'And if anything occurs to you?'

'I will, of course, bring it directly to your attention,' he said.

'So you've received no threats recently?'

'I would worry if I didn't receive threats. Success breeds envy from weak-minded individuals.'

'But ...'

'Look, I hear what you're saying, DI Moore. And believe me, I'm grateful.'

He stood up to leave and shook her hand.

'You'll keep me posted.'

'A Family Liaison Officer has been assigned to the case.'

'That's not what I asked.'

As she looked into his flinty grey eyes, DI Moore saw beyond the predatory shark to the grieving father within.

'I'll do what I can,' she assured him.

'Consider me in your debt,' he replied, releasing her hand.

She watched him leave then sank back into her seat. Had she really just received an IOU from a member of the Sicilian Mafia? She hoped she'd never have need of it. Wearily, she tucked a few wisps of hair that had escaped her severe bun behind her ears. She felt simultaneously exhausted and buzzing from adrenalin.

She wasn't sure how she felt about their station being invaded by the MIT team. While it was good to see Frank, Mhairi and Dave again it was also a reminder of their last case. Memories that she had fought hard to repress were now trying to bubble to the surface. Letting her guard down back then had been the biggest mistake of her life never mind her career.

Seeing the time, she realized she should eat something. She opened her desk and took out a packet of edamame beans. Unexpectedly she felt a wave of nausea. Jumping to her feet she threw open her door and rushed along the corridor to the toilets, where she retched painfully. Taking in her skeletal frame beneath the harsh lighting she noticed for the first time how thin she had become. She slid her eyes away from her reflection, feeling slightly ashamed though not entirely sure why. Thank goodness no one had heard her.

Once safely back in her room, she bent her head to her work trawling through the web for information on Mario Lombardo's legitimate business interests. She doubted she would find anything much there as the last thing he wanted was to do anything to crack his veneer of respectability. She would need to sink deeper into his world. With a sigh she picked up the phone to a contact in organized crime. He owed her one and she had no hesitation in cashing in this particular chip.

Chapter 16

Farrell and Mhairi paused next to a gleaming brass plate with 'Gabriel Ferrante' written on it, outside a small office near the court.

'This isn't going to be an easy conversation,' Farrell said.

'Being around all these lawyers is making me twitchy,' said Mhairi. 'Normally, we're the ones with the upper hand.'

'*They* don't come with handcuffs as standard,' he said, as they climbed the steep stairs to the door marked 'Reception'.

A thickset burly man, sitting behind the desk, welcomed them with a decidedly unfriendly look.

'Can I help you?' he asked, looking as though his first impulse had been to push them back down the stairs. Farrell could only guess that he had them pegged as coppers, but why should that bother him?

'DI Farrell and DS McLeod,' he said stepping forward, hand outstretched, leaving the other man no option but to meet it with his own rough mitt.

'And you are?' he asked, as no introduction was forthcoming.

'Joe Capaldi. I'm afraid you've just missed him,' he said with a smile.

Gabriel Ferrante chose that moment to walk through from his office.

'Oh.' The smile died. 'He must have slipped in without me noticing him,' he muttered.

Gabriel Ferrante grinned at them and walked over. He was a ruggedly handsome man who looked to be in his late forties with more than a little charisma about him. The jagged scar down one side of his face seemed to add to rather than detract from his charm.

'Don't mind Joe here, officers. He's paid to be my gatekeeper. When you're in court as much as I am, office time to catch up on your paperwork is a precious commodity. How can I help?'

'We're here to ask you some questions in relation to the murder of Gina Campbell,' said Farrell.

'I see,' he said. 'Won't you come this way? Joe, could you bring us coffee?'

'Sure thing, boss,' he replied, looking like butter wouldn't melt.

Farrell was intrigued. His gut was telling him there was something a little off about this set-up.

They sat in two chairs in front of the cheap plywood desk. It was strewn with files and correspondence. This was the office of a grafter. There were no frills.

Coffee arrived in the shape of three mugs and a packet of own-brand gingernuts. No expense spared, thought Farrell, glancing at the tough-looking lawyer across the desk.

'I want to be straight with you, Mr Ferrante. It has come to our attention that you may have been having an affair with Gina Campbell.'

Ferrante sat back in his chair and looked at them, his gaze inscrutable.

'Who else knows?' he eventually asked.

'So, you admit it?'

Ferrante sighed and ran his hands through his hair.

'Yes, I admit it. I have no desire to obstruct your inquiry. I'm as keen to find the bastard who murdered her as you are. I'll ask you again. Who knows?'

'We're not at liberty to say,' said Mhairi. 'When did your relationship start?'

'The very first night that we met. A year from the date that she was killed.'

'When was the last time you saw her?' asked Farrell.

'It should have been that night. She'd arranged for her kids to stay with their nanny and we were to celebrate together. I went around there as planned at around 9 p.m. The door was locked and the lights were off. It looked like there was nobody in, so I gave up and went home.'

'So you were at the locus close to the time she was murdered,' Farrell said.

'Yes. Only one problem, DI Farrell. I didn't do it.'

'Did you see anyone else in the vicinity?' asked Mhairi.

'No. My focus was on not being seen myself. I never thought for a second something had happened to her. I assumed her husband had come home unexpectedly and they'd gone out.'

'Is it possible that her husband could have got wind of your affair?' asked Farrell.

'No. I'm sure of it. I'd been sat beside him in court all day. Look, I'm not proud of sleeping with another man's wife. I begged her to leave him, but she was having none of it.'

'So why did you?' said Farrell bluntly.

'What can I say? We had a connection. What else is there? When I heard she'd been killed, I wanted to come forward, but what good would it have done? Fergus is a bit of a cold fish but he's a decent bloke. I didn't want to hurt him needlessly.'

'Can anyone vouch for your whereabouts that night?' asked Mhairi.

'No. I went straight home. Do with that what you will.'

Farrell sat back in his chair and stared at him. Ferrante stared right back.

Farrell got to his feet, closely followed by Mhairi.

'I appreciate you being so candid. I'll send an officer down to take your statement. Fergus Campbell is going to find out about you and his wife, but he won't hear it from us.'

'Thank you, I appreciate that,' said Ferrante, escorting them from his office.

Once out in the warm May sun, Farrell and Mhairi grabbed some coffee from a deli in Irish Street and walked back to the car.

'That was almost too easy,' said Farrell, taking a long slug of coffee.

'He offered it up to us on a plate.'

'I found him hard to read,' said Farrell.

'He's very charming, but there's something about him ... I can't quite put my finger on it,' said Mhairi.

'I know what you mean. He's not your bog-standard lawyer. He's got a fair bit of life experience behind him, I'd wager.'

'He's bound to know we'd be coming for him. His openness could have been a strategy to deflect suspicion. Although, weirdly, I liked him,' said Mhairi.

Farrell looked at her.

'Not like that. I just thought he seemed like a decent bloke. And yes, before you say it, I know that doesn't necessarily bode well.' She glared.

It was true, Mhairi didn't have the best taste in men. After what he hoped was a tactful silence, Farrell changed the subject.

'Joe Capaldi's a bit of an odd choice as office manager.'

'You can say that again. He comes across like a bouncer in a seedy nightclub,' said Mhairi. 'I wonder how Gabriel Ferrante got that scar?'

'He may have been glassed at some point.'

'Grateful client?'

'Someone wasn't happy with him that's for sure.'

Chapter 17

Their next port of call was Jack Kerr's house, a former council house in Locharbriggs. The paintwork was flaking off the windows. He clearly wasn't as well off as his two friends. As they walked up the path, the door burst open and a lanky youth with pockmarked skin and a murderous expression stormed past them. A woman appeared on the doorstep bellowing after him.

'Get back in here this minute, Aaron!'

The youth ignored her and headed off down the street, shrugging up his black hoody so that it covered his face, shoulders hunched in the manner of teenage boys everywhere.

The woman, still looking flustered, attempted to rally.

'Can I help you?'

'DI Farrell and DS McLeod. We're investigating the murder of Gina Campbell and wonder if we might ask you a few questions.'

'Yes, of course,' she said, opening the door wide.

'Please excuse the mess, it looks like a bombsite. Aaron gets upset sometimes, tears through the place like a hurricane,' she said with a weak grin. 'He's had a rough time. We're hoping we can turn things around.'

'It's a difficult age,' said Mhairi.

'Is he your only child?' asked Farrell.

'We foster him. Have done for the last five years. We've had a stream of boys through the house, but felt Aaron would do better if he had our whole attention. We're in the process of adopting him.'

'Do you work as well?' asked Mhairi, sympathetically.

'Yes, I'm a midwife,' she replied, pasting on a bright smile even though she was clearly struggling.

'I still can't believe what happened to Gina. You don't expect it to happen to someone you know.'

'Murder?' said Mhairi.

'Yes! It's so shocking. So out there.'

'I understand that your husband is friendly with Gina's husband.'

'He's been tight with Fergus and Max for years.'

'They seem very different,' said Mhairi.

'Nobody gets it. I'm not even sure that I do. All I know is that ever since that poor girl burned to death in Jedburgh, they've been inseparable. It was so awful and they were all so young that it seemed to weld them together.'

'Peter Swift was her fiancé at the time, but he doesn't tend to hang out with them as much?' said Mhairi.

'He's a great guy and they get on really well but, given that he's a fiscal and they're on opposite sides of the court, it's probably easier if they're not joined at the hip. I'm so glad that he's with Beth now. She's a lovely girl.'

'What can you tell us about Gina Campbell?' asked Farrell.

'She wasn't terribly popular among the legal wives. At first I was under the impression she was really snooty, thought she was better than everyone else. Fergus himself is a bit of a toff in case you haven't noticed. However, in the last few months I had come to quite like her. We got drunk together one night after we snuck off from some boring Faculty cocktail party. She'd a wicked sense of humour. She cracked me up.' Her eyes filled with tears. 'That was a good night. It's how I'm going to remember her.'

'How did she get along with Fergus?' asked Mhairi.

'Well, I'm sure there was plenty of drama. Gina was highly combustible. Fergus seemed to take it all in his stride though. He worshipped her.'

'I'm sure that you're aware of the rumours,' said Farrell.

Sarah dropped her eyes.

'Yes,' she admitted. 'I didn't know who but she hinted at it that night. I mentioned it to Jack, but he decided not to say anything to Fergus in the hope it would blow over. If he finds out now in such devastating circumstances it'll destroy him.'

'What can you tell us about the night of the murder?'

'Very little, really. I was at home with the kids and Jack stayed the night with Max. I only found out what had happened the morning after when Fergus phoned at the back of seven.'

Farrell glanced out of the front window and saw Aaron slouching along the pavement with an older lad who looked vaguely familiar. They parted company at the gate and a minute later the front door opened and heavy feet thudded up the stairs followed by the bang of a door.

'The prodigal returns,' said Mhairi with a grin.

Sarah laughed.

'Do you happen to know the name of that lad he was with?' asked Farrell.

'I'm afraid not. Why? Should I be worried?'

'No, not at all.'

'I'm always on at him to invite his friends back, but he never does.'

'This phase will pass,' said Mhairi.

'I know. My main concern is trying to keep him safe until the clouds lift. Teenage boys are such a worry. Jack was a product of the care system himself. Bounced around from pillar to post. Then he got lucky with his last foster parents. He ended up with a scholarship to one of the best private schools in Scotland, Morrington Academy. He wants to do the same for other kids, but Aaron sure isn't making it easy. His behaviour is getting worse, not better. I don't understand it.'

'He's probably testing your commitment to him with the adoption looming,' said Mhairi.

'Yes, I'm sure you're right,' Sarah said with a quick smile as she showed them out to the accompaniment of loud music from upstairs.

Chapter 18

'That woman is a saint,' said Mhairi, as they were driving away. 'Rather her than me.'

'Don't you want kids one day?' asked Farrell, slightly warily, as it was something they had never discussed before.

Mhairi paused a little before answering.

'I used to want them. With my parents losing my brother, the way they did, I wanted nothing more than to present them with a grandchild. Now, though, I just don't know. Most of the men I've met have turned out to be complete bastards. I reckon some part of me has given up on the idea.'

'You could always go it alone,' said Farrell, aware that he was wading dangerously out of his depth.

Mhairi snorted.

'Frank Farrell, you never cease to surprise me,' she grinned. 'What about you? There's nothing stopping you either.'

He thought about Lind's four kids. The kids that might have borne more than a passing resemblance to him, if he hadn't gone off to the seminary when he did. He thought of his aching loneliness. The punishment he felt driven to inflict upon himself, the anger he struggled to contain, the whisky he self-medicated with.

Suddenly aware that he'd taken too long to reply and that Mhairi was staring at him curiously, he resolutely shook his head.

'Nope, I don't consider myself to be father material.'

'I think you're wrong about that,' said Mhairi, staring straight ahead.

'Let's take a drive by Fergus Campbell's house.' Farrell pulled his mind back to the job. 'I want to look at the garden across the road where the prowler was reported.'

Within a couple of minutes they pulled up by the row of modest terraced houses in the Edinburgh Road.

Farrell knocked on the door and within seconds it was flung open by a sprightly lady in her sixties.

'DI Farrell and DS McLeod, here about the prowler you reported.'

'I'm surprised you're even bothering with that, given what happened across the road,' she said, nodding towards the Campbells' house.

'There's an outside possibility it might have been someone watching the Campbells' comings and goings,' said Farrell. 'Equally, it might have been someone looking to break in.'

'Did the crime prevention officer visit you to give advice on how to make your house more secure?' asked Mhairi.

'Yes, he did, I'm all sorted now,' she said.

'Pleased to hear it,' said Farrell. 'Mind if we take a look in your garden?'

'Help yourselves,' she said and retreated back inside. They heard the sound of a bolt and chain being drawn.

Farrell carefully moved around the garden behind the trees bordering the pavement.

'I reckon this is where he stood,' he said finally, pointing to a patch of earth behind a rhododendron bush which offered concealment as well as a view of the driveway and upper windows of the Campbells' house across the road. There was also an empty crisp packet and a couple of cigarette butts that had been pushed into the interior of the bush.

'We'd best get those fag ends sent for DNA analysis just in case,' he said, rejoining Mhairi on the path, and sealing them into an evidence bag.

Mhairi caught a glimpse of movement at an upstairs window across the road in Fergus Campbell's house as they were moving away. She nudged Farrell.

'Look! Somebody's in.'

They went up the driveway and rang the bell. A few seconds later it was opened and the nanny, Jane Pearson, stood before them in bare feet and a silver ball gown.

She reddened as she took in their shocked expressions.

'What do you want?' she asked, tilting her chin.

'May we come in?' said Mhairi.

'I suppose so.' She turned her back to Mhairi. 'Could you sort this zip for me?'

Mhairi duly obliged. To say the dress was a snug fit was an understatement.

Jane Pearson took off up the stairs to change after showing them into the lounge.

When she returned she was wearing her usual attire of jeans and a jumper. She was holding Teddy's hand and carrying baby Amelia.

'I'm sorry if we've called at an inconvenient time,' said Mhairi, her eyes alight with curiosity.

Jane Pearson sighed.

'It's fine. The Faculty dinner is coming up soon. Fergus has asked me to come along. He can't face going on his own but doesn't want people to think he's hiding away because he's got something to feel guilty about. I didn't have a dress, so he asked me to find one from Gina's wardrobe.'

'We were wondering if we could have a poke around, get a feel for who Gina was as a person?'

Jane bit her lip, unsure.

'We didn't want to bother Fergus with it, but we can give him a call if you'd rather,' said Farrell, getting out his phone.

'No, don't worry, you go ahead. It's time I was getting this pair off for their nap anyway. Just pull the door shut behind you when you leave.'

Once they were alone, Farrell turned to Mhairi.

'Interesting.'

'Trying on his dead wife's clothes is a bit creepy,' she said.

'So is asking the nanny to go with you to a black-tie event before your wife is even buried.'

'I reckon we ought to keep our eyes on her,' said Mhairi. 'She was the last known person to see Gina alive.'

'Agreed. It's possible that she killed Gina after Fergus left the house then sailed off with the kids. She could have kept them upstairs then left the house without going through the kitchen.'

'If only the pathologist could pin down the time of death more precisely. We're working with too big a window.'

'Maybe the toxicology results will help,' said Farrell.

Looking around the various photos of the dead woman, they tried to get a sense of her personality, but she remained an enigma. Even when smiling, her eyes remained cold. Her face was unnaturally smooth. Although glamorous, she seemed distant as though she wasn't really present, even in the photos with her children. There were no casual photos on display. Every one of them was carefully posed and taken in a photographer's studio. There was one of her with Mario Lombardo at a black-tie event with some smirking politicians.

'Mario Lombardo's connections seem to run pretty deep,' said Farrell.

The place was spotless with no trace of the violent death that had occurred there.

'Maybe the two wine glasses are a false trail,' said Farrell. 'There were no prints on them. I could see why the killer might wipe his own glass but why hers? Someone could have rinsed the glasses out with wine and poured the rest down the sink. Fergus Campbell could have stumbled on the affair and decided to murder her. He could have been waiting for his moment for months. Framing the man she'd been having the affair with would be the icing on the cake.'

'What if he and the nanny are in it together?' asked Mhairi? 'I'm starting to feel as if there's a hive of bees buzzing in my head.'

'You and me both,' said Farrell. 'So much for wrapping up this case quickly.'

They went upstairs into the master bedroom. Judging from the contents of the two bedside tables, Fergus and Gina Campbell appeared to have shared a bedroom at least.

Mhairi looked inside the wardrobe and gave a low whistle.

'Everything in here is designer. God knows where you'd wear any of this stuff in Dumfries.'

They found nothing of particular interest. In contrast to his wife, Fergus's side of the wardrobe was sparsely populated.

'I'll drop you off at the station,' said Farrell. 'Can you bring Dave up to date and post a briefing for six? I've got somethin to attend to before then.'

As Mhairi hurried into the station, Farrell glanced behind him and did a U-turn. He couldn't put it off any longer. For Lind's sake he had to touch base with Laura and find out what was going on. According to the nursing staff she hadn't been up to see him for a couple of months. Maybe she was depressed? Maybe she was angry at how things had turned out? Maybe she blamed him? He sure as hell blamed himself.

As he parked across the road from the Victorian sandstone house, he noticed with a pang that the front garden lawn had been concreted over. His friend must have been the gardener. The house looked colder now, somehow withdrawn.

Bracing himself he walked up the driveway and rang the bell.

The door opened and he came face to face with Laura.

'I was wondering when you'd show up,' she said, sounding less than pleased to see him.

'Aren't you going to invite me in?' he asked.

She kept the door half closed.

'Now's not a good time. I'm busy.'

He stared at her.

A muffled voice shouted from inside.

'You might as well let him in and get this over with.'

Laura swung the door open with a sigh.

Farrell charged past her in the direction of the voice. He'd know it anywhere.

'You!' he snapped, as he burst into the living room. And stood aghast in the open doorway. Everything looked the same as the last time he visited his friend here, except that Byers was now sitting in John's chair with his stockinged feet on the hearth. 'How could you do this to him? John's lying up there in a hospital bed and you're sitting here as if he's already dead and buried.'

Byers stood and took a deep breath, clearly struggling to hold on to his temper. Laura walked over and stood by his side, staring at Farrell defiantly.

'It's not like that, Frank,' Byers snapped. 'To all intents and purposes, John is already gone. You have to accept it. He would be the first one to tell Laura to move on and you know it. I had the greatest of respect for him as a man and as my boss. You're not going to walk in here and make me feel like shit.'

'He's right, Frank. It was all right for you. You took off to Glasgow. I had to stay here. The kids needed stability and routine. I was left on my own with them. If it hadn't been for Mike, I wouldn't have coped. He was a kind and supportive friend, which is more than I can say for you. Over time we became closer and it just happened. There's nothing I can do for John now except put a pillow over his face.'

'How can you even say that?' shouted Farrell.

'If you were any kind of friend to him you would have done it already,' she shouted back in his face. 'Now get the hell out of our house. I never want to see you again.'

Farrell felt a surge of fury almost lift him off his feet. He spun around on his heel and strode out of the house.

Chapter 19

Back at the station, Mhairi and Dave Thomson were hard at work in the MCA room ensuring that all the statements and rolling information about the case were collated and inputted into the HOLMES system. Now that the investigation was gathering momentum it was important to make sure they didn't miss any developing connections.

'You know,' Mhairi mused, 'one of the problems with this case is that the main players are in court most of the time. We can't get at them to try and trip them up. They see our moves coming before we've even thought of them. We need a way to get on the inside and see what's really going on.'

'How do you propose we do that?' asked DC Thomson, rubbing his screen-sore eyes.

'Well, they already know what Frank and I look like, so we can't do it. You could, though.'

'Tell me you're not suggesting what I think you're suggesting.'

'Go undercover? Why not?'

'Are you kidding me? Last time I ended up taking a bullet.'

'You're such a drama queen,' she said, narrowing her eyes

at him. 'I only mean you could be substituted for the regular police officer who works there.'

'What about a social event? Something I might not need to wear a vest for. The Glasgow Bar are always throwing some shindig or other. I've even been invited to a few.'

'Look at you, all grown up and consorting with the enemy,' she mocked. 'Actually, on reflection that's not a bad idea. If you contact Peter Swift at the fiscal's office, he'll be able to send you over a list of events. The nanny did mention there's some kind of big dinner coming up.'

'Now that's more like it,' he grinned.

Mhairi continued sifting through the statements. She paused as something occurred to her.

Both of the wives had mentioned the significance of an anniversary as a prompt for the solicitors meeting up the night that Gina Campbell was murdered. Something about a young solicitor dying tragically in Jedburgh? They were all such different characters. It seemed odd that it could have welded them together to that extent. Could there have been more to it than that? It was a long shot but she made a note to look into it further. She glanced at her watch. It was nearly 6 p.m. Where the hell was Farrell? He should have been back before now.

She slipped out her phone and pressed speed dial.

'Frank, it's nearly six. If you're planning to take the briefing you'd better get a wiggle on.'

She stood up, her face draining of colour. Hurriedly, she left the room, watched by a curious DC Thomson.

Once safely in the corridor, she hissed.

'Have you been drinking? You visited Laura? Have you taken leave of your senses? Look, save it! I don't have time for this ... Where are you? Right, I'll come straight there after the briefing ... Stay put!'

She ended the call and slumped against the wall, fatigue rolling over her.

He'd obviously caused some kind of scene at Laura's house. Before Lind's catastrophic injury on their last case, Farrell had been one of the most conscientious officers she'd ever come across. Now, without his faith to anchor him, he seemed to be hell-bent on self-destruction. He'd never blown off a briefing in all the time she'd known him.

It was already six. She threw her shoulders back and marched along to the briefing, her heart hammering.

'Fake it till you make it,' she muttered as she threw open the door.

As she walked to the front and cleared her throat the room grew silent. She noticed that DS Byers was also absent.

'DI Farrell has an appointment so asked me to take this briefing. We've made some progress today,' she announced. 'We've ascertained that another member of the local Bar, Gabriel Ferrante, was having an affair with Gina Campbell.'

'Does he have an alibi?' asked PC Rosie Green.

'No. He claims he was going to meet her at her home at 9 p.m., but there was no answer, so he left.'

'So he could possibly be our killer?' said DI Moore.

'Yes,' said Mhairi. 'It's impossible to determine whether his apparent candour is a sign of innocence or part of his defence strategy. Maybe she tried to dump him and he lost control?'

'I read DI Farrell's notes from the post-mortem,' said DC Thomson. 'Bartle-White reckons that the knife recovered at the scene wasn't the murder weapon. Could we get a search warrant for Gabriel Ferrante's house and office based on his admission?'

'Possibly,' said Mhairi. 'There are pros and cons to doing that at this stage. Fergus Campbell claims that he had no idea that his wife was having an affair. His alibi is a bit leaky despite the best efforts of his friends.

'Another avenue of enquiry should be the nanny, Jane Pearson,' she went on. 'She clearly loathed Gina Campbell and was the last person we know of to see the dead woman alive. She also seems very cosy with Fergus, who comes across as a bit of a prickly pear.'

'They could even be in it together,' said DI Moore.

'Exactly,' said Mhairi. 'Have you heard anything back from your contacts in organized crime?' she asked.

'No, not yet. It's a bit early for that. I'll keep pushing, though.'

'PC Green, how are you getting along as FLO? Do you have any insights to share with the team at present?'

'To be honest, I've been struggling a bit to win their trust. Fergus Campbell shuts down whenever I call on him. I get the feeling he's just itching to show me the door.'

'Try and get the nanny, Jane Pearson, on board,' said Mhairi. 'I'd frame it as concern about Fergus and the kids. That might appeal to her. Maybe take the little boy a small toy or something.'

'It seems so ... calculating,' said PC Green, doubt written all over her face.

'If you feel the role is too challenging we can appoint someone else?' snapped Mhairi.

'No, it's fine, I didn't mean ...' stuttered PC Green, her cheeks reddening.

'Good. That's it for now,' said Mhairi, already ashamed of her harsh words. She was so worried about Farrell she couldn't bear to stay at the station a minute longer than she had to. He was skating on thin ice already. The last thing he needed was for Laura to put in a complaint about him harassing her.

She was almost out the door when she felt a light hand tap her on the shoulder from behind. She spun around ready to snap, but it was DI Moore, looking as worried as she felt.

Mhairi stepped to one side with her until the others had left.

'There's something I need to tell you,' said DI Moore. 'Laura Lind has been seeing DS Byers. In fact, he's recently moved in with her.'

Mhairi leaned against the wall for support.

She knew that DI Moore, despite her aloof exterior, was as fond of Farrell as she was and could therefore be trusted.

'He went to visit her this afternoon. I gather it didn't go well. He phoned me from the pub. I'm heading there now before he digs himself into an even deeper hole,' said Mhairi.

'Call me if you need any help,' said DI Moore. 'There's something else you should know, if you don't already.'

'What's that?'

'He and Laura used to be involved a long time ago. He left her behind when he went off to the seminary.'

'He told you this?' asked Mhairi, trying not to show how hurt she was that he had never shared this information with her. This was even worse than she had imagined.

'No. Laura did, when the twins went missing a few years ago. I never told anyone. But given today's events, I think you need to know.'

'Thanks, I'd best go and find him.'

As Mhairi left the station she saw a sight that filled her with dread. Moira Sharkey, tabloid journalist and bane of their lives, was walking into the police station. Her stooped posture and long beaky nose were unmistakable. The vultures were starting to circle. She put her head down and marched along the street.

Chapter 20

Farrell sat slumped at a small table in the corner of the Pig and Whistle. It was tacky with beer and the carpet was scarred with cigarette burns. The pub was a dive and mainly used by those down on their luck and needing to drown their sorrows in a vat of beer. The misery hung in the air like a toxic cloud. Tonight, he felt completely at home. Knocking back the whisky chaser, he smacked his lips together as the fiery amber liquid burned its way to his stomach. His life had been one long struggle to get to this point and what did he have to show for it? A poxy flat in Glasgow. A lost vocation and a career that no longer satisfied him. As if that wasn't enough, the only two women he'd ever loved were lost to him for ever. He raised his pint and gulped greedily, desperate to silence the scathing voice in his head. Had he taken his lithium this morning? He couldn't remember and was past caring.

'Is this a pity party for one or can anyone join in?' asked Mhairi, making him jump and almost drop his glass. Damn, he'd forgotten she was on her way. He winced as he saw himself through her eyes, a washed-up has-been that was becoming a liability. She seemed to be swaying from side to side but then he realized that was him.

'Seriously, Frank, I know that you're upset but you have to get a grip. You need to accept that Laura has done her best for John but now needs to move on. It's been nearly two years. There's nothing more they can do for him. There's nothing more any of us can do for him. John would be the last person who would want Laura to spend the rest of her life alone.'

'And I haven't been there for her? Is that what you're trying to say?' he snapped, thumping his beer down so hard some slopped on to the table. The barman slid a look in their direction and made a move as if to come over, but Mhairi shook her head at him.

'I know why you've given her a wide berth. You were too scared that you'd be tempted to fill John's shoes yourself.'

'That's ridiculous,' he scoffed.

The accusation stung, but he wasn't so drunk that he couldn't recognize the truth in it. As if he needed to feel more guilty than he already did.

'You're not the only one who misses him.' She reached out and covered his hand with hers. 'But turning to drink isn't the best way to honour his memory. Nor is falling down on the job that he used to take such a pride in.'

He knew she was right.

He stood up, rocking slightly on his heels.

'Come on, let's get out of here. I need some coffee.' He strode away from her, pushed through the pub door and disappeared.

Mhairi thought quickly as she gathered up her stuff from the back of the chair. She could hardly take him home in this state. Yvonne Farrell would lay an egg. Best to grab some coffees from the chippy and head out of town.

As she was leaving, her head turned in the direction of raised voices at the other end of the pub. It was Aaron, Jack Kerr's foster son. He wasn't old enough to be in here drinking. He was sitting with that slightly dodgy young guy, Barry McLeish, from outside the court who was already well-oiled. Their eyes met. Barry lurched out of his seat and came towards her.

'Did your sister end up in the pokie, then?' he asked, grinning lopsidedly.

Her mind went blank then she remembered: Aaron hadn't seen her when she visited his mum, so it might be useful to play along.

'Six months, she got. He's a right ballbreaker that sheriff.'

'Fancy a drink, hen?'

'Maybe another time,' she said. 'Stick your number in my phone. You never know your luck.' She grinned, striving to look like she meant it.

Barry did as she asked then swaggered back to the table.

Mhairi flew out the door before Frank could stagger back in and blow her little scheme to smithereens. She almost collided with a burly man on his way in and muttered an apology, realizing as she swiftly walked on that it had been Joe Capaldi, Gabriel Ferrante's office manager.

Frank was waiting around the corner by her car looking perplexed and slightly less drunk.

'What took you so long?'

'I'll tell you later.'

She opened her car and shoe-horned him into the passenger

seat, chucking all the stuff on it haphazardly into the back. Her next port of call was the chippy on the Whitesands where she bought two fish suppers and a couple of coffees. The smell improved the air quality in her car. She really needed a new air freshener.

Farrell sat quietly, staring out of the window, his gaze unfathomable. Mhairi felt the first beats of a headache pound behind her eyes. As she left the town behind, she wound down the window and sucked the clean country air deep into her lungs. How she missed the scent of the open countryside in Glasgow. She drove for a few miles then parked the car at Mabie Forest. It was still light and the air was balmy, though Mhairi could smell a change in the atmosphere. It felt like a storm might be coming. They walked across the wooden bridge and along the path to a picnic bench in the shade of a giant sequoia tree beside a stream. They sat eating in companionable silence, the scent of the pine forest and the wild flowering garlic adding to the taste.

After he'd finished eating, Farrell turned to her.

'Sorry, Mhairi. I've been a bit of a prat.'

'Don't sweat it, Frank. I know that the last two years haven't been easy. What about getting in touch with Father Murray? You could talk to him about stuff. Religious stuff.'

'I saw him recently. I'm not quite the man he used to know. It's difficult.'

'Give him some credit,' retorted Mhairi. 'I doubt he'll be phased by anything you've got to dish up to him. What about all that prodigal son and Mary Magdalene stuff right there in the Bible?' She said, dredging deep in her memory.

Farrell threw his head back and laughed.

'What's so funny?'

'You are, Mhairi McLeod.'

'Anyway, enough about me. The grease has mopped up the alcohol. My head is back in the game. Tell me about the briefing.'

She filled him in on what he had missed and also her encounter with Barry McLeish. He looked worried.

'I didn't see young Aaron until I'd had a few drinks so I felt I couldn't intervene,' he said. 'He must be only fifteen or so.'

'He was only drinking a Coke or I'd have had to do something,' said Mhairi. 'They'd the remains of a meal on the table as well and McLeish is an adult, so technically no licensing rules were being broken. We've got bigger fish to fry and I didn't want to draw attention to the fact we were coppers. It might be an idea to give Sarah Kerr a heads-up, though.'

The light had almost gone by the time they finished talking and headed back to the car. Yvonne Farrell's neat bungalow was in darkness as Mhairi drew up beside it.

Farrell turned his head and smiled at her, the deep sadness in his eyes made her want to hold him close, but she had determined never to walk across that invisible line. He meant too much to her for that.

'Night, Frank,' she said.

'Night, Mhairi. See you bright and early in the morning.'

She watched him let himself in the door, then drove away, her mood sombre. A flash of lightening lit up the sky as the first bloated drops of rain started to pelt her windscreen. A crack of thunder made her jump as the rain intensified. Hurriedly she turned her car in the direction of her temporary home.

Chapter 21

Farrell groped around blindly in the dark for his phone. It was 5.30 a.m. He grabbed it and swung his legs out of the bed in one fluid movement.

'DS Byers,' snapped the voice. 'There's been another murder.'

'Who?'

'Aaron Kerr, Jack Kerr's foster son. He was found under the Buccleuch Street bridge by a dog walker. He's been stabbed.'

'On my way.'

The nausea that made his stomach churn had nothing to do with the amount of alcohol he had consumed last night and everything to do with the horror and guilt he felt at the possibility their failure to remove Aaron from the pub had somehow cost the lad his life. Both he and Mhairi might be caught up in this investigation. His boss would be less than impressed.

Filled with a sense of urgency, he jumped in the shower, then threw on his clothes and grabbed a banana from the fruit bowl on the way out of the kitchen. It was already light and the dawn chorus was raucous. The storm last night had cleared the air. The morning felt fresh and teeming with life. For Jack and Sarah Kerr it would be the first day that didn't have their cherished foster son in it. Sometimes having a ringside seat at all this suffering felt unbearable.

'I should do you lot for breach of the peace,' he muttered at the birds, as he slid into his old car, which was cleaner than he had left it thanks to the rain.

DS Byers was at the scene, the cordon already in place. He gave him a curt nod. Farrell suited up and joined him on the other side, keeping his distance so that he didn't contaminate the scene. Janet White and Phil Tait were both quietly and efficiently preparing to get to work with all the accoutrements of their trade. Even after all this time, Farrell realized, he still knew very little about them. They had always held themselves apart from the rest of the team. With a grim expression, the duty police surgeon stooped over the body which was sodden from a recent downpour. It had been left propped up against the underside of the bridge among the rubbish like it too was disposable. Police tape cordoned off the area from the few members of the public who might be around at that time of the morning. The elderly woman who had found him was sitting on a nearby bench beside the river with a small dog peering anxiously up at her, wrapped in a blanket and with a paramedic in attendance.

'The witness stated she didn't touch the body,' said Byers. 'It was clear that there was nothing to be done for the lad, so she called it in and waited for us.'

The police surgeon straightened up and came over to them.

'Rory McAllister,' he introduced himself to Farrell. 'Life extinct. Believe it or not, the body is still warm.'

'Cause of death?' asked Farrell.

'There's a stab wound in his side. Beyond that, it will be up to the pathologist to determine.'

The sound of raised voices intruded on the scene echoing under the sandstone bridge.

Farrell retraced his steps to investigate. As he moved from underneath the shadow cast by the bridge, he discovered two uniforms on the edge of the outer cordon embroiled in a fierce struggle with Jack Kerr, whose eyes were red-rimmed and angry. The deserted children's playpark on the grass beyond the cordon served as a stark reminder of what had been lost.

'Let me through, goddammit!' he yelled at Farrell, spittle flying from his mouth.

'You know I can't do that. If the scene is contaminated, the bastard who did this to Aaron could end up walking right out the court. Think about it. Do you want your last memory of Aaron to be seeing him here?'

Kerr stopped struggling and sagged at the knees as the adrenalin started to leave his system.

Farrell nodded at the two officers to release him and gently took Kerr by the arm and walked him over to a picnic bench outside the perimeter.

'I can't believe it,' he said. 'What in hell's name happened?'

'He was stabbed. Not that long ago, either.'

Kerr half rose to his feet and stared around wildly. Farrell tugged him back down.

'The killer's long gone. What do you know about his movements last night? The company he was keeping?'

'My wife, Sarah, will know more about that than I did. I tried to guide him, keep him on the straight and narrow. We fostered him from the age of ten. Maybe by then, the damage had already been done. The care system is brutal. He used to be on his computer constantly so we nagged him to get out more, see his friends. I don't know what we were thinking. Boys are a bloody danger to themselves at that age. We should lock them in a room at fourteen and not let them out until they're twenty-one.'

'He was seen in the Pig and Whistle last night with a man called Barry McLeish,' said Farrell.

'In a pub? Was he drinking?'

'That's yet to be determined.'

'Shit! There's no way the barman should have served him,' he snapped.

'He's been keeping company with a Barry McLeish. Tell me what you know about him,' said Farrell.

'I didn't know he was hanging out with Aaron. He's got a list of priors as long as my arm. Breach of the peace, burglary, reset, a bit of dealing. No violence, though. He's Fergus Campbell's client. You think he's involved?'

'Not necessarily,' said Farrell. 'We're going to be some time here. I suggest you get away home meantime. I'll keep you in the loop as much as I can, I promise,' said Farrell.

Kerr left quietly. His rage would be replaced by the type of grief that could break a man.

Farrell walked over to Mhairi McLeod who had arrived as he'd been talking to Jack Kerr. Their eyes met and he saw that she was as white as a sheet. She moved to one side with him.

'Shit, Frank. That poor kid. We knew he was underage but we did nothing!'

'We did nothing because I was too busy drowning my sorrows,' said Farrell.

'We were off-duty,' said Mhairi.

'I'll mention it to Byers,' said Farrell. 'This is just the type of thing that would give the press a field day.'

'Talking of the press, I saw Moira Sharkey waltzing in to the station yesterday.'

'That's all we need. That woman won't rest until she has my head on a pike for something.'

'Joe Capaldi was entering the pub just as we were leaving,' said Mhairi. 'I wonder who he was planning to meet there?'

'There's something off about that man. My antennae twitched the minute I first laid eyes on him.'

DS Byers approached. 'SOCO will be a while yet. There's no sign of the murder weapon, but I've drafted in uniforms from a number of outlying stations to search the area. DC Thomson is already at the station setting up this new investigation. Since you guys are down anyway, I'll take all the help I can get.'

'You might want to interview Joe Capaldi,' said Mhairi. 'He was in the pub at the same time as the deceased. You might also want to send a couple of constables to bring in Barry McLeish and the barman from the Pig and Whistle.'

'How do you know that?' asked Byers.

Mhairi glanced at Farrell.

'Because we were there too.'

'What the hell were you doing there? It's a total dive. Wait a minute, the dead boy was underage. Tell me you brought that to the attention of the barman?'

Mhairi bit her lip and shook her head.

'Well that's just peachy,' snapped DS Byers. 'I was going to request you be SIO on this case, but that's out the question now you've placed yourself slap bang in the middle of it.'

'It was my fault,' said Farrell. 'At the time the boy was sober and drinking Coke.'

'And you weren't, I take it?'

'I was off-duty. I'm entitled to a life.'

Farrell noticed a big news truck edging along the Whitesands. Byers saw it too and swore.

'Right, I'll wait until SOCO are finished. Are you pair fine to get back to the station and post a briefing for 8 a.m.?'

'Yes,' said Farrell. 'I'll update DCI Buchanan in Glasgow.'

'I'll call in Andy Moran, the civilian press officer, to deal with that lot. Now there's been two separate murders in the area, the press will be all over us.'

Chapter 22

By the time Farrell arrived back at Loreburn Street it was bright sunlight. The golden girl of local TV news, Sophie Richardson, was setting up outside the station, but he managed to dodge her by slipping in the rear entrance.

Taking the stairs two at a time, Farrell headed straight to the MCA room, where Dave Thomson already had fresh coffee brewing. Farrell poured himself a mug and grabbed a Mars Bar from his secret stash. He put one out for Mhairi too as he heard her feet clattering up the stairs. Still looking upset, she took it from him with a nod of thanks.

DI Moore was already hanging stuff about the new case up on the walls and whiteboard. She walked over to Mhairi.

'I gather you and DI Farrell happened to be in the Pig and Whistle last night,' she said as if that fact was stretching her credulity to fresh bounds.

'Yes, we went there after he popped in on Laura,' said Mhairi.

'I see,' she said. 'So you know about Byers, Frank?'

'I do now. Anyway, that's all water under the bridge. We saw Aaron in there, drinking a Coke with one of Fergus

Campbell's clients, a Barry McLeish. The barman didn't seem fussed, so we left it,' said Farrell, his matter-of-fact words belying the guilt twisting his guts like origami.

'That's unfortunate, but you weren't to know. If he'd been turfed out of the pub it probably wouldn't have made a difference.'

There was an awkward pause.

Farrell approached a harassed-looking DC Thomson who was coordinating the flow of information in relation to both cases.

'We need to post a briefing for 8 a.m.,' said Farrell.

'Got it, boss.'

'I'd also like you to do some digging into Joe Capaldi, Gabriel Ferrante's office manager. See if he has any priors. I want whatever background you can get.'

'Jack Kerr and his pals are sure as hell unlucky,' said DC Thomson.

'What do you mean?' said Farrell.

'Well, death seems to follow them wherever they go. That girl who burned to death ten years ago. Then Fergus Campbell's wife was murdered and now Jack Kerr's son has met a similar fate. That only leaves Max Delaney unscathed, doesn't it?'

'So it would seem,' Farrell replied. Could there really be a link between all these disparate cases?

He turned on his heel, went up to the Super's office and tapped lightly on the door. It was still before seven, so he was pleased to find Crawford Cunningham already installed behind his desk looking like he'd been there for some time.

'DI Farrell,' he said in the cut-glass public school accent which sounded so alien in these parts. 'Come in, man, come in. Another murder, eh? What's DCI Buchanan saying about that? Is she planning to send down another MIT team or additional resources?'

'I'm going to speak to her as soon as I'm done here, sir. I suspect she won't be able to spare much in the way of bodies. One possibility that occurred to me is that Ronnie Stirling might be persuaded out of retirement to join us as a consultant. He's got some serious experience in major crimes. I could also do with a couple of bright constables to boost our manpower.'

'I'll see what I can do. Sounds like you're planning on being here a while.'

'As long as it takes, sir. Make no mistake, though, I'm as keen to return to Glasgow as you'll be to have your station back to normal.'

'We understand each other then. I have a couple of uniforms in mind. I'll get them seconded.'

Farrell noticed a picture on the bookcase depicting a school class photo.

'I see you went to Morrington Academy, sir. Jack Kerr went there too.'

'He did? Well, that does rather surprise me. Must have been a scholarship boy. There were a couple in every year, poor blighters.'

'Why do you say that, sir?'

'Don't get me wrong, it was a wonderful opportunity for them. Jack Kerr is clearly one of the success stories. However, some of the more objectionable parents didn't like it. Said if they wanted their kids to mix with riff-raff, they'd have sent them to a state school. There were some bad cases of bullying over the years.'

'The press is converging outside. Sophie Richardson and Moira Sharkey are particularly persistent. Are you going to schedule a press conference, sir?'

'Not yet. I've instructed Andy Moran to release a brief statement saying as little as possible. It won't stop them attempting to whip the public into a frenzy, though.'

Farrell retreated to his office and video-called DCI Buchanan in Glasgow.

'DI Farrell,' the brisk no-nonsense voice of his superior came over the link.

'Morning, ma'am. I take it you've heard about the second murder?'

'Yes. Two stabbings in such a short time frame is most unusual in Dumfries. I gather, though tenuous, there is a possible link between them?'

'Yes. Both are close family of two local criminal defence solicitors and both were stabbed but we've yet to recover the knife used.'

'How soon can the post-mortem be arranged?'

'I'm hoping later today. The pathologist here is Roland Bartle-White. He can be a bit touchy. Sandy Gillespie is travelling back down from Glasgow to assist.'

'Would you like me to call this Bartle-White character. Put a hustle on him?'

Farrell winced at the likely response from Bartle-White.

'Thanks, but I can handle him.'

'Are you all right for manpower? I'd send down another team, but we're stretched a bit thin as it is.'

'I reckon Mhairi, Dave and I have it covered. DI Moore and DS Byers are extremely competent and the new Super seems fairly receptive. I might need you to put the squeeze on for lab results from time to time. For example, we still don't have Gina Campbell's toxicology results.'

'You want me to be your muscle, DI Farrell?' she said with a combative gleam in her eye.

'Something like that.'

'Happy to oblige. I've sourced a flat for the three of you to live meantime. It's the most cost-effective solution.'

Farrell hesitated. He was keen to get out from under his mother's feet, but living with Mhairi? He wasn't sure.

'DI Farrell?'

'Yes, ma'am. That should be fine.'

'Keep me posted,' she said, terminating the connection.

Chapter 23

The small lecture room was bursting at the seams and there were a host of unfamiliar faces. The Super had clearly made good on his promise to scare up some more bodies to help out on the two investigations.

Farrell cleared his throat and the room fell silent.

'We now have two local criminal defence lawyers who have suffered the murder of a close family member.'

A hand went up. Farrell nodded at the young PC.

'PC Joanne Burns, sir. Wasn't Aaron Sullivan simply being fostered?'

'Yes, but there were adoption proceedings in hand. These two murders may be unrelated, but despite the differing victims there could well be a link between them.

'So far, we haven't been able to uncover any eye witnesses to this morning's murder, which isn't surprising given the secluded nature of the kill site. The victim was stabbed and we've yet to recover the knife. After the briefing, I'd like those of you not already tasked to join DS Byers in a search for the missing weapon.

'Aaron Sullivan attended Bruce Academy. I need someone

to go to the school and speak to his head of year, get a feel for the type of crowd he was hanging out with and identify anyone at the school he was particularly close to. PC Green?'

'Yes, sir. I'll get right on it.'

'DC Thomson, did you find us any information relating to the death of that young solicitor in Jedburgh ten years ago?'

'Yes, sir, I have the case summary here.'

There was a quick murmur of interest round the room.

'The reason I asked for this is that it seems to have been responsible for the strong bond between the solicitors whose families are now being attacked. The night that Fergus Campbell's wife was murdered was the ten-year anniversary of her death. It may be completely unrelated or the anniversary could have served as a trigger.'

DC Thomson cleared his throat. 'Colette Currie was a twenty-five-year-old solicitor who was in Jedburgh along with the other three to represent one of four accused in charges involving a breach of the peace. The three males were staying in a guest house opposite the court, but Miss Currie was staying in a cottage on the outskirts of town. During the night the property was destroyed by fire. Colette Currie didn't make it out alive.

'She was discovered near the door, but for some reason, hadn't managed to open it and get out. It was thought she'd been confused and disoriented. Her blood alcohol level was high and there were trace amounts of cannabis as well as ecstasy found in her system. It was ruled to be a tragic accident. I'm obtaining the reports and analysis from the fire authority.'

'Who benefitted from the insurance on the house?' asked Farrell.

'The estate of the late Judith Fox. She was a spinster, so her estate went to her nephew, Peter Swift. He was Colette's fiancé, which is why she ended up staying there. It wasn't worth a whole lot so unlikely to be a motive in itself for murder.'

'What did the three men have to say about it at the time?' asked Farrell.

'They claimed to be devastated and told the police they'd been playing poker together at their lodgings.'

'Interesting,' said Farrell, feeling a twinge of unease that they'd trotted out the same alibi then too.

'Barry McLeish is still in the wind,' he went on. 'We have a team of uniforms out interviewing all known associates and places he might be hiding out.'

'I have his cell number in my phone,' said Mhairi, remembering. There were a few titters that made her scowl. 'Here it is,' she said, handing it to DC Thomson.

'In the meantime, the barman at the Pig and Whistle has been picked up. DI Moore, would you like to do the honours on that one along with DC Thomson?'

She nodded.

'DI Moore, has Gina Campbell's father identified any additional suspects in relation to his daughter's murder?'

'He said he couldn't think of anyone, but I'm not sure whether I believed him,' she said. 'I hate to muddy the waters even more, but it looks like Gina Campbell's father didn't move down here to retire. My contact in organized crime has sent me an extensive file. He's been charged multiple times over the years but nothing ever stuck,' she said.

'What types of crimes are we talking about?' asked Farrell.

'Extortion and drugs, mainly.'

'What a charmer,' said Mhairi.

'He deals in information,' said Moore. 'He's rumoured to have compiled dossiers on most of the power brokers in Scotland. Here's the interesting bit: they reckon Gina Campbell may have worked hand in glove with her father over the years.'

'So, if she was instrumental in blackmailing someone it could have got her killed,' said Farrell.

'Or, she might have had a little extortion scheme of her own going on,' said Mhairi.

'Lots to think about there,' said Farrell. 'And now, I'd like those of you who are helping with the search for the knife to head towards the Whitesands, near the toilets. DS Byers will meet and brief you there.'

Everyone filed out, leaving him with DI Moore, DC Thomson and Mhairi.

'Dave, I'll need you in the MCA room to coordinate both investigations. Try and get a location for Barry McLeish's mobile phone. I'm not sure yet if he's running scared or if he's a guilty party. I've requested that Ronnie Stirling be approached to assist as a consultant, which would free you up to help us with the legwork.'

DC Thomson's face brightened at the prospect.

'His Vera will have your guts for garters,' said Mhairi. 'We'll never hear the end of it.'

Chapter 24

Farrell and Mhairi swung by the Sheriff Court first, nodding to Bob, the Bar officer as they went in search of Max Delaney or Fergus Campbell. To their surprise they found all three of the lawyers huddled in a corner of the agents' room, engaged in a heated conversation.

The fiscal, Peter Swift, was sitting at the table, deeply engrossed in a large file of papers, a look of intense concentration on his face.

They all glanced up as Farrell and Mhairi walked in.

Jack Kerr rose to his feet expectantly.

'Sorry, I'm afraid we have no more news for you at the moment,' Farrell said.

'Then why are you here?' he asked, his face white and strained.

'We came in search of your two colleagues. Is there no one who can cover your cases today?' asked Farrell.

'It's best if I keep busy. It seems less real that way.'

Max clapped an arm on his friend's shoulder.

'Don't worry, officer, we'll keep him right.'

Peter Swift looked up from his files. 'Hey, if you guys

need an adjournment for any trials or other issues, I'll do what I can. Sheriff Granger, on the other hand, I can't answer for.'

'Cheers,' said Jack Kerr, 'I appreciate that.'

'What are you all doing down here anyway?' said Mhairi. 'Shouldn't court have started?'

'The sheriff had something to deal with in chambers,' said Max Delaney. 'It wasn't on the list, but the clerk wasn't about to argue with him.'

'There's something I need to talk to the three of you about anyway,' said Farrell. He glanced apologetically at Peter Swift who good naturedly took the hint, gathered up his files and left the room.

'We're somewhat concerned that two out of three of you have had someone close to you harmed, possibly by the same perpetrator.'

'You think it's the same person?' said Fergus Campbell.

'We have to consider that possibility,' said Farrell.

Max went pale.

'You think my wife or daughter could be next,' he stated.

'I'd rather err on the side of caution. We're going to send someone round to advise on enhancing your home security.'

'Why would someone target us?' asked Fergus Campbell, clearly puzzled. 'It makes no sense.'

Farrell walked over and closed the door. Then he sat down at the large table with Mhairi and motioned to the three men to join him.

'Could it relate to what happened in Jedburgh?' he said.

All three men glanced at each other uneasily.

'You know about that?' said Fergus Campbell. He broke eye contact and looked away.

'Is it possible that someone blames you three for what happened to your friend, Colette?'

'How could they?' asked Max Delaney. 'It wasn't our fault. The fire was ruled to be accidental.'

'Tell us exactly what happened that night, every little bit of it,' said Mhairi.

They all shifted uneasily in their seats, avoiding eye contact with them and each other.

It was Max Delaney who broke the sudden silence.

'Am I correct in assuming you aren't interested in any youthful transgressions, DI Farrell?'

'I'm only interested in solving these murders and preventing any more. That trumps anything else in my book.'

'Come on, you guys, they could be coming for my wife or little girl next,' pleaded Max Delaney.

'Fine,' sighed Jack Kerr. 'We'd been stuck in the back of beyond for two weeks doing a piss-boring trial with multiple accused.'

'Can you remember their names?' asked Mhairi.

'Mine was Scott Murray,' said Kerr.

'Kyle Rogers,' said Delaney.

'Danny Heaton,' added Campbell.

'And Colette Currie's client?'

'Barry McLeish,' added Fergus Campbell. 'He's my client now. He was a first offender back then, only sixteen.'

'Are the others you mentioned still kicking around?' asked Farrell.

'Scott Murray is dead, drugs overdose,' said Kerr.

'Danny Heaton left the area years ago,' supplied Campbell.

'Kyle Rogers is serving a stretch in Barlinnie for armed robbery,' stated Delaney.

'Walk me through what you did after leaving the court that day,' said Farrell to Max Delaney.

'It was the back of four when we got out,' said Max Delaney. 'We headed back to our digs to get changed and dump our files then met Colette at the pub. We had a couple of beers there but then left because our clients, who'd been allowed bail for the night, pitched up and started taking the piss.'

'Then?' asked Farrell, noticing that the other two were looking increasingly tense.

'We went for a meal at the local Italian, got some booze and headed back to Colette's cottage.'

He too started to look on edge.

'And then?'

'We downed some drinks and headed back to the guest house before midnight. Then we played a few hands of poker there before turning in. We didn't find out what had happened until we pitched up at court the next morning.'

'What happened to your clients?' said Mhairi.

'We were all in shock, including the clients. Barry McLeish was in tears when he heard. Even the sheriff seemed upset. I reckon he'd been going to convict them, but he just came on and pronounced them not guilty like he couldn't get off the

Bench fast enough. They were free to walk. It hit everyone real hard.'

'Why was she staying in a cottage and not staying with you guys at the guesthouse?' asked Mhairi.

'The cottage belonged to Peter Swift's aunt. She'd died recently so it was empty.'

'He wasn't in Jedburgh for the trial?' asked Farrell.

'No, he was working down here by then. It took him a long time to get over it,' said Jack Kerr.

'The toxicology report highlighted that she'd consumed a lot of alcohol as well as cannabis and ecstasy,' said Farrell.

They looked at each other, clearly uncomfortable. Delaney, as ever, was their spokesman.

'We couldn't possibly comment on that. Like I said, officers, we were young at the time.'

'Which one of you was the last to see her alive?'

'That would be me,' said Jack Kerr, his eyes on the floor, a slight flush spreading across his face. 'I popped back into her room to check she was OK and didn't want one of us to stay with her that night.'

His two friends looked at him. This was clearly news to them.

The door opened suddenly making Mhairi jump. It was Peter Swift.

'Sorry to interrupt, the sheriff's about to come on the Bench.'

All three men jumped to their feet, gathered up their files and followed him out of the room.

'That was intense,' said Mhairi, rubbing her neck.

'It's obvious that Colette Currie and Jack Kerr were more

than just friends, but whether it started that same night or had been going on before they went there, I can't say.'

'I'm not sure the others knew until now,' said Mhairi. 'You really think that this might be the key to these murders?'

'I can't yet rule it out,' said Farrell.

Chapter 25

PC Rosie Green pulled into the car park at Bruce Academy. Although it was only mid-morning she already felt her cotton shirt sticking to her back. She removed her sunglasses and headed for reception. These investigations were growing arms and legs. Her husband had been moaning he hardly saw her these days, but she paid no attention. Her plan was to make herself invaluable to the investigating team, so that she could be Glasgow-bound herself. If her husband couldn't handle that, well, she might have to leave him behind. It would maybe be different if they'd been able to have kids but, as it stood, she'd no intention of languishing in Dumfries.

Once she was registered and attired with the obligatory visitor pass she didn't have long to wait before being claimed by Mr Layden, the guidance teacher she had come to see.

Sitting across from her in a hot, stuffy room not much bigger than the size of a cupboard, she noticed that he looked genuinely affected by Aaron's death.

'I still can't quite believe it,' he said, sitting back in his chair. 'A young life snuffed out in the blink of an eye.'

'What was Aaron like as a pupil?' she asked.

129

'Don't get me wrong, he could have a bit of a temper on him, but most of the time he was just a regular kid. He was smart but at pains to hide it sometimes. He wanted to fit in with his friends, which was probably a bit of a survival mechanism after being bounced around in care when he was younger. The crowd he hung with were fairly rough diamonds. I guess he felt more comfortable around them given the home he came from originally.'

'Was there any contact with his birth family?'

'No. His mother died from a drug overdose before he entered care. His father scarpered when she was pregnant. He had a great home with the Kerr family. I don't know Jack well but Sarah was very involved in the life of the school.'

'Can you think of any recent problems he had with anyone here? Any bad fallout with another kid? Girl trouble?'

'No, nothing like that. His work had fallen away a bit in recent months and he'd become a bit more mouthy with a few of the teachers, but he was a teenage boy so that was all fairly par for the course. No red flags as far as the school was concerned.'

'Did he have a best friend? Someone he was especially close to?'

'He did. A lad called George McLeish. They were inseparable until he contracted meningitis six months ago. Dead within the week. It affected Aaron badly.'

'McLeish? I don't suppose you know whether George had a big brother called Barry?'

'Yes, he did. He came through the school as well. Always in trouble of one sort or another. No real badness in him, though, and he always had a twinkle in his eye. Both lads came from quite a volatile home environment.'

'Did Aaron have a locker at the school?'

'Yes, all the kids do.'

'Can you open it for me?'

'I shouldn't really,' he said.

'Aaron was murdered. It could provide crucial evidence. I could come back with a search warrant, but it will only delay matters further.'

'Very well, come with me.'

The corridors were quiet as they walked through the school, hearing snatches of lessons leaking out from the classrooms.

Mr Layden paused in front of Aaron's locker and inserted the key. The inside of the door was personalized with gig tickets. PC Green felt a lump in her throat at the thought Aaron had opened it up only yesterday, not realizing it would be his last day alive and that these tiny trophies would be among the final traces of his existence.

She gloved up before examining the contents. In it was a clean gym kit, folders, jotters and a maths text book. There was also a schoolbag which she would have thought should have gone home with him yesterday. She unzipped it and peered in. Her heart started pounding as she realized that she was probably staring at wraps of cocaine with a street value of well over two thousand pounds.

Chapter 26

Farrell and Mhairi grabbed two coffees from The Waterfront and took them across to a bench overlooking the river where they couldn't be overheard. A couple of swans glided serenely past and the seagulls whooped and plunged all around them. Mhairi slipped her jacket off and turned her white face up to the sun like a plant seeking salvation. Farrell lit a cigarette, and she wrinkled her nose in distaste.

'Frank Farrell, when are you going to give up that disgusting habit?'

He inhaled deeply as though he was trying to drag every last molecule of nicotine into his lungs.

'You sound like my mother.'

She thumped him on the arm.

'Don't ever say that to me again.'

He grinned at her then turned to look out over the sparkling waters of the River Nith which ran through the town.

'Can I ask you something?'

'Like I could stop you,' he retorted.

'Do you feel happier now you've turned your back on the Church?'

133

He froze. She bit her lip and pressed on. 'I mean now you're smoking, boozing, fornicating ...'

His startled eyes met hers.

'Just kidding. That got your attention.'

'Mhairi, I don't think it's any of your—'

'It's just that you don't seem happier to me. I admit I never had much time for God myself, but you were different. It lit you up.'

'Like Ready Brek,' he said, always one to deflect with a joke.

'Something like that.' She smiled. Oh, what was the use? It was like trying to pry open a clam. Some things were just too broken to fix.

Farrell glanced at his watch.

'Right then, time to head for the mortuary. Don't say I never take you anywhere nice.'

Mhairi groaned.

She was dreading this one. Post-mortems were bad enough but this time it was a kid.

Once suitably attired they walked through to join Roland Bartle-White. Sandy Gillespie was also in attendance, but there would be no jokes today. As his serious eyes met hers, Mhairi nodded. He looked as sad as she felt about the violent death of a young lad who had barely started living.

The young pathologist removed the sheet and Mhairi tensed. She took an involuntary step closer but retreated when Bartle-White held up his hand.

'Is that a Panopticon tattoo on his hip?' she asked.

'It is indeed,' Bartle-White replied. 'Done relatively recently, I should think.'

A digital image of the tattoo was taken by Sandy Gillespie and the two men completed their painstaking external physical examination before turning to the stab wound.

'As expected, cause of death is one incision but inflicted with enough force to penetrate the spleen. He would have bled out in minutes,' said Bartle-White into his Dictaphone.

'Can you determine whether the same knife stabbed Gina Campbell and Aaron Sullivan?' asked Farrell.

Roland Bartle-White straightened and stared at them with his chilly grey eyes. He got annoyed when they interrupted his flow, but he had to understand this was a murder investigation not a lecture hall.

'I am not engaged in the realm of speculation, DI Farrell. It is impossible to say without having the actual knife employed. However, I can say that if it wasn't that knife, it would likely be a fairly similar one in terms of size and blade. Will that suffice?'

'Any sign of drug use?' asked Farrell.

Bartle-White straightened up after a few minutes.

'None that I can see. No obvious signs such as track marks or injection sites. No sign of damage to the nasal membranes. Perhaps he hadn't gone that far yet. Toxicology might throw some light on that. I'll also test some of his hair, which can give a fairly accurate indication, not only of what he ingested but how long ago.'

Despite the temperature-controlled chill, sweat trickled and pooled down at the base of Mhairi's back. The room began to sway a little. The smell of formaldehyde and blood was overpowering. She swallowed and excused herself under the pretext of having a call to make.

Once outside, she sat on a wooden bench and took several deep breaths until the nausea subsided. Despite the beauty of the morning she felt wretched. Was there no end to the pain and suffering around her? Maybe she should take a leaf out of Farrell's book and become a nun, join a contemplative order. She imagined wafting about in gilded serenity. Then she thought of the unflattering headgear and sensible shoes. Not a chance. She was still smiling to herself when Sandy Gillespie rushed out the door she had just come through, his brows creased in worry.

'Oh, there you are.' He sounded relieved, as he sat beside her. 'Are you all right? I didn't quite buy the phone-call thing.'

'Sorry to be a walking cliché,' she smiled. 'I've attended loads of these. It just got to me because it was a kid. That and the smell.'

'Not to mention Bartle-White droning on in his boring monotone.'

'I don't know how you stand it day in and day out.'

'That's only one part of the job. I find pathology fascinating, a bit like being a detective but all your clues are in one place. I think your job's far harder. Dealing with people who are alive? No thanks. Give me a nice juicy corpse any day of the week.'

'You do know who you're talking to, right? Next thing you'll be telling me you live with your mother.'

'Er, I do live with my mother.' He looked away.

Mhairi felt her skin flush. Her and her big mouth.

He turned back to her with a grin.

'Just kidding.'

'You're as bad as Frank Farrell.' She glared at him.

'I choose to take that as a compliment,' he said, getting up. 'Well, I'd best get back in. I'll see you around. If you have any questions or you'd like to meet up sometime for a drink, here's my card.'

Mhairi took it dumbfounded. The cheek of the man! It didn't stop the small smile twitching at the corner of her lips.

She had no intention of calling him. However, she placed it carefully in her jacket pocket, just in case she had some burning question on forensics that needed answering.

Keep telling yourself that, Mhairi, whispered the annoying little voice in her head that sounded eerily similar to her mother.

Taking a deep breath she followed him back in.

Chapter 27

They headed gratefully out into the sunlight after the post-mortem. There had been no further insights gained, pending the remaining results coming through, which wouldn't be for some time yet.

'I think you've got a fan there,' said Farrell, shooting her a sideways glance.

'Bartle-White? I think he's a bit old for me,' she said.

'You know perfectly well who I mean.'

'Oh,' she said, pulling his card out of her pocket and waving it at him. 'You mean Dr Sandy Gillespie?'

'He didn't waste much time. Are you going to meet up with him?'

'Nosey much?'

'Sorry, none of my business. He seems harmless enough, if you like inane chatter.'

'I must do or I wouldn't be partnered with you,' she snapped.

Farrell's face tightened but he said nothing further.

'What on earth is the deal with that Panopticon tattoo?' asked Mhairi, keen to get back on to safer ground, as they

139

got into the roasting hot Citroen. She quickly opened the windows before they became mummified corpses themselves.

'It's so creepy,' she went on. 'The idea that someone is watching you all the time and knows everything you're up to. Of course, I'm sure that the watcher would find some of us a little lacking in excitement,' she said.

He turned to her, startled.

'What did you just say?'

'I was only joking,' she said, glancing at him.

'No, not that, I meant "the watcher". Do you think that's what it is? He's watching them and stalking them like a voyeur?'

Mhairi shuddered.

'God, I hope not. Could the tattoo be a gang thing?'

'Possibly.'

'It could just be the latest fad,' said Mhairi.

'True, maybe we're reading too much into it,' said Farrell. 'We need to canvas any local tattoo shops, and if it's a current fad or fashion, they'll be able to tell us.'

As they drew near the Kerr household they could see that the street had been overrun by public school media types rushing around with cables and furry microphones and hair that didn't move in the breeze. One of these unlovely creatures was shouting through the letterbox.

Farrell leapt out the car, with Mhairi at his heels, and roared at the spotty youth with the slicked back hair and no manners.

'What do you think you're playing at? Get back to the pavement before I charge you with a breach of the peace. Move it!' he yelled looking sufficiently wild-eyed and unpredictable for the suit to decide discretion was the better part of valour and leg it down the path.

It would not keep them at bay for long.

Farrell rang the doorbell and himself shouted through the letterbox, the irony not lost on him.

'Sarah, it's DI Farrell and DS McLeod. Can you let us in?'

For an awful moment they thought she wasn't going to and they would have to beat a humiliating retreat, but the door opened a crack and her white face peered out. This triggered a burst of camera flashes from frustrated journalists. She admitted them and quickly slammed the door, sliding the chain across.

'Those bastards have been here all morning,' she shouted. 'They're doing my head in. Can't you make them leave or something?'

The phone was lying in bits on the floor after she'd clearly thrown it against the wall in a fit of rage.

Farrell felt bad for her. They should have foreseen this. Trouble was they were severely overstretched.

'I'll get a Family Liaison Officer over and an officer to stand guard at your gate,' he said.

Mhairi took out her phone and walked into the hall.

'Thank you. Sorry. It's all been a bit much,' she said, collapsing onto the sofa. 'I've been up all night. Aaron stormed out again yesterday. After you two had gone I'd got on at him about his exams, how he had to work harder if he wanted to get on in life. If I'd only known that would be our last conversation.' She broke down in tears.

Farrell felt helpless in the face of her grief.

Mhairi came back in. She sat beside Sarah and enfolded her hand in two of her own.

'PC Joanne Burns is on her way along with another officer to prevent access by the press.' She glanced at Farrell. He nodded.

'PC Rosie Green went to the school this morning to gain access to Aaron's locker. There was a backpack inside.'

She showed Sarah a picture on her phone.

'Have you ever seen this before?'

Sarah looked.

'Yes, but it's not his schoolbag, it's just an old one he uses for going to the gym or to stay with a mate.'

'There's no easy way to say this, but I'm afraid it was full of drugs,' said Mhairi.

'What? That's impossible! They can't have been his.'

Farrell and Mhairi said nothing, allowing the information to sink in.

'What kind of drugs?' she whispered after a few moments.

'We won't know for sure until tests have been carried out,' said Mhairi. 'But it looks like cocaine.'

'I'd like to search his bedroom, if you don't mind,' said Farrell. 'We're also going to need to remove any electronic devices or computers.'

'Do what you have to, DI Farrell. It's up the stairs and first on the left.'

'Is there anyone I can call for you?' asked Mhairi.

'My husband should be here,' she said with a tinge of bitterness. 'He always manages to put his clients before his family. Our son was dealing drugs? How could we have missed this?'

'I'm sure your husband will get away just as soon as he can,' said Mhairi, giving her hand a squeeze before getting to her feet.

'Oh, one more thing. Did you know that your son had a tattoo?'

'No, I didn't. What kind of tattoo?'

Mhairi showed her an identical image of the one from the post-mortem.

Sarah shook her head and shrugged.

'It means nothing to me. Hardly seems to matter now, does it?' Her lips pressed tightly together to avoid crying.

Aaron Kerr's bedroom showed that he wanted for nothing. There was an expensive laptop sitting on a study desk and the latest games console with a good selection of games beside it. The wardrobe was well-stocked with all the latest teenage gear.

Farrell groped along the high shelves and on top for anything concealed from prying eyes. Mhairi crouched down and raked about carefully on the bottom of the wardrobe and under the bed, pulling everything out to examine it. Together, they lifted the mattress and extracted some computer magazines.

'At least it's not porn,' she said.

'All that stuff is online nowadays,' said Farrell. 'Or so I'm led to believe.'

Mhairi was about to put them back when a twenty pound note fluttered to the floor. Farrell replaced the mattress and she carefully flicked through the magazines. They were stuffed with well-pressed twenty pound notes.

'I reckon we've found his drug money,' said Farrell.

They bagged up the computer and games console and also removed the magazines.

By the time they returned downstairs, PC Joanne Burns was installed and a bulky uniform was stationed outside the front gate looking suitably menacing.

Farrell took a moment to show Sarah the magazines and the money contained within. Given her husband's occupation he didn't want any suggestion that he had planted evidence to rear its head.

Sarah Kerr shook her head in disbelief.

'But there's hundreds of pounds there. What did he need all that money for? It's not as though we kept him short. He could've come to us if he was in trouble.'

'I'm hoping that once our techs get into his computer and social media accounts we'll get a better idea of what was going on,' said Farrell.

'You mustn't blame yourself,' said Mhairi. 'Teenage boys his age are notoriously secretive.'

144

Chapter 28

It was hot and stuffy in the interview room. Farrell and Mhairi stared at the barman from the Pig and Whistle. Hamish McTaggart was a thickset, mulish man in his late forties with a gut that strained against the buttons of his polyester shirt. He folded his arms defensively.

The two detectives glanced at each other in frustration. This guy was absolutely determined not to play ball. Talk about hear no evil, see no evil.

Farrell leaned across the table and stopped the tape.

'Interview suspended at 14.06.'

'Look, Hamish, I get that you're no fan of the police. However, a young lad of fifteen lost his life last night, so I'm at a loss to understand why you won't tell us what happened.'

The man shifted in his seat. 'That was nothing to do with me. I know what you coppers are like. I open my mouth, you'll be charging me with all sorts.'

'Look, if you're simply worried about serving someone underage, then I can take that off the table right now. When I saw the lad he was quiet and sober. Murder trumps underage drinking. Answer our questions fully and we can guarantee no criminal charge for that.'

'Equally,' said Mhairi, 'if you choose to hinder our investigation we've got no reason to do you a favour.'

'I don't give a toss about that. It was before 8 p.m. and the lad was in with an adult having a meal. It's not as though I served him alcohol.'

'What's your problem then?' said Farrell.

'Some proper hardmen come in the boozer. If word gets back to them I've been squealing to you lot, I'm going to be in far more trouble than you can dish out.'

'Names?'

'Not a chance,' he scoffed.

'Look at it this way,' said Farrell. 'Whoever you're worried about is bound to realize we'd haul you in for questioning. If you cooperate we'll make sure the source can't be traced back to you. If you don't ...? Well, we'll just shrug our shoulders and who knows what conclusions they'll jump to?'

'Fine, but I don't know what I can tell you.' Hamish ran a sweaty hand through his thinning hair.

Farrell switched on the tape.

'Interview resumed, 14.09. How many times had Aaron Sullivan been in the Pig and Whistle while you were working there?'

'About half a dozen. He showed me ID. Not my fault if it was fake.'

'How often did he come in and who did he meet there?'

'He was in every Friday for the last few weeks. He always

met up with Barry McLeish. He's one of the regulars. I never saw him talking to anyone else.'

'What about Joe Capaldi?'

'What about him?'

'Well, the night that Aaron died, Joe Capaldi was in the pub too.'

'So were a lot of people. He wasn't with Aaron and Barry. He was with an old boy. Silver hair, expensive watch. I hadn't seen him in there before. I do remember one thing: Barry went up to Capaldi and said hello. He blanked him and Barry scuttled away with his tail between his legs. It was bloody hilarious.'

'You've no idea who the man with the silver hair was?'

'Not a clue. There was something about him that made me want to keep my distance though.'

Farrell terminated the interview and thanked him for coming in.

He walked to the canteen with Mhairi to grab his usual caffeine and Mars Bar combo. Mhairi grabbed a bottle of water and an apple.

'I need to counteract the effects of Vera's cooking.' She patted her stomach.

'About that,' said Farrell. 'DCI Buchanan wants the three of us to save costs by moving into a house owned by the police for the duration of the investigation. We can move in tonight.'

'What did you tell her?'

'I said it was fine by me, but if you don't want to that's not a problem.'

'I didn't say that,' she said. 'I suppose it makes sense.'

Why did it feel so awkward then? Farrell quickly moved the conversation back on to the job.

'I suspect that our elderly gentleman was Mario Lombardo,' he said as they sat down at a table.

'I doubt that Joe Capaldi will admit the association.'

'The Pig and Whistle doesn't have CCTV either,' said Farrell.

'Perhaps, that's why he chose such a dive. He doesn't strike me as someone accustomed to roughing it from what DI Moore has said.'

'This whole thing is going to take way longer than we thought,' said Mhairi.' Just as well we brought the moggs with us.'

'Between the attentions of Vera and my mother, we'll be lucky if we can persuade them to come back to Glasgow,' said Farrell. 'Right, come on. We'd best head to the court and see if we can catch Jack Kerr.'

'Barry McLeish is still in the wind,' said Mhairi. 'I'd have thought they'd have picked him up by now. His mobile phone hasn't been active either, so we haven't been able to trace him that way.'

'He's either gone to ground or something's happened to him.'

'You don't think he had anything to do with Aaron's death?'

'No. He might have an idea who did kill him, though.'

'And that information could cost him his life,' said Mhairi.

Chapter 29

They walked into the court and made a beeline for Bob, who was perched behind his wooden desk as though he'd never moved from the last time.

'Hey,' said Mhairi. 'We're here to catch Jack Kerr. Has he left yet?'

'Believe it or not, he's still here.' He shook his head. 'That poor laddie, I couldn't believe it. What's the world coming to, eh?'

'God only knows,' said Mhairi, shaking her head along with him.

Farrell kept quiet. Small talk wasn't his forte.

'Court Two, top of the stairs,' said Bob. 'The sheriff's off the Bench at the moment.'

As they pushed open the door at the top of the stairs, the first person they clapped eyes on was Beth Roberts. She was sitting on a chair outside the door hyperventilating, tears spilling from her eyes, as she struggled to breathe. Peter Swift was crouched beside her, his expression furious.

'Don't give that bastard the satisfaction,' he said, squeezing her hand so tightly she tried to pull it away from him.

The court clerk and the defence agents stood in a cluster apart, with concerned expressions.

He looked round and saw Farrell and Mhairi.

Mhairi, who was trained in first aid immediately moved in to help.

Farrell placed an elbow under the fiscal's arm and helped him to his feet. He looked as if he wanted to resist for a second, but then he moved to one side with Farrell.

'I'm guessing Sheriff Granger has been up to his tricks,' said Farrell.

'He's an absolute shit!' hissed the enraged man. 'I can take his crap and let it wash over me, but he gets inside Beth's head. Every day I have to watch him torment and undermine her. No wonder the Glasgow Bar ran him out of town. He's a bully through and through. I don't know how much more of this Beth can take.'

'It must be painful to watch,' said Farrell. 'Has she thought about moving into another area of law?'

'She says she's damned if she'll let him drive her from a job she used to love.'

Mhairi stood up and Beth too got to her feet with an embarrassed smile. She came over to them.

'Sorry, a little too hot in there. That, coupled with missing lunch, seems to have triggered a panic attack.'

Brave lass, thought Farrell, smiling warmly at her. He extended his hand and she passed her own small clammy one across for him to shake.

'DI Farrell. The heat's a devil at the moment; we're not used to it.'

They left her with Peter Swift and went in search of Jack Kerr, who emerged from the warren of interview rooms with a client in tow. His client shook his hand and walked through the glass doors and down the stairs.

'Another happy customer?' said Farrell.

'He bloody should be,' said Kerr. 'By rights he should be banged up right now. I assume you've come back about Aaron. That was my last case. We can go through here, if you like.'

They followed him into a small airless interview room that reeked of body odour and pine air freshener. The heat was stifling, as there were bars on the window, preventing it from being opened.

'We spoke to your wife earlier,' said Farrell.

'How was she?' he asked, looking guilty.

'Not good,' said Mhairi. 'The press has turned up outside your house and she was struggling a bit.'

'I know I should have been there,' he said.

'Everyone copes with things in their own way,' said Farrell. 'We sent an officer round to keep them at bay and she has our FLO, PC Joanne Burns, with her now.'

Jack Kerr sighed. 'I know she'll be poking around as well as making cups of tea. But let her, we've got nothing to hide.'

'You haven't heard then,' said Farrell.

'Heard what? I've been in a trial all day. My phone's been off.'

Farrell broke the news to him about the cocaine discovered in Aaron's school locker then paused to allow him to take it in.

Jack Kerr sat back in his seat and exhaled, as though he was trying to get a grip on himself.

'Were you aware he was mixed up in anything like this?' asked Mhairi. 'Did he have issues with drugs? Sometimes it starts off as just selling enough to manage your own addiction.'

'No, I had no bloody idea. Is that what got him killed?'

'It's something we're looking into,' said Farrell. 'I hate to ask you this but are you a recreational drug user yourself?'

Kerr's eyes slid away from them and he said nothing.

'If I ever did something like that, then I would make damn sure that my son would never know,' he said.

'If you were ever to do something like that, is it likely you might obtain it from a local source?'

'No comment,' he snapped.

'Were you aware that your son was hanging out with a known criminal, Barry McLeish?'

'What? Fergus's client? No, I had no idea. Clearly, I was the shittiest father on the planet as I don't seem to have been aware of much,' he said, his voice laced with self-loathing.

'You can't blame yourself,' said Mhairi. 'Your boy took a wrong turn but would most likely have righted himself, given time. That's teenagers the world over.'

'I do blame myself, DS McLeod,' he said. 'If I hadn't been so busy defending other people I might have been a big enough presence in my son's life to have saved him. Now, if you'll excuse me, I need to get home to my wife.'

Chapter 30

DC Thomson looked up from the computer with an expression of triumph.

'Guess what?' he said to Stirling and Byers who had their noses buried in the files.

'I'm a bit old for guessing games, laddie, spit it out,' said Stirling, peering at him over his new reading glasses. He'd settled back into the team as if he'd never been away.

'Joe Capaldi has a criminal past.'

'Is that right?' said Byers, perking up.

'He's been in and out of gaol for most of his life until his last stretch in Barlinnie that ended eight years ago. Since then, he seems to have kept his nose clean, so far as I can tell. I found him under the Italian version of his name, Giuseppe.'

'What kinds of crime?'

'Well, get this, possession with intent to supply features heavily, along with multiple assaults, some to severe injury.'

'I wonder if Gabriel Ferrante knows?' mused Stirling.

'Maybe he was a former client and Ferrante decided to give him a break when he came out the pokey,' said DC Thomson.

'He might be a criminal defence solicitor, but it would still be a highly unusual thing to do. It's possible he doesn't know. However, I would doubt it,' said Stirling. 'Pretty decent thing to do if he is aware, all the same. No wonder Capaldi is loyal to the man.'

'That degree of crime is a bit bad ass for this neck of the woods,' said DS Byers. 'I'm wondering if it's possible that Mario Lombardo has recruited him to do his dirty work. He could have threatened to blow his cover if he didn't play ball.'

'Plus they may have been meeting each other in the Pig and Whistle,' said Stirling. 'If that's the case, it's likely he's on the trail of Gina Campbell's killer. Mario Lombardo isn't going to let that go unavenged. If he thinks it's one if his business rivals, I don't think much of their chances. He might have leaned on Capaldi to be his enforcer.'

'Any joy on tracing those tattoos, Dave?' asked Byers.

'Some progress. I visited the local tattoo shops and they all have it as part of their portfolios. One of them looked proper shifty when I showed him a picture of Aaron and denied doing the tattoo. I reckoned he was lying because the boy was underage. I pushed him and he said the boy produced ID. Apparently Aaron said he didn't want the tattoo to be visible, as if he was reluctant to have it done. It struck him as odd because half the point for young lads is the bragging rights in showing it off to their mates.'

'And where's your tattoo, Davey lad?' said Stirling, with a wink at Byers.

DC Thomson blushed to the delight of the two older men.

'Need to know basis only.' He grinned, tapping the side of his nose.

'I wonder if the tattoo signifies being part of a gang?' he asked

'But how does that explain the transfer on Gina Campbell?' said Byers.

'Has she ever been inside?' asked Stirling.

'I would doubt that,' said Byers. 'I suspect that if she came within a whisper of charges, Daddy would have hired the best lawyers to ensure that she walked. No harm checking it out, though.'

At that moment, Farrell and Mhairi arrived.

'Great to see you back, Ronnie,' said Farrell. 'You'll be able to whip DC Thomson back into shape in no time.'

'I'm surprised you recognized him with his new trendy haircut,' said Mhairi, ruffling Dave Thomson's hair as he batted at her hands in annoyance. 'The amount he spends on clothes to go clubbing makes even my eyes water these days.'

PC Rosie Green followed them in.

'Great to see the team back together.' She smiled. 'Just like old times.'

The words hung leaden in the air as everyone froze for a split second then started talking all at once. PC Green looked away.

'I'm absolutely gagging for something to eat. Rosie, if you come with me down to the canteen, I can tell you a few things I need you to look into that might help us,' said Mhairi.

'Grab me a Mars Bar,' said Farrell, his mouth smiling but his eyes someplace else.

* * *

155

As they were heading downstairs Rosie bit her lip.

'I'm so sorry,' she said. 'I didn't think.'

'It's not your fault,' Mhairi said. 'It was a long time ago. You didn't know him as well as we did. Anyway, no one has a worse case of foot-in-mouth disease than me, so don't worry.'

Once in the canteen they grabbed two coffees and a table.

'Is Barry McLeish still on the run?'

'Either that or someone higher up the food chain has decided he needs to be silenced. Permanently,' said Mhairi.

'I don't know how we're going to stay on top of all this,' said PC Green. 'DI Moore ...'

'Yes?' said Mhairi, leaning forward.

'Well, she's only got back to work recently. She was off work with depression.'

'I hadn't realized,' said Mhairi guiltily. 'If I'd known I would have come down and seen her.'

'She didn't want anyone to know. The official story was that she was on unpaid leave to help look after an elderly relative.'

'How did you find out?' asked Mhairi, feeling bad that she had been so wrapped up in her Glasgow bubble that this had got past her.

'Let's just say I was in the right place at the right time. I don't want to say any more than that.'

'Who else knows?'

'Only DS Byers. He smelled a rat and went round to see her. I thought you three should know as you were all so close before. I thought maybe DI Farrell could help her.'

Chance would be a fine thing, Mhairi thought. He can barely take care of himself at the moment.

'I really don't think she's doing all that well. You guys coming down. Well it's stirred everything up again. And now with this increased workload. Well, I'm worried ...'

Mhairi patted her hand.

'I'm so glad you told me. Leave it with me and I'll speak to DI Farrell. I'll not let on it was you who told me.'

'Phew, I've been nerving myself to have this conversation for ages.'

'And now I need you to do something for me. Can you go up to Tech and sit on someone up there till they manage to get into Aaron's social media accounts and messages? We're waiting on his mobile phone records as well. When we get a picture of who he was talking to or interacting with things should become clearer.'

'On it,' PC Green said, and exited the canteen looking a lot brighter.

Mhairi's face darkened as she allowed her coffee to get cold. Farrell and DI Moore were both in trouble and it was down to her to sort things before they blew apart. Oh, and solve a couple of murders while she was at it.

'No, biggie,' she sighed, leaving her coffee and trailing back upstairs.

Her phone pinged. It was Sandy Gillespie, the young pathologist, inviting her out for a drink. Automatically, she typed a polite refusal. It was not the first time he had asked. Then she thought about his kind eyes and smiling face and hesitated. It would be good to have a friendly drink and a few laughs for light relief. Before she could change her mind she texted back to meet him later that night. What harm could it do? She thought about where he put his hands for a living and shuddered. She hoped he was a big believer in soap and water.

Chapter 31

The following day, Farrell sat across from Joe Capaldi in Ferrante's legal office, trying to obtain a measure of the man. He might as well have been staring at a rock. Capaldi's eyes were blank and his meaty arms were folded across the breast of his cheap shiny suit. His boss had already left for court so there was no one to disturb them.

'We appreciate you agreeing to assist us with our enquiries,' said Farrell.

'Whatever helps you sleep at night, officer. I can't imagine how you think I might assist you.'

'We know about your criminal record,' said Farrell, eyeballing him.

'Is that so?' said Capaldi, staring at him with barely concealed contempt. 'Then you also know that I served my time.'

'Did you disclose your past to your boss, Gabriel Ferrante?' asked Mhairi.

Capaldi hesitated for a split second as if debating internally with himself how to play this.

'Yes, I did. When I applied for the job I hoped he might

take a chance on me anyway, what with him being a defence lawyer. Seems only fair,' he said with a glint of humour.

'Mr Ferrante had set up shop in a rough area of Glasgow. No point having a wee lassie on reception when you've got some nutter high on crack trying to muscle his way in. I suppose you could say I started as a bit of a bouncer and my job continued to evolve.'

'When did you move down here?' asked Farrell.

'About a year ago.'

'Why would your boss shut up shop and move from the fast lane down to Sleepy Hollow here?' asked Mhairi.

Capaldi shrugged.

'Reckon he had a knife pulled on him one too many times.'

'The scar on his face?' asked Mhairi.

'Dumfries seemed a safer bet.'

'Until now,' said Farrell.

Capaldi's gaze dropped, anticipating from years of shadow boxing around coppers that they were about to get down to the nitty-gritty.

'You appreciate that we have to ask you some questions in relation to the murder of Gina Campbell?' said Farrell.

'I can't tell you what I don't know,' he said.

'Were you aware that Gabriel Ferrante was having a relationship with Gina Campbell?'

'Not at the time. He told me after you lot came sniffing around. Reckoned it would soon be doing the rounds.'

'Were you surprised?' asked Mhairi.

'Can't say I gave it much thought,' he replied. 'None of my business. I keep my head down, do my job, go home.'

'Did you know Gina Campbell yourself?'

Again that miniscule hesitation.

'No. Why would I?'

'Well, you certainly know her father, Mario Lombardo,' said Farrell, leaning forward and fixing him with an unflinching gaze.

An expression of fear flitted across Capaldi's features.

'The hell, I do. What the fuck is this? I'm not saying nothing without a lawyer.'

'Sorry,' said Mhairi. 'Did we strike a nerve?'

'And what if I were to suggest to you that someone at the Pig and Whistle saw you deep in conversation with Mario Lombardo,' said Farrell. 'Would he be lying to us, do you think?'

'I can't categorically state that I haven't passed the time of day with some bloke in the boozer, but I wouldn't have felt the need to know his name or anything about him. That's just what blokes having a pint do. Bit of a chat about the footie or the weather and that's it. Been a proper bloody party.'

'Have you ever been involved in working for Mario Lombardo at any time in the past?'

'Look, I have no idea who he even is,' he snapped. 'Either charge me and get me a lawyer or I'm walking. You have nothing on me. This is a total piss-take. I'm done being helpful. You'd be better off spending your time catching the person who murdered that woman and kid.'

'You think that they were killed by the same person?' asked Mhairi. 'What makes you say that?'

Capaldi rolled his eyes.

161

'For the umpteenth time, I don't have a friggin' clue. Stop trying to twist my words.'

'Where were you on the night Gina Campbell was killed?' said Farrell.

'I finished work, had a pint in the Pig and Whistle and went home. Microwave dinner for one and watched telly. It's a wonderful bloody life, all right? Can I go now?'

'And how about the night of Aaron Sullivan's death?'

'What? You're trying to pin the death of that kid on me too? Not a chance.'

'Just answer the question,' snapped Farrell, his patience wearing thin.

'Work, Pig and Whistle then home around nine. Satisfied? In fact, now I think of it you were bloody there too, the pair of you. I passed you at the door.'

He glared at Farrell. 'You were bloody staggering as I recall and it was only half past bloody six.'

Mhairi went hot and cold.

Shit, this wasn't good. Just as well this interview wasn't being taped.

Undeterred, Farrell pressed on. 'Did you know Aaron Sullivan, the boy who was murdered?'

Capaldi lost his combative air. 'No, I didn't. I saw a kid in there sitting with that wanker, Barry McLeish. I thought he looked a bit young at the time. It should never have happened.'

'What do you mean?' asked Farrell.

'Whatever shit is going down you don't kill kids that age. I hope you get the bastard that did it.'

Farrell changed tack.

'Have you ever known your boss, Gabriel Ferrante, to lose his temper? I mean dealing with criminals, some of them can be a bit mouthy if things aren't going their way, right? It'd be only natural to lose your rag once in a while.'

Capaldi laughed.

'You're barking up the wrong tree there, mate. My boss is as cool as a cucumber. If you're thinking crime of passion, I'd forget it if I were you.'

'Thank you, Mr Capaldi. We appreciate you giving up your time to talk to us.'

'What do you reckon?' asked Mhairi, once they had emerged onto the street and were out of earshot.

'He'd follow Gabriel Ferrante off a cliff,' said Farrell. 'He's completely loyal to him. If he thought Ferrante had killed Gina Campbell in a lovers' tiff, he would help him cover it up in a heartbeat. The kid, though, that's a different story.'

'Agreed,' said Mhairi. 'The most likely scenario then is that those murders weren't related.'

'The fact that Aaron had a load of drugs stashed in his locker makes that more likely. Although, it does seem rather odd that two of three friends have recently had someone close to them stabbed. We mustn't forget that the victims share the same mode of death.'

'Mind you, death by stabbing isn't all that exotic these days,' said Mhairi. 'If Aaron was working as a drug runner for Mario Lombardo and Gina was his daughter, the common link could be someone with a vendetta against him rather than the three lawyers.

163

'By the way, the barman didn't say that Joe Capaldi and Mario Lombardo were deep in conversation in the pub.'

'I know. I used a classic cross-examining technique. Most perps walk right into the trap.'

'Sneaky,' said Mhairi. 'But I like it.'

Farrell's radio crackled into life. It was DS Byers.

'I'm at the court,' he said, sounding as if he had been running. 'A fight's broken out between some lawyers. I need assistance.'

'On our way,' said Farrell as he and Mhairi dodged the traffic crossing across Buccleuch Street and sprinted into the court building.

Chapter 32

They ran up the stairs to Court Two where they found a full-blown brawl in progress. Sheriff Robert Granger had already been escorted off the Bench into chambers, and Bob stood beside a handful of other solicitors, all watching the action unfolding through the glass doors into the court.

'I don't know what started them off,' said Bob, turning to Farrell. 'It all happened so fast and then the lot of them were going at it hammer and tongs. The two officers in the dock opened the hatch and got the three accused back down the stairs to the cells. We couldn't do anything about the spectators. We figured they'd be safer staying where they were.'

'Mhairi, you wait here,' said Farrell as he burst open the door and plunged in to assist DS Byers in breaking up the fray.

'As if,' she muttered, running after him. She grabbed Jack Kerr, who was scrapping with the procurator fiscal, Peter Swift. With a howl of rage he swung round to punch her, but she neatly dodged, used his weight against him and had him face down and handcuffed in a matter of seconds.

Swift held up his hands in surrender and collapsed onto

a chair. He was breathing heavily and red-faced with exertion. Max Delaney was furiously trying to resist arrest, maintaining he'd been acting in self-defence, but he was no match for Byers's superior strength and inferior patience.

Mhairi left Byers to cuff Swift and Delaney, sprinting across to help Farrell who was having a much harder time trying to subdue Gabriel Ferrante. He had Fergus Campbell bent backwards over the agents' table, punching him with brutal efficiency. There was blood spattered everywhere and Campbell's face was beginning to resemble tenderized meat. Where had he learned to fight like that? He was solid muscle. Mhairi raced round the table in front of them, leaned over, grabbed Ferrante by the ears, and dug her very sharp nails in as far as they would go. He yelped and his fist shot out and landed with a loud smack on her nose, sending her reeling backwards. Her head cracked against the wooden sheriff's Bench. Briefly, she saw stars before sliding down onto the floor. Farrell grabbed Ferrante's fist from behind. Realizing what he had done the fight went out of him and his body softened, enabling Farrell to handcuff him. It was over.

'Don't you ever do anything I say?' yelled Farrell with a worried glare as he took in Mhairi's burgeoning black eye. 'There was no need for you to jump in. Byers and I had it under control.'

Mhairi grimaced in pain, gingerly checking her nose was still in the right place, as Byers helped her to her feet.

'You keep telling yourself, that, Frank Farrell,' she snapped.

The paramedics arrived and immediately rushed to the aid of Fergus Campbell who had slid off the table, onto the floor, apparently unconscious. After a few seconds they pronounced him stable and stretchered him out to the waiting ambulance, winding carefully down the steep flights of stairs. Within minutes more paramedics arrived to patch up the other combatants before they were cautioned by the police and escorted, still cuffed, through the open trap door in the dock down to the cells.

The motley crew of spectators laughed and jeered as Farrell stood grimly at the side of the dock.

Peter Swift the fiscal was furious that he was being treated the same as everyone else.

'DI Farrell, this is outrageous,' he hissed. 'I was trying to break up the fight not involved in it.'

'Not from where I was standing,' replied Farrell, unmoved.

'You're completely undermining my authority in this court,' he hissed, as a more enterprising and audacious member of the public benches leaned forward to take their photo.

'I think you did that all by yourself, when you took the decision to throw a punch.'

The hatch opened and Swift was led away, still huffing and puffing.

'Right, that's the lot,' said Farrell. 'And here's the cavalry. About time.' He dispatched the uniforms surging through the door to interview the dozen or so witnesses who were being funnelled out the court.

His keen eye spotted an anomaly. He hurried over to Bob.

'That guy at the back of the queue, Bob, talking to the woman, I'm sure he wasn't in here before?'

Bob peered across at them.

'You're right, he definitely wasn't.'

'He'll be one of Sophie Richardson's assistants,' muttered Farrell through clenched teeth. He strode over to the trendy young guy in his thirties in the designer gear who avoided eye contact on his approach.

'You can tell Ms Richardson that if she wants information, she'll need to go through the proper channels. I'm sure that Andy Moran, the civilian press officer, will be only too pleased to assist.'

'I don't know what you mean,' he attempted to protest. 'It's a public gallery. I'm entitled to be here.'

'Not if you're attempting to interfere with a criminal investigation you're not.' Farrell beckoned to a couple of young uniforms to come over.

'Please show this gentleman out and don't permit him to talk to anyone on the way down,' he said.

The young whippersnapper had the cheek to slip his card into the bag of the woman he'd been talking to and mouth, 'call me', to her as he was being led away. Farrell became aware he was grinding his teeth.

He walked over to Mhairi and frowned at the bruised mess her face had become.

'I hope you're happy. I told you not to wade in.'

'You can talk,' she snapped right back, pointing to his burst lip and matching black eye.

They glared at each other, then grinned as the absurdity of the situation hit them.

'That almost matched a typical Friday night in Glasgow,' said Mhairi.

'I've never seen the likes of it,' said Farrell. 'I suppose there's a first time for everything.'

'We'd best take the back entrance, or you'll get pounced on by Sophie Richardson and her media darlings.'

'I'd take a good old-fashioned punch-up any day of the week,' groaned Farrell.

They were leaving the court room when Bob came rushing out of the door to Sheriff Granger's private chambers.

'The sheriff would like a word with you,' he said apologetically.

'What, now?' said Farrell, exasperated.

'I'm afraid so. And he doesn't like to be kept waiting,' he whispered, glancing nervously at the closed door behind him.

Farrell sighed. He loathed bullies with a passion and this sheriff seemed to rule his little fiefdom with an iron fist.

'Fine, let's get it over with,' he said.

'I'll come,' said Mhairi. 'You might need backup.'

Chapter 33

Sheriff Granger sat in his gown minus wig and contemplated them with an ugly expression.

'DI Farrell, I will not tolerate this behaviour in my courtroom. I want you to know that all of these solicitors will be found in contempt of court, punishment to be determined. I also want Miss Beth Roberts held in custody.'

'On what grounds, my Lord?' asked Mhairi, staring him straight in the eye.

'I can't hear you,' he said, bouncing with anger in his seat.

'Would you like me to shout, my Lord?' asked Mhairi, knowing perfectly well what he was getting at but choosing to be obtuse.

Bob and Farrell sent her worried looks.

'I cannot hear you, young woman, because I have not yet invited you to speak! DI Farrell, perhaps you can teach your subordinate some courtroom etiquette when you have a few moments.'

'Yes, my Lord,' said Farrell, earning a glare from Mhairi. 'Might I enquire on what grounds you wish Beth Roberts to be detained? When we arrived she was nowhere to be seen.'

'Don't let her looks fool you. That young woman is an absolute menace. She's not only sly and deceitful but grossly incompetent. You can't trust a word that comes out of her mouth. Apparently she's been running around with Jack Kerr behind Peter Swift's back. That's what caused the whole thing to kick off in the first case. She incited the entire anarchic event.'

'I'm not sure I follow, my Lord,' said Farrell. 'I can understand a dispute occurring out of the court but when you were on the Bench? How could that possibly have arisen?'

Bob cleared his throat.

'If I may, my Lord?'

'Go ahead,' said the sheriff, with a majestic wave.

Bob removed two letters from his jacket and handed them to Farrell, who put on gloves to examine them. One envelope was addressed to Fergus Campbell. The enclosed photo clearly showed Gabriel Ferrante and Gina Campbell in the throes of passion. The note read:

Enjoy the show.
I did.

The other envelope was addressed to Peter Swift. The photo was grainier this time and showed Jack Kerr entangled with a woman on a rumpled bed. Her face was hidden beneath him. The note read:

Jack Kerr and your fiancée are having an affair.
SUCKER

Farrell bagged up the evidence carefully.

'Each of the solicitors involved found an envelope with their name on it waiting at their usual seat after lunch,' said the Bar officer. 'Peter Swift threw the first punch and seconds later they were all fighting.'

'Tell them who placed the notes on the table,' said the sheriff, with a malicious gleam in his eye.

'It was Miss Roberts,' admitted Bob, looking distinctly unhappy. 'I saw her do it, as I came in from the sheriff's chambers to place a witness list on the Bench.'

'Now do you see?' demanded Sheriff Granger.

'You have my word that we'll look into her involvement, my Lord,' said Farrell. He bowed his head and Mhairi reluctantly followed his lead as Bob ushered them out into the corridor.

'Tosser,' she muttered.

'Careful, he'll hear you,' whispered Bob with a worried backwards glance at the closed door.

'I'm not scared of him,' she said.

'Maybe you should be,' he replied.

Byers was waiting for them along the hall, looking somewhat the worse for wear too.

'That soft bastard, Max Delaney, ripped my new shirt,' he complained. 'I'll be sending him the bloody bill.'

As they got closer he took in Mhairi's battered face and Farrell's split lip.

'Christ, looks like I fared better than you two,' he said.

Farrell brought him up to speed with what had been said in chambers and showed him the notes and photos.

Byers shook his head in disbelief. 'Ferrante and Gina Campbell, fair enough, but if Beth Roberts is having an affair with Jack Kerr why would she want to advertise the fact to her fiancé of all people?'

'Can you hand off these letters and envelopes to Janet White or Phil Tait?' Farrell said, passing across the bag. 'I want copies for the 6 p.m. briefing. See if they can get any useful prints or DNA off them.'

'What do you want to do about the lawyers, boss?' asked Byers.

'I'd like them all cautioned and charged for now,' said Farrell. 'I reckon we should keep them in overnight. I want them to have absolutely no contact with each other until we can work out what's been going on.'

'What about Beth Roberts?' said Mhairi.

'I've not seen her,' said Byers. 'She seems to have left before we got here.'

'She can keep,' said Farrell. 'I'm going to take Mhairi to the hospital to get her checked out properly like the paramedic wanted.'

'I beg your pardon,' said Mhairi, affronted.

'You can beg all you like but my mind's made up,' said Farrell. 'As a little inducement we can also pop in on Fergus Campbell and get a first crack at him when he might be feeling more vulnerable.'

'Oh well, why didn't you say that in the first place?' huffed Mhairi and set off down the stairs.

Both men looked at each other and shook their head in a rare moment of accord.

'That one is something else,' said DS Byers.

'Enough to turn a man's hair grey,' agreed Farrell.

She turned back and gave them a lopsided glare.

'Come on, what are you waiting for?'

They exited the building the same way they had come in, thus avoiding the unstoppable Sophie Richardson whose media truck was now impeding the flow of traffic. Farrell opened the rear door of the airless basement, which contained the cells beneath the court. They were halfway across the car park when a cloud passed over the sun and they were caught on camera by Farrell's nemesis of old, Moira Sharkey, with whom he had occasionally had a very uneasy symbiotic relationship.

She stalked towards them, her vulpine features twisted with pleasure. She was dressed in her trademark shaggy black shapeless coat with her thick black fringe falling over hooded eyes. Even the warmth of the day had not caused her to shed any layers.

Farrell felt a shiver run up his spine.

'DI Farrell and DS McLeod. I see you've been having quite the day.' She smirked. 'Now, there's two ways I could feature those photos. Heroes of the hour or heavy-handed police brutality. Any preference?'

'Ms Sharkey,' said Farrell, refusing to rise to the bait, even though he could feel his blood pressure climbing, 'I'm afraid I'm in a hurry. My colleague has been injured in the course of duty. I need to get her to hospital.'

Mhairi tried to rock the damsel-in-distress look whereupon Sharkey laughed with real enjoyment.

'DS McLeod is about as fragile as I am,' she said.

Mhairi straightened up not sure whether to feel insulted or complimented.

'I won't keep you long. I have some information that might be of interest.' She passed her card to Farrell with a bony finger.

'And let me guess, you want something in return?' he said, pocketing the card.

'I'll be in touch,' she said, walking away fast, her shoulders hunched.

Chapter 34

Farrell enquired at the hospital reception as to Fergus Campbell's whereabouts and was told that, although he had come around, he still appeared to be suffering from concussion as well as a fractured cheekbone and bruised ribs. He was being admitted to a ward once his injuries had been attended to.

That established, Mhairi McLeod condescended to have her own injured nose examined. Once the doctor had left, Farrell pushed aside the curtain.

Both eyes were colouring up nicely either side of her swollen but thankfully reasonably straight nose. She looked somehow defenceless and vulnerable in her blue hospital gown. He sat down beside her and enfolded her hand in his own. To his surprise, she let him. He knew perfectly well that she talked a big game but wasn't quite as tough as she liked to make out. She was also no fan of hospitals. She wrenched her hand away with a scowl after a couple of minutes.

'Come on,' she said swinging her legs out of bed. 'There's no time to waste. Let's get up and see Fergus Campbell.'

She was already pulling her trousers on and he turned his back until she was done.

There were two old ladies in the lift up to the wards and they tutted in disapproval at Farrell, assuming he was responsible for Mhairi's injuries. Escaping on to the second floor they were soon directed to a private room. They peered through the window and Farrell quickly pulled Mhairi out of sight.

'Well, look who's here?' muttered Farrell. 'Fergus Campbell and Jane Pearson looking very cosy.'

'She certainly didn't waste any time,' said Mhairi, sidling along the wall to take a quick peek through the glass. 'Look! She's holding his hand.'

'Doesn't necessarily mean anything,' said Farrell, 'I was holding yours a couple of minutes ago.'

'Tell anyone that and you're dead to me.' She glared.

They walked into the room, and Fergus Campbell and Jane Pearson shot apart as though they'd been electrocuted. Both officers pretended they hadn't noticed anything amiss.

'How are you feeling?' asked Mhairi.

'Not much worse than you, by the looks of things,' said Campbell. 'Are you here to take my statement?'

'Yes,' said Farrell. 'Would you mind giving us a minute?' he said to Pearson who seemed way more than professionally concerned about her boss.

'I'll grab a cup of coffee,' she said at once as though eager to get away.

'Where are the children?' Mhairi asked.

'They're with my family,' Campbell said. 'The hospital notified them as my next of kin and for once they decided to be of some use.'

'What's the damage?' asked Mhairi.

'A fractured cheekbone and some bruised ribs. I've also lost a couple of my front teeth, as you can see,' he grimaced. 'I hope you've charged that bastard Gabriel Ferrante?'

'From what we understand, you threw the first punch,' said Farrell.

'You're telling me this was self-defence?' He pointed to his ruined face. 'A tad excessive, wouldn't you say? That bastard barely has a scratch on him.'

'I honestly don't know what is going to happen,' said Farrell. 'I imagine a procurator fiscal from Glasgow will be sent down to manage this mess given that one of their own was also caught up in it.'

Campbell gave a mirthless laugh.

'I don't know what set Peter Swift off. He's normally so easy-going.'

Farrell didn't mention what he had read in the note left for Swift, as he was still unclear who had orchestrated the fracas.

'I'd like to remind you, you're still under caution,' Farrell said.

Campbell settled back on his pillows with a sigh. 'Get on with it then.'

'Tell me what happened.'

'I came back in after lunch and took my usual seat at the table. There was an envelope on the table with my name on it. I opened it at once in case it related to that afternoon's business.'

'Did you see who put it there?'

'No.'

He paused and swallowed, his face twisted with emotion.

'Go on,' said Farrell.

'Inside there was a picture of my wife and Gabriel Ferrante. They were ... they were ... going at it.'

'You mean having sex?'

'Yes. And the bastard was sitting right beside me making small talk like nothing had happened. It was a shock. I defy anyone not to lash out in those circumstances. My wife was barely cold in her grave. I'd only just started to come to terms with the fact she might have been having an affair let alone that it was one of my colleagues.'

'Where was the photo taken?'

'It was fairly dark and the quality wasn't great. It looked like the inside of a garden shed. I don't know where. All I can say is that it wasn't in my garden. I could see them both quite distinctly. If my wife wasn't already dead I might kill her myself. I can't believe she would betray me like that.

'I thought she loved me,' he said, turning his face away.

Chapter 35

Despite going through the motions of kicking up a fuss, Mhairi was relieved when Farrell insisted on dropping her at their new accommodation. He said he would bring back some shopping on his way home from the station. The police house was comfortably furnished and perfectly adequate for their needs. She doubted they would see much of Dave who had hooked up with some of his old mates and kept late hours. It felt weird living in such close proximity to her boss, but she would get used to it.

Mhairi fed Oscar and Henry and flopped on to the couch pulling the throw over her. Suddenly she remembered she was meant to be meeting Sandy Gillespie for a drink.

She glanced at her watch in alarm and realized he was probably sitting there now waiting on her. Shit! Quickly, she pulled out his card from her purse and called his mobile.

'Hello?' he said in his warm highland burr.

'Sandy, I'm so sorry! I was involved in a bit of a fight today and my face simply isn't fit for public consumption. I'm only just back in the door. Can we do this another night? I'm honestly not blowing you off, I have two black eyes and a busted nose.'

'Poor thing, you've been in the wars,' he said, sounding so concerned for her that she had to fight back a tear. It had been a long time since anyone apart from Frank had spoken to her like that.

'You can come round for an hour or so if you like,' she offered, wishing she could stuff the words back in her mouth the moment she said them. Her cheeks burned. He'd think she was a sad loser now, for sure.

'Of course, you shouldn't be alone. I'll pick up a couple of things on my way.'

While she was waiting, Mhairi managed to have a shower and wash her hair. She debated what to wear but thought he might as well see her warts and all. After the day she'd had she wanted to be comfy above all else. She got into her fleecy pyjamas and dressing gown, stuck her feet in her slippers and laughed as she caught a glimpse of her battered face in the mirror. Well, if this didn't put him off, she didn't know what would.

The doorbell rang and she opened it.

He looked so worried as he gently enfolded her in a big hug that she felt those treacherous tears start to prickle again.

'Let's get you comfortable,' he said as he led her over to the sofa.

She always forgot that pathologists were also medical doctors so could tend the living as well as the dead.

Gently he pushed her hair back from her face and probed her injuries with long, delicate fingers, his warm brown eyes crinkled with concern. Mhairi had never felt so exposed. Normally, she would have been totally freaked out, but for some weird reason she felt incredibly comfortable and safe around him.

'Good,' he said. 'Nothing that shouldn't heal nicely when the swelling goes down.'

He reached inside the carrier bag he had brought with him and pulled out a large jar of emollient cream, together with some arnica tablets and anti-inflammatories. He brought her a glass of water and after she'd taken the tablets, he opened the tub and gently stroked the soothing cream in a thick layer all over her face. Mhairi sighed with pleasure.

'You are absolutely wasted on the dead,' she murmured.

'Ah, but at least they can't answer me back.' He grinned.

He then made her two boiled eggs mashed in a cup with a slice of toast cut into soldiers and produced a romcom from the carrier bag.

They settled down to watch it, Henry and Oscar between them, purring loudly.

The front door opened and Farrell staggered in laden with groceries. He looked startled and not entirely pleased to see Sandy sitting on the couch but greeted him politely.

'Sandy, I'm glad you're here to keep an eye on this one. I have to head back to the station. Make sure she doesn't get herself in any more bother while I'm gone.'

'I'll have my work cut out there.' He smiled.

'Sitting right here, guys,' murmured Mhairi.

She could feel her face redden under the cream. This whole situation was beyond awkward. What had she been thinking inviting Sandy back here? It must have been the pain meds talking.

As Farrell left, she realized she had tensed up again. Sandy grinned at her.

'I take it DI Farrell doesn't get out much,' he said.

'He's a bit reserved, that's all. Just trying to give us some space.'

'For this?' he said, leaning over and gently touching his lips to her bruised ones.

It felt good but this wasn't the time and it certainly wasn't the place.

She pointed the remote at the TV. As first dates went it was either a total bust or the best she had ever had.

Time would tell.

Chapter 36

Farrell and the remaining members of the team had been working tirelessly for hours. A while ago they'd ordered in pizza. Looking at the greasy, stressed faces around the table, Farrell knew that they mirrored his own, but without the split lip. The vinegar on his chips had been a bad idea.

As if their limited manpower hadn't been stretched enough without this brawl erupting today. The strands of this investigation were starting to resemble a multiverse. There were just too many unexplored avenues spooling out in all directions. Unless, of course, that was the idea? Maybe they were being played by a master manipulator using smoke and mirrors to cover something up. That whole carry on in court today had clearly been an orchestrated distraction, but who had been pulling the strings? Was Beth Roberts as meek as she seemed, or was it all an act? Why did Sheriff Granger seem to hate her so much? Was it just her or was he like that with all women? He clearly wasn't crazy about Mhairi, but he wasn't stupid enough to take her on either.

'The Dean of Faculty has just got back to me,' said DC

Thomson. 'The Faculty dinner is on Saturday night at The Cairnsmore Hotel.'

'I reckon we should arrange to turn up en-masse,' Byers said.

'Agreed,' said Farrell. 'I've been invited to a few of these over the years. Once the formal part is over, it turns into a right old piss-up. We might catch some of them off-guard.'

'I could bring Laura,' said Byers, avoiding Farrell's glare. 'The only reason I'm suggesting it is because we can't all turn up as blokes without a partner, or we might as well have "on the job" tattooed on our foreheads.'

Farrell sighed. Byers was right. Besides, there'd been enough aggro today already.

'I could team up with DI Moore and Dave can attend with PC Rosie Green.'

'What about Mhairi?' asked Byers.

'Let's see how she is first. We can't all sit together. We need to be interspersed among the various firms' tables. Perhaps the Dean of Faculty could arrange that by having a discreet word in the ears of the senior partners. The procurator fiscal will also have a table. It must be emphasized that discretion is key, however.'

'On it, boss,' said Thomson.

'I reckon we need to get Beth Roberts in for questioning,' said Farrell. 'If Sheriff Granger and the Bar officer are to be believed, she may have been the one who placed those envelopes on the table in court today. I want to know whether they originated with her or whether someone told her to do it on their behalf.'

Donald Sloan, the custody sergeant, popped his head round the door.

'Are you sure we can't release those bloody lawyers on police bail, boss? They're doing my bloody head in with their moaning. Bloody divas, the lot of them.'

Farrell shook his head.

'Sorry, Sergeant. They're having to bring down a senior procurator fiscal from Glasgow to decide how best to play things. If charges are to be brought another sheriff from outwith the area will have to be bussed in as well.'

'The two old lags we've got in custody are proper loving life,' Sloan grumbled. 'Everything those lawyers are demanding they're piping up with too. Like a bloody echo chamber, so it is. Ah, well back down to the seventh circle of Hell.' Sighing, he trundled away.

Farrell continued typing out separate reports on the two investigations to date for both DSup Crawford and also DCI Buchanan. He hadn't been able to face speaking to her on the phone and knew that Mhairi wouldn't have done so either, in the circumstances.

While he was typing the word 'distraction' kept rumbling round his mind like wind. Assuming this whole carry on had been a diversionary tactic, who was behind it and for what purpose? For some reason Max Delaney popped into his mind, along with a burgeoning feeling of unease. Could an attack be launched on Max Delaney's wife or daughter while he was tucked away in custody out of the way and unable to protect them? Could that be what this was all about?

He was so shattered he could hardly think straight and

was craving a drink to settle him after the events of the day. It was already gone nine and he would need to be in at the crack of dawn tomorrow.

DI Moore put her head round the door. 'I'm calling it a day,' she said. 'Night all.'

Kate had declined the offer of a takeaway earlier and Farrell assumed she had had nothing to eat yet. In fact, now he thought about it, he hadn't noticed her eat at all since they'd been in Dumfries. He didn't want to go back to the house yet, in case he walked in on Mhairi and her new bloke up to God knows what. The mere thought made him feel sick. If he hurt her in any way ... He gave himself a mental shake. She was a grown woman. Her love life was none of his business. Why was he feeling so twitchy about this? Making a decision he jumped to his feet.

'Hold on, Kate and I'll walk you out.'

He grabbed his jacket and followed her.

Chapter 37

'Fancy grabbing a bite to eat?' he said.

'But you've just eaten,' she said. 'That pizza you put away would fill a family of three.'

'I'm happy to have something light while you eat, keep you company.'

She stopped and turned to him, stony-faced. 'Frank, really, I'm not hungry. I've been on a bit of a health kick recently and feel much better for it.'

You could have fooled me, thought Farrell, taking in the sharp planes of her face and emaciated frame. Time to try another tack.

'Okay, forget dinner, that was just an excuse. I really need to talk to you about some stuff. Is there anywhere we can go? I would welcome your advice.'

She smiled at him with those level grey eyes that always seemed to see straight through him. He turned away, fearful of what she might find. He wasn't the same man she had known before. He didn't know if he would ever be that person again.

'Come to mine for a coffee then. I can't promise I'll manage to stay up for long.'

With a start, he realized, as he followed her out of the police car park, that he didn't even know where she lived. Fiercely private, Kate Moore was something of an enigma and liked to keep it that way. Since the very public hurt and humiliation she had suffered at the hands of an art critic two years ago, she had built a carapace so thick he doubted she would ever allow anyone to pierce it again.

To his surprise, they ended up at the luxury apartments near the rowing club overlooking the river. The very same apartments where his former girlfriend, Clare Yates, had lived. He fervently hoped they didn't run into her.

'I didn't know you lived here, Kate,' he said as she let him into her first-floor flat.

'After that business a while back I felt like a change.' She shrugged. 'I like the fact that there's a secure entrance and CCTV. I don't have any need of a garden, really. Not when I have this magnificent view.'

'I see what you mean,' said Farrell with as much enthusiasm as he could muster, though, in truth, he felt sad for her, entombed in her safe room.

'Does Clare Yates still live in the building?'

'Yes, although I doubt she will for much longer. She's engaged now, to a local GP. They're looking for a new house, I believe, with a view to starting a family.'

She looked bleak once more. Ever since she was shot in the line of duty in her twenties, she had known she would be unable to have children. It was a private sorrow she bore with fortitude. Her massive payout, small consolation.

As she went through to the kitchen to make some coffee,

Farrell looked around him, trying to obtain some clues as to her state of mind. The interior was immaculate with a quiet understated elegance.

She came back through and placed a tray on the coffee table and sat beside him.

'Byers told me you know that he's living with Laura Lind now. It must have been a hard thing for you to accept,' she said.

'It seems like a terrible betrayal,' said Farrell. 'I don't know how either of them could do that to John.'

'If it makes you feel any better, I don't think it was intentional. Due to the timing, with Police Scotland coming into being, you, Mhairi and Dave Thomson headed for Glasgow within weeks of Lind being struck down, I was all over the place and barely able to look after myself. The Super and Ronnie Stirling retired more or less right away. I think Byers felt we owed it to Lind to support his wife and kids and he was the only one capable of doing so at the time.'

That did put a somewhat different complexion on things, Farrell admitted to himself, feeling ashamed of his recent outburst. The shock of seeing Byers installed in John's house had blinded him to reason at the time.

'Byers used to go there on his day off to be with the kids so that Laura could spend time with Lind. Eventually, as the news coming back from the hospital grew less and less hopeful for a recovery, they became closer. It was a gradual thing. Lind wouldn't want Laura to struggle on alone with four kids to raise.'

It was hard to hear but she was right. He felt the truth of it now that he'd had the opportunity to reflect. He had been consumed with anger for so long, but the reality was that Farrell had abandoned them. He had also abandoned God. Had he been wrong about that too?

He reached across and squeezed her hand.

'I've missed you, Kate.'

'I thought Mhairi McLeod would have been keeping you in order.'

'She does her best but subtlety isn't exactly her strong suit.'

'More wrecking ball than diplomacy.' She grinned.

'What do you think is going on with these murders?' he asked, keen to steer the conversation back to safer waters.

'I wish I knew. The points of intersection seem to be as follows:

'Both victims were stabbed and related to a member of a small friend group.

'Both victims are connected to Mario Lombardo. One is his daughter and one may have been embroiled in one of his criminal enterprises.'

'There's a third possibility,' said Farrell. 'It may relate in some way to the death of that girl who burned to death ten years ago in Jedburgh.'

'It certainly explains how tight they are,' said DI Moore. 'But what are you suggesting? That they murdered her?'

'I'm not sure, yet,' said Farrell. 'It's odd that the first victim was murdered on the tenth anniversary of the fire in Jedburgh. The fire was ruled an accidental death. But was it? I think there's a strong possibility that those three men are harbouring a guilty secret about that night.'

'And someone might want to avenge the dead,' said DI Moore.

Chapter 38

It was gone ten but Farrell didn't feel like heading back to the house yet. He felt lighter as though something hard and brittle inside him had been released. Sometimes all that was needed was to view an issue from a different perspective. Something slid into the periphery of his mind. Before he went back with Kate, he had been concerned that Max Delaney's family might be targeted next. He could swing by there on the way home and check that all was as it should be.

Sliding the car into gear he headed over to Max Delaney's house. He parked a couple of streets away. His senses heightened as he walked quietly along the deserted streets, inhaling the scent of heavy-headed roses in the warm summer air. Closer to the Delaney house he melted into the hedgerows and paused. There was a single light on upstairs, presumably in the master bedroom. As he watched, the silhouette of a woman appeared and drew the curtains. Farrell relaxed, about to retrace his footsteps. Everything seemed to be in order.

Suddenly, he heard a muffled cough nearby and his heart skipped a beat. He froze, scarcely daring to breathe, trying to ascertain where the sound had come from. Was someone else watching the house? He couldn't call for backup or he'd scare them off. He would have to handle this himself. Slowly he crept forward, the lengthening shadows as the light diminished helping to conceal him. Could someone be waiting with a knife, watching him advance? Farrell delicately probed his pockets, but found only a biro. He halted as he saw the red tip of a cigarette. The watcher was behind a tree at the foot of the next garden. Hopefully, he'd caught him unawares. Farrell crept forward inch by inch until he was almost upon the watcher.

Breaking cover at the last moment, he launched himself forward.

'Police, stay where you are,' he yelled, vaulting over the wall and bringing the suspect to the ground.

He grappled with the man, determined not to let him get away. A vicious punch connected with his ear, as the man fought to wriggle out from under him. Light spilled into the garden as the door to the property swung back to reveal an elderly couple in their dressing gowns.

'Call the police!' yelled Farrell. 'And get inside.'

He rolled around the ground expecting to feel the hot piercing stab of a knife wound at any moment. A sudden searing pain caused Farrell to yell. The bastard had sunk his teeth into the fleshy part of his hand. A red mist descended and he stopped fighting clean and fought to win, landing several hard punches of his own. When he heard the crunch of broken cartilage from a punch to the nose, he knew he had gained the upper hand. By the time he heard the screech of the sirens, he had the guy cuffed, searched and subdued.

There was no sign of a knife, but that didn't mean he hadn't thrown it down in the scuffle. It was too dark now to enable a thorough search. Still shaking, he felt the energy drain from his body. He had no idea who the man was that he'd arrested but he'd clearly been targeting Max Delaney's house.

DS Byers and DC Thomson piled out of the first car and took the prisoner into custody.

'He hasn't said a word to me,' said Farrell, as Byers walked back to him. 'He's been in this garden watching the Delaneys' house. I don't know for how long. I don't know if he's a sole operator or working for someone else. I've done a cursory search and found no weapon, but you'll need to instruct someone to search the garden and bins here, just in case.'

'You all right?' asked Byers, taking in his filthy clothes, ripped shirt, scratched face and split lip.

'I'm fine. I'll drive my own car back to the station. It's parked not too far from here. I'm going to speak to Chloe Delaney now, and I'd like the officers in the second car to remain here for the night as a very visible presence.'

'Do you reckon we should release Delaney on police bail till the procurator fiscal decides what to do with them?' asked Byers.

'Yes, and release Jack Kerr too. The last thing I want is for something to happen to their wife or kid while they're in custody. That could be what emboldened this guy tonight. I'll take full responsibility.'

'What about the fiscal, Peter Swift?'

'I suppose we have to let him out too,' said Farrell.

'I'm still a bit unclear about what's going on with Beth

Roberts. Hopefully, we'll be able to track her down first thing in the morning.'

Farrell stood up and his head swam. This really had been one hellish day.

'Are you sure you don't want me to go and speak to Chloe Delaney? No offence, boss, but you look like shit.'

'None taken. I need to do it myself. She's the only spouse I've not met yet. If Rosie Green can get here in the next ten minutes she can come with me. It might be best to have another woman there rather than me turn up alone at this time of night looking like this, when she doesn't know me.'

Byers reached into the glove compartment of his car and brought out baby wipes. He handed the pouch to Farrell.

'Here, these should help take the worst off. I'll get the duty police surgeon to give you the once-over at the station.'

'There's no need,' snapped Farrell, wiping away what dirt and blood he could from his face and hands.

'Look, don't be an ass. I have to call him for this custody anyway. It's protocol,' sighed Byers.

'Fine,' said Farrell. 'The bastard bit me. I might need a rabies shot.'

He turned to PC Green who had just arrived and come running across to them.

'Right, Rosie. Will I do?'

She looked doubtful but nodded.

Five minutes later, they rang the doorbell.

Chloe Delaney swung back the door, looking alarmed.

'I heard all the commotion. What's happened?' she asked.

'DI Frank Farrell, Mrs Delaney. May we come in?'

'At this time of night?' she asked, confused, then sighed and stood back to let them enter.

'I still can't believe that you arrested Max,' she said.

'He and his colleagues didn't leave us a whole lot of choice.'

'Is that why you're here? Couldn't this have waited until the morning?' she asked, once they were all seated in the pristine lounge.

'I'm afraid not,' said Farrell. 'I caught somebody watching your house not long ago.'

'The sirens?'

'Yes, he's been arrested and taken to the station for questioning.'

Chloe Delaney went pale.

'Is he the one who killed Gina Campbell and Jack and Sarah's boy?'

'Impossible to say at the moment,' replied Farrell. 'We've arranged for Max to be released on bail, and I've stationed an officer outside your home. PC Rosie Green here will remain with you tonight for added protection, assuming you have no objection.'

'No, none at all.'

At that moment a little girl came running through the door and made a beeline for her mother. She came in holding a soft pink blanket to her cheek, her long hair tousled and blonde, just like her mother. Farrell frowned slightly. Instead of being dressed in cartoon stuff like most little kids her age, she was wearing dusky pink silk PJs and a dressing gown that were a perfect replica of those worn by her mother. He glanced across at PC Green and noticed a look of concern there too.

'Mia and I like to dress alike. We've got a huge following on Instagram,' said Chloe. 'It's perfectly harmless and she loves dressing up like mummy, don't you darling?' she said giving her daughter a gentle squeeze.

'Would you mind showing me the account, please?' asked Farrell.

Chloe looked surprised but lifted her iPad off the coffee table and pulled up the account.

Farrell leaned over so that PC Green could see the images too as he scrolled through.

'We're in the process of getting Mia her own YouTube channel,' said Chloe, her eyes flashing with excitement. 'Isn't that right, darling?'

The little girl snuggled further into her comforter and nodded her head.

'These posts have hundreds of thousands of likes,' said PC Green.

'Yes, I'm what they call a social-media influencer. Mia is a big part of mummy's success, aren't you, darling?'

The little girl was no longer listening. She looked tired and withdrawn.

There were so many pictures that Farrell wondered that Mia had time for any kind of life at all other than posing for the camera. They showed no tantrums or mess to mar the perfection. As Farrell continued to scroll down there were also swimwear shots of them at the beach building sandcastles and frolicking in the waves. He felt a sinking feeling in the pit of his stomach. Although they were innocent enough, he could imagine they could excite a lot of interest from predatory paedophiles. Perhaps the lurker outside was nothing to do with these cases at all but some obsessed stalker.

'Have you had any unsavoury interest expressed in any pics in relation to this account? Any dubious messages or indication that your followers might have tracked down where you live?' he asked.

'Well of course, I have lots of fans. That's the whole idea. Once you become an influencer, companies basically pay you to promote their products online. To be honest, my little "hobby" brings us in more money than Max does. There are so many messages I couldn't possibly go through them all myself. I pay someone to do that for me. They filter them out and forward a number for me to react to every month.'

'And what about your daughter?' asked PC Green, clearly struggling not to show her disapproval. 'Does she interact with the fans too?'

'Sometimes, but only with my help. It's usually little girls asking about where she gets a particular top or toy or hairband. It's all very harmless,' she said, starting to sound annoyed.

'I'm going to need the name of the person who filters your messages, to ensure that things are monitored a bit more closely for the next few weeks.'

'You think this could have put us in harm's way?' asked Chloe.

'I hope not,' he replied, 'but I suggest that you close it down for a while until we've looked into this further.'

'It's not as easy to do that as you think, DI Farrell.'

Farrell looked at her adorable little girl and thought that, if she was his, he would find it the easiest thing in the world.

Chapter 39

Walking away from the Delaneys and their life lived through the prism of a lens, Farrell had to force himself back to the station. He was exhausted beyond all reason, but he had to keep pushing. The fear that little Mia might be on some hit list spurred him on. Two punch-ups in one day? That was a record even for him. His muscles were already stiffening and his split lip had swollen. His suit was filthy and one of the buttons was hanging on by a thread. At this rate he'd be injecting the drycleaners in Dumfries with enough capital to expand.

He headed straight for the locker room and had a brisk shower. As he towelled himself dry he flinched as the towel passed over the welts he had inflicted on his back. Twisting round, he noticed signs of infection. He needed to stop this before things went too far. He knew he could no longer tell himself that his guilty little secret was all about religious observance.

He broke out a new shirt from its cellophane. His mother had restocked his drawers since he'd returned, as if she was belatedly trying to make up for her historical coldness towards him.

Walking into the MCA room, he helped himself to the fresh pot of coffee that Dave Thomson had thoughtfully made.

'Cheers, Dave,' he said, greedily slurping the strong brew and feeling his nerve endings perk up to the stimulus.

'I reckon if they cut you, coffee rather than blood would leak out, boss.' Dave grinned.

'You could be right about that,' said Farrell, draining his coffee and pouring another one. 'Right then, let's head down to the cells and see if we've netted ourselves a murderer.'

As it was now after eleven, the cells were heaving with the usual assortment of drunks and human driftwood that came in on the tide of having a good time. Farrell leapt aside to avoid projectile vomit from a drunk man in a shiny suit. DS Byers, who was filling out some paperwork, was not so lucky and stormed off cursing. Farrell tried not to laugh, but he was only human.

'That's your perp been processed,' said DS Donald Sloan, shouting above the ruckus. 'Refused to give his name or any details. His solicitor is on her way.'

DI Moore appeared, trailed by Jack Kerr, and the fiscal depute, Peter Swift. The latter was tight-lipped with anger.

'I'll remember this next time you lot are looking for a favour,' he snapped, to jeering from one of the drunks who was laughing and pointing him out to his buddies.

'Look,' said Farrell, exasperated, 'we didn't want to do this, but you left us very little choice. Sheriff Granger was spitting nails. You're being released on police bail pending appearance in court tomorrow.'

'Before Sheriff Granger?' asked Jack Kerr, looking worried.

'No. They're sending another sheriff from Glasgow,' said DI Moore. She glanced at Peter Swift. 'Your boss has also arranged another fiscal from Edinburgh. The case will be called in Court 3 at 8.30, which should ensure you don't have an audience, at least.'

'That's something I suppose,' said Swift.

At that moment, in walked Beth Roberts.

'What took you so long?' snapped Peter Swift.

'I'm not here for you, I've been called out to another case,' she said, looking embarrassed and sliding her eyes from his.

'Of course, you have,' Swift said. 'Never you mind about me.'

'Take it easy, mate,' said Jack Kerr.

'If I wanted your opinion I'd have asked for it,' Swift said.

This was getting ugly again. Farrell raised his eyes at Donald Sloan who nodded back and bent his head with some urgency to the paperwork. A few minutes later, they were sent grumbling on their way.

'He's just embarrassed,' said Beth Roberts to Farrell.

'I can understand that,' he replied with a quick grin, though he hadn't liked the way the man had spoken to her. 'I'll pop you in to an interview room and we'll be along with your client shortly. After that, I'd like to interview you about the carry on in court today. I need you to clear something up for us.'

She coloured but met his eyes and smiled.

'Sure, no problem.'

Next up were Max Delaney and Gabriel Ferrante.

Delaney was taut with anxiety. He stopped in front of Farrell. 'Thank you. I owe you one. And I'm a man who pays my debts. If anything had happened to them ...'

'We'll keep an eye on them for the time being,' said Farrell. 'Try not to worry.'

Gabriel Ferrante nodded. 'Nice one, DI Farrell. A pleasing novelty to meet a decent copper.'

'From you, I'll take that as a compliment,' said Farrell.

He stood and watched both men as they were processed at the desk. Ferrante was something of an enigma to him. He couldn't figure him out at all.

DI Moore walked up behind Ferrante, carrying a jacket, and tapped him on the shoulder. To everyone's shock he spun round and grabbed her throat with one hand, the tip of a pen pressed against her neck. His face was devoid of emotion and his eyes blank. Suddenly, his expression changed to one of horror, as though he had woken from a trance. He released his grip immediately and DI Moore staggered backwards. Two burly uniforms rushed to grab him, but DI Moore, coughing, held up her hand to ward them off.

Ferrante was ashen and shaking.

'I'm so sorry,' he mumbled, 'I don't know what came over me. How I could have ...?' He shook his head and held out his hands, wrists together, as if begging her to cuff him.

'Don't worry about it,' she said, with a strained smile. 'I startled you. You forgot your jacket.'

He took it from her with murmured thanks and the two men were sent on their way.

Farrell motioned to DI Moore to follow him into an interview room around the corner. He too had been shocked by Ferrante's reaction.

She flopped into a chair and he could see the imprint of Ferrante's fingers round her throat as well as a red mark where the pen had been pressed against her neck.

'That's what I get for coming back in,' she said.

'Are you sure you're okay?' he asked.

'Really, I'm fine,' she said. 'I admit it was a bit of a shock but it was my own stupid fault. I should've known better. My dad was a marine and I was always told never to jump out on him as a kid because they are trained to react first and think later. I forgot once and he spun round and knocked me clean off my feet. I broke my arm.'

She attempted a hollow laugh. This was the first time she'd ever mentioned her family. He could see that she was already starting to regret it.

DC Thomson stuck his head round the door.

'Boss, that's our man in Interview Room 4,' he said.

Farrell got to his feet.

'I suspect that's all the drama over for one night, Kate. You might as well get yourself home.'

She glanced at her watch and sighed.

'You're not wrong there. If I don't get home now, I might meet myself coming back in. The multiverse in action, courtesy of Police Scotland.'

'I didn't have you pegged for a Sci-fi fan, Kate.'

'Need to know,' she said, tapping the side of her nose with a small smile.

Chapter 40

The man sitting across the table from them was heavy and thickset. This was clearly not his first rodeo. Beth Roberts looked more nervous than he was. Farrell leaned over and switched on the recording device.

'Interview commenced at 11.52 p.m. Please identify yourself for the tape.'

'Ian Maxwell.'

Farrell, DC Thomson and Beth Roberts did the same.

'I'd like to remind you that you're still under caution,' said Farrell.

'Address and date of birth?'

'At 5 Green Court, Lincluden, Dumfries: 13. 4. 87.'

'Can you tell me what you were doing in the garden of 27 Terregles Court at 10 p.m. tonight?'

'I was having a quiet smoke until you bloody jumped me.'

Beth Roberts put a restraining hand on his arm and he shook her off roughly.

'Steady on, sir,' said DC Thomson.

'Fine, I admit I shouldn't have stepped into the garden, but I wanted a smoke and a bit of a rest, like.'

'You can't smoke and walk like the rest of us?' said DC Thomson.

'I needed a breather. I'd walked there from town.'

'And why exactly was that?' asked Farrell. 'You were nowhere near your home. Bit out of your way, wouldn't you say?'

'I like to go for a long walk every now and then. Last I checked that wasn't illegal.'

'Cut the crap,' said Farrell leaning across the table. 'You were watching the Delaney house. We know it and you know it. The real question is why?'

'I've no idea what you're talking about,' said Maxwell. 'Who are the Delaneys? Never heard of them.'

'What are you? Some kind of twisted pervert who gets off on spying on little girls?'

'What? Where the bloody hell did that come from?'

Maxwell looked startled. Either he was innocent or he'd simply been watching the house on someone else's instructions, thought Farrell.

'You know what they do to child molesters round here,' said Farrell, sensing this was Maxwell's weak spot. 'Even being charged with a crime like that is something you'll never get out from under.'

Maxwell wasn't acting so cocky now. A fine sweat had broken out on his face. He sent a desperate look towards his solicitor. She couldn't help him.

'Look, I'm no pervert, all right? Folk like that are the scum of the earth. I admit I was watching the house. I thought it was for some bloke who suspected his wife was playing around. Nobody said anything about watching a little kid. I just had to report on their comings and goings, that kind of stuff.'

'If that's all it was then I'm sure we can come to some arrangement,' said Farrell. 'Who asked you to watch the house?'

Beth Roberts stood up.

'Don't answer that. I need a moment alone with my client, DI Farrell.'

Farrell ground his teeth in frustration, but had no choice other than to suspend the interview and leave the room with DC Thomson.

'What the hell's she bloody playing at, sir? If she was going to shut him down, shouldn't she have done so earlier? He was just about to spill his guts and then he would probably have been given a deal. I don't get it.'

'Me, neither. Maybe she's realized she has a conflict of interest and that the client she's acting for at the moment could implicate one of her other clients.'

Beth Roberts stuck her head out of the interview room.

'We're ready for you now, officers,' she said.

They went back in and Farrell switched the recording device back on.

'Interview resumed at 11.26 p.m. So, Mr Maxwell. Where were we? We were about to offer you a deal if you can reveal to us the details of who instructed your little surveillance project?'

'On the advice of my solicitor, I have no comment.'

'Really?' said Farrell, looking at Beth Roberts, who refused to meet his eyes. 'That's where you're going with this? I don't know what advice your solicitor has given you, but I can't imagine how it can improve upon the opportunity you're being given here. Tell us what we need to know and you can walk right out of here without charge.

'Why would you possibly want to turn that down?'

Maxwell shot his solicitor a look of absolute loathing. She looked right back at him, her face expressionless, though flushed.

'On the advice of my solicitor, I have no comment,' he said, through gritted teeth.

'Fine,' said Farrell. 'Well, you leave me with no choice but to infer you were in that garden unlawfully for the purpose of committing theft. You'll be remanded overnight to appear from custody in court tomorrow.'

'What? You're keeping me in? You told me this wouldn't happen!' he shouted to his solicitor, as DC Thomson led him from the room.

'Trust me, everything will be fine,' she shouted after him. 'I'll meet you at court tomorrow.'

She shifted restlessly on the hard chair and looked across the table at Farrell.

'Do we really have to do this now, Inspector? It's been rather a long day,' she said.

'It won't take long,' he said.

DC Thomson returned and sat beside him.

'I understand that you were at court immediately prior to the afternoon session,' he said.

'Yes, that's right. I had a watching brief on a trial.'

'So why did you leave before we got there?'

'I left as soon as the fighting started. I knew the case I was interested in couldn't possibly proceed once it all kicked off and I had no intention of getting involved either as a witness or a participant.'

'You weren't worried about Peter Swift, your fiancé?'

'Peter? Hardly, he can handle himself.'

'We've received an allegation that it was you who placed the letters on the table in court. Is that the case?'

She sighed.

'Yes, it was me. I saw them on the court officer's desk outside the court. I thought it was probably instructions for the afternoon's court, so I put them on the table at their usual seats. If I hadn't lifted them, most likely someone else would have.'

'Are you saying that you had no idea what was in them?'

'That's exactly what I am saying.'

'Are you aware that one of them alleges that you have been having an affair with Jack Kerr?'

'Yes, I heard. That's laughable. He's not my type at all.'

'Your fiancé seemed to believe it at the time. He was knocking lumps out of Kerr.'

Her face clouded over.

'He can be a little jealous sometimes. I've given him no cause. He's apologized for doubting me. Is that it, DI Farrell? I really am rather tired.'

Farrell stood.

'Thank you for clearing that up for us, Miss Roberts, I appreciate you taking the time.'

He showed her out and exited via the back door with DC Thomson.

'Do you believe her boss?'

'I'm not entirely sure,' he said.

He'd decided to stay the night at his mother's house rather than risk getting in Mhairi's way. He wondered how her date with Sandy had gone. His gut twisted. He hoped she had finally met someone worthy of her. As he drew up outside Yvonne Farrell's neat bungalow, he dreaded the thought of going inside. Even though he and his mother were getting on better these days, she still made him feel as though he wasn't quite up to scratch. A failed priest wasn't the kind of thing that earned you bragging rights down at St Margaret's, where she was quite the mover and shaker. This new bloke seemed to have softened her, though. The more Farrell came across him the more he warmed to the guy. Even the exterior of the house somehow had a more cared-for look.

He slipped in quietly and tiptoed up the stairs, not wanting her to see him in such a state. As he heard her acerbic tones and answering laughter from Dermot Reilly, he felt an unexpected surge of loneliness. Reaching his room, he sat on the bed and slowly peeled off his clothes. His muscles still ached and the bruising already darkened his skin. Lifting the covers he slid between the crisp cotton sheets.

Chapter 41

Mhairi woke up and groaned as she remembered the events of yesterday. The phone had woken her, but not in time to answer it. She sat up gingerly and glanced in the mirror. I'd be a shoo-in for Hammer House of Horror, she thought, gingerly stroking her poor swollen nose. The bruising had really come out under her eyes but looked worse than it felt. Yip, she was good to go.

There was a quiet knock at the door. To her surprise, Sandy walked in with a fully laden breakfast tray and a couple of newspapers.

Mhairi smiled tentatively then wished she hadn't.

'Ouch!'

'That'll teach you to go wading in to the middle of a fight,' he said.

'That's kind of my job. This looks amazing, Sandy! But, er, what are you doing here? How did you get in?'

'I thought I'd pop in on my only live patient on the way to work. Dave let me in on his way out the door.'

There was a slightly awkward pause.

'DI Farrell phoned a few minutes ago. I hope you don't

213

mind me answering your phone, but I saw it was him so thought it might be important. He said to tell you to take as long as you want. Apparently, he was involved in some fisticuffs last night as well.'

'How on earth did he manage that?' asked Mhairi, starting to gobble down her food to enable her to get in to the station quicker. Clearly there had been some developments.

'Look, Mhairi. I hope I haven't overstepped ...?'

'No, honestly, it's fine. I appreciate the concern,' she said.

Sandy kissed her cheek and departed. It felt weird, like they'd suddenly been catapulted into a relationship, rather than had only one date. She wasn't even sure how she felt about him yet. Things were moving a bit too fast. God knows what Frank had thought when Sandy answered her phone. She glanced down at the headlines in the papers.

LOCAL LAWYERS BRAWL IN COURT

FEMALE POLICE OFFICER PUNCHED IN FACE

Mhairi bristled at the portrayal of her as a helpless victim instead of the truth – which was that she had kicked ass and arrested the buggers. They'd even managed to get a shot of her in her hospital gown looking small and defenceless.

'Bloody outrageous,' she muttered under her breath.

She picked up the other one and growled in rage. It was even worse.

DUMB(FRIES) COPPERS IN COURTROOM BRAWL WHILE CRIMINALS GET AWAY WITH MURDER.

Mhairi finished her breakfast, had a quick shower and got dressed. She remembered to apply the arnica cream and gulp down the anti-inflammatories before she left.

She fed Oscar and Henry and left them curled up in the warm sunny kitchen.

It was going to be another scorcher. To her disgust, she noticed the media scrum at the entrance to the station was getting larger. Despite the gate to the car park being code only, one or two of the leeches had the cheek to try and thrust their tape recorders in her face as she quickly punched in the code. Viciously she rammed up the electric window hoping for a finger or two to be chopped off. No such luck.

Chapter 42

Mhairi headed straight for the MCA room. There were more than a few covert glances at her nose and black eyes, but her thunderous expression did not invite comments.

'DS McLeod, a word?' said a firm voice behind her.

'DCI Buchanan!' she said, jerking like she'd been electrocuted. 'This is a ... a ...' she couldn't think what the hell it was.

Her boss must think she and Farrell had royally screwed up to be schlepping it all the way down here. She followed her out of the room and showed DCI Buchanan into a nearby empty office.

'Relax, Mhairi. I'm not here to give you a bollocking. I simply want to assess where we are with this investigation and to see what additional resources and manpower are required. I take it you got a little too close to the action, yesterday,' she said, with a wry nod to Mhairi's bruised face.

'You could say that, ma'am. The trouble is that what started off as a straightforward murder has become two murders that may or may not be related.'

'Related how?'

'They were both stabbed, but no knife or weapon was recovered at either scene.'

'Isn't that a bit of a stretch? The victims are a different age and sex. Surely, it's more likely to be two separate killers?'

'Perhaps, but the victims are both immediate family of two members of the local Criminal Bar.'

'A disgruntled client, perhaps?'

'That was one of the first things we checked. There's no commonality in their client base. Down in this neck of the woods criminal clients tend to stick with their lawyers for years. Fergus Campbell and Jack Kerr are both competent lawyers with excellent reputations, so it's unlikely anyone would feel they'd had a bum steer off either of them.'

'Other theories?'

'Well, it's possible that there's one killer who is targeting the three men because of something that happened ten years ago in Jedburgh. All three men were there for a criminal trial along with a young female lawyer, Colette Currie.'

'What happened?'

Mhairi filled her in on what had transpired.

DCI Buchanan put her head in her hands and sighed.

'When I asked if you needed more resources, I didn't have in mind that they would be required for an investigation of this scope. I'm not sure I can authorize what sounds tantamount to a wild goose chase.'

'DI Farrell and I can do some digging around in our spare time,' she pleaded. 'It's possible the tenth anniversary was some catalyst in the killer's mind.'

'Very well, poke around *discreetly* as long as it doesn't

jeopardize any other more logical lines of enquiry and keep me in the loop.'

'There's something else, ma'am. Late last night DI Farrell arrested a man outside Max Delaney's house.'

DCI Buchanan leaned forward in her seat.

'What's he got to say for himself?'

'Not a lot. He got his lawyer down here pronto.'

'Do you think that Max Delaney's wife and child are in serious danger?'

'Honestly? It's impossible to say. It could be someone targeting those close to the three friends. Or some pervert who has got too attached to Mia, the little girl, through their Instagram account.'

'What have you done to mitigate the risk?'

'We've advised her to suspend the account for the time being but we can't force her. We posted PC Rosie Green to stay with them overnight and posted a squad car outside the house.'

'We can't keep up that level of security indefinitely,' said DCI Buchanan.

'There's a possibility that Mario Lombardo is supplying drugs in the area and using kids like Aaron Sullivan to move them around. Aaron hung around with one of his low-level stooges, Barry McLeish.'

'I'm not liking Mario Lombardo for the murder of the kid,' said DCI Buchanan. 'If he found out who murdered his daughter, he'd snuff them out in a heartbeat, but he's more ruthless businessman than killer.'

'I agree. Unless, Aaron threatened to expose what was

going on to the police. Barry McLeish is still in the wind as well.'

'Dead?'

'Who knows?' said Mhairi.

'There's something else,' said DCI Buchanan. 'The reason I wanted to speak to you on your own first.'

'Go on,' said Mhairi, her body tensing.

'It's DCI Lind. He's been showing signs of increased awareness. His next of kin has specifically requested that DI Farrell *not* be informed.'

'You mean Laura?' snapped Mhairi. 'Lind is his best friend. He has a right to know.'

'Maybe if he hadn't gone round there shooting his mouth off ...'

'You know about that?'

'The Super here, Crawford Cunningham, gave me a heads-up. Look, Mhairi, it's not as if he's sitting up in bed talking. It's early days. He could continue to progress or he could sink back deeper.'

'I wish you hadn't told me. How can I keep this from him?'

'You must. If he finds out he'll be tearing up to Glasgow and it could completely destabilize him. He was already clinging on by a thread before coming down here.'

Chapter 43

Farrell had managed to speak to the senior fiscal depute sent down from Edinburgh to deal with the accused lawyers. Fortunately, it had been someone sensible who agreed with him that given the recent stresses the court lawyers had been under and the apparently deliberate nature of the provocation, nothing was to be gained from throwing the book at them.

It was agreed that the best and most expedient course of action was to charge all five of them, including the fiscal depute, with a simple breach of the peace. Sheriff Granger wouldn't be happy, but the sheriff clerk discreetly conveyed to him that the sheriff principal had already been on the phone and seen off that likely rebellion with judicious use of both carrot and stick.

Farrell waited in Court 3 as all five accused were led up from the cells directly into the dock to protect them from prying eyes. With no ceremony, the visiting sheriff came onto the Bench and fixed the embarrassed lawyers with a penetrating stare as the sheriff clerk read out the charge.

'How do you plead?' the sheriff clerk asked each of them in turn.

'Guilty,' they all murmured, one by one.

'Anything to add, Fiscal?'

'No, my Lord, this has been utterly disgraceful behaviour from Officers of the Court. However, there have been mitigating circumstances, as my Lord has no doubt been made aware. In light of these, the Crown would respectfully ask for as lenient a disposal as possible, given the circumstances.'

'Anything to add?' the sheriff scowled down at them.

'No, my Lord,' they all chorused.

'Very well, each of you is fined £100 payable within seven days. I also expect each of you to apologize personally to Sheriff Granger for your conduct. Is that clear?'

'Yes, my Lord,' they said.

'You're skating on very thin ice, gentlemen,' the sheriff snapped. 'I expect you all to be of exemplary behaviour from now on or the consequences will be dire.'

Four lawyers exited the dock leaving Gabriel Ferrante standing alone. He was calm and composed despite what was to come. He was to be charged with assaulting Fergus Campbell to his severe injury. His actions had gone way beyond self-defence. He was also to be charged with assaulting Mhairi and resisting arrest. It would likely mean the end of his legal career.

'Call the case of Gabriel Ferrante,' said the sheriff clerk. He read out the charges.

'How do you plead?'

'Not guilty,' replied Ferrante.

'Trial fixed for 15th August,' said the sheriff clerk.

'I move for bail, my Lord,' said Ferrante, looking tense.

'Any opposition, Fiscal?' asked the sheriff.

'None, my Lord.'

'Very well, usual conditions apply,' said the sheriff.

'All rise,' shouted the sheriff clerk, as the sheriff left the Bench.

It was done.

Farrell walked up to Ferrante who was standing apart from the others. They were understandably wary of him now that they had seen what he was capable of.

'Rough morning' he said.

'One of many, DI Farrell.' He sounded tired and strained, his face grey with exhaustion.

Joe Capaldi barrelled into the court through the public entrance but relaxed on seeing his boss and took a seat in the now-empty court to wait for him.

'Tell me, how is Fergus Campbell? I phoned the hospital but no one would give any information. He swung at me first, but I deeply regret losing my temper. I wish it was me in that hospital bed. I lost control. I couldn't even allow him the dignity of beating me after he found out I'd been sleeping with his wife.'

'I phoned before coming in to the court,' said Farrell. 'The injuries to his face will heal. The injury to his pride is another matter.'

'I fear I may have lost my moral compass, DI Farrell. It's something I've held fast to for a long time.'

Farrell couldn't help warming to the man. He was convinced that despite his recent transgressions, he had a good heart.

'I've heard you were a Roman Catholic priest,' said Ferrante.

'I was raised a Catholic. Sometimes I crave the luxury of unburdening myself.'

'Confession can provide a welcome release for a troubled soul,' said Farrell, uncomfortably aware that this conversation was veering off course. 'You can't go far wrong with Father Jim Murray at St Margaret's,' he said. 'It might bring you a measure of comfort. I imagine you're missing her?' he said, looking deep into Ferrante's eyes and seeing no guilt reflected back at him.

'More than I can say. Goodbye, DI Farrell.'

He left with Joe Capaldi.

Farrell sat down on a pew at the back of the small court for a few minutes. It wasn't as imposing as the other two courts and most punters didn't even know it existed on the top floor of the courthouse.

His brief chat with Gabriel Ferrante had moved him in some way he had yet to fathom. He felt a sudden surge of longing for the faith that he had abandoned. An urge to realign his own moral compass.

Chapter 44

Farrell landed back at the station to find Mhairi looking pale and subdued. The events of yesterday must have got to her more than she had let on. The bruising round her eyes was really coming out now. Mind you, he was a bit frayed round the edges himself.

'Let's grab a roll from the canteen,' he said. 'I can update you on what happened in court.'

'Sure,' she said, attempting a smile. 'I've posted the briefing for 11 a.m.'

They made their way downstairs and were soon sitting at a table with their rolls and coffee. Farrell wanted to ask her about her date with Sandy, but didn't like to pry. If he was still there this morning when he phoned, they must have really hit it off. He wanted to be happy for her but felt instead a pang of anticipatory loss.

'Well, how did it go?' asked Mhairi.

'They were done for breach of the peace and fined. Given the severity of Fergus Campbell's injuries, Gabriel Ferrante was charged with assault to severe injury and also for resisting arrest and assaulting you.'

'He didn't mean to assault me. I thought I'd made that clear in my report.'

'You sound like you want to give evidence for the defence.' He smiled. 'It's not up to us, remember.'

'I take it he pleaded not guilty then?'

'Yes. If he's convicted, he'll be disbarred. Probably needs time to put his affairs in order.'

'The look in his eyes,' Mhairi shuddered. 'It was as if he'd taken complete leave of his senses.'

'That's what I thought too,' said Farrell. 'Like a switch had flipped in his head and he was somewhere else entirely. He seems genuinely remorseful.'

'You missed DCI Buchanan,' said Mhairi, casually.

'She was here?'

'Yes, I caught her up with the investigations and she touched base with the Super. She's given us the green light to poke around into the case of Colette Currie in Jedburgh. It's to be done in our own time unless we discover something material to the present cases.'

'Maybe we can nip up to Jedburgh first thing tomorrow morning?'

'Fine by me.'

'Is she sending more bodies down?'

'No, they're stretched at the moment. She promised to have someone put a hustle on all our outstanding test results though, particularly toxicology and the drug analysis of Aaron's hair.'

'Anything else?'

'Nope,' she replied, springing to her feet. 'Come on, it's time for the morning briefing.'

Farrell followed her out of the canteen, his antenna twitching. What wasn't she telling him?

Farrell walked to the front of the MCA room and held up his hand for silence. The heat was already oppressive.

'Despite an extensive search, the murder weapons still haven't been found. Accordingly, we can't yet say with any certainty whether the murders of Gina Campbell and Aaron Sullivan are linked. It's perhaps safer to assume for the present that there is a connection given that Max Delaney's household was clearly being watched. PC Rosie Green stayed with the family last night but is returning to other duties in the investigation from today. We're installing a panic button just in case.'

'Barry McLeish switched his phone on briefly a few minutes ago, sir,' said DC Thomson. 'We got a ping on his location and a couple of uniforms have been sent to pick him up.'

'Excellent. Perhaps he can shine a light on what happened to Aaron Sullivan. Mhairi and I will handle the interview. I'm hoping we can persuade him to talk.'

'Do you think he could have done it?' asked Thomson.

'It's possible but unlikely,' said Farrell. 'Any samples obtained from the letters Beth Roberts placed on the court table?'

'There was only one set of fingerprints,' said DS Byers. 'Also, no saliva; the flaps were tucked in to the envelopes, not sealed.

'One of the two letters said that Jack Kerr had been sleeping with Beth Roberts. It seems unlikely that she would be the instigator in those circumstances,' he said.

'Unless that's what she wants us to think,' said Mhairi. 'That aside, is there any evidence to suggest that Jack Kerr was in fact sleeping with her? He doesn't seem the type.'

'He was questioned about that last night,' said Byers. 'He looked so astonished, I tend to think it never crossed his mind.'

'The whole thing could have been staged to act as a diversion but from what? The fight is starting to seem more and more orchestrated,' said Farrell.

'This time Peter Swift was targeted. That could be another potential connection to the death of Colette Currie in Jedburgh,' said Mhairi.

'How so?' asked Byers. 'He wasn't even in Jedburgh then.'

'No, he wasn't,' said Farrell. 'But it was his fiancée who died in his aunt's cottage, and he was the sole beneficiary of his aunt's estate, so someone could have been targeting him. His fiancée might have been collateral damage.'

'DI Moore, have you got anywhere with Mario Lombardo?'

'Yes, Organized Crime reckon that the whole retiring to be near his daughter version was just to save face as he'd been burned in Glasgow. The rumour was he'd been extorting someone high up in the judiciary and bitten off more than he could chew. Whoever it was apparently took out a hit on him and he was lucky to escape with his life. Since then, he's been keeping a relatively low profile. His house is like Fort Knox: CCTV, electric gates and the kind of dogs that don't want their tummy rubbed.'

'So, it's conceivable that this person he tried to extort went after his daughter and his business distribution network as part of a wider vendetta,' said Farrell. 'If only we knew who that might be?'

'Our only hope is persuading him to tell us, but he's not likely to do that as he'd be looking at serious jail time himself. I'll have another crack at him,' said DI Moore.

'Have you developed any rapport with him as FLO, PC Green?'

Rosie shook her head.

'Sorry, sir, I've done my best, but he's giving me nothing. Either he's being super cagey about his daughter, Gina, or they weren't all that close. He seems more angry than upset.'

'What about his grandchildren?' said DI Moore. 'He's never mentioned them. Does he see them?'

'I don't know,' replied PC Green. 'All I can say is that he's never mentioned them to me. Thinking back, I can't recall seeing a single photo of them in the house.'

'That's rather odd,' said DI Moore. 'Like I say, I'll pay him a visit and see what I can dig out of him.'

Chapter 45

'Toxicology results have come in for Gina Campbell,' said DS Byers as he came in to the MCA room after lunch.

'And?' said Farrell.

'They found faint traces of barbiturates in one of the glasses but not the other one. So, she likely shared a glass of wine with her killer and then was stabbed once she'd become unconscious.'

'If that's the case then the killer was definitely someone she knew well enough to let into her home,' said Mhairi. 'There were two wine glasses, but no bottle that I could see. Dave can you look up the inventory of stuff from the house?'

DC Thomson typed for a few seconds.

'There were no empty bottles either in the house or in the rubbish. The only wine bottles inventoried were full and unopened.'

'There were snacks on the table too, weren't there? Olives and chorizo,' said Mhairi. 'Things that would make it harder to detect the barbiturates in the wine. Whoever killed her obviously didn't have the nerve to tackle her without overcoming her resistance first,' she said. 'Maybe it was a woman?'

'It certainly rules out an attack in the heat of the moment,' said Farrell. 'This murder has been carefully planned and executed down to the last detail.

'I'm not liking Gabriel Ferrante for this now,' he said. 'However, if the husband, Fergus Campbell, had found out about their affair he might have been angry enough to plot his revenge in cold blood. He did come across as very unemotional, given what had just occurred.'

'It's odd that Campbell wasn't hitting back at Gabriel Ferrante, yesterday,' said Mhairi. 'Think about it, you've discovered your colleague was running around with your wife. Are you really just going to lie there and take it when he thrashes you in public? I'd have expected to see real rage there.'

'Don't forget we got there at the tail end of that particular battle. By all accounts Fergus Campbell swung first. Taking a beating from Ferrante might have been a strategy to deflect suspicion away from himself for the murder,' said Byers.

'Or Ferrante might simply be a better fighter,' said DC Thomson.

'The victim was strong and fit. She might have been willing to sit down and have a drink with the nanny, Jane Pearson,' said Farrell.

'She's certainly got motive,' said Mhairi. 'I suspect she was eaten up by envy. She could have planned to get Gina out of the way, so she could take over her life.'

'I can't see them sitting down together,' said Byers. 'Pearson couldn't stand Gina and, more importantly, it sounds as though Gina couldn't stand her either.'

'Yes, but we only have Jane Pearson's word for that, don't

we?' said Mhairi. 'She might have been acting alone or she could have planned it all with Fergus Campbell.'

'Equally, he could simply be a product of his upbringing,' said Byers. 'All that stiff upper lip stuff could have prevented him from reacting in what we would perceive as a normal way.'

DC Thomson looked up from his computer.

'I've heard back from the fiscal's office. They've arranged for us to be invited as guests to the dinner with the help of the Dean of Faculty.'

'I'd forgotten about that,' said Farrell. 'Tomorrow night, isn't it? Mhairi, I assume you'll be partnering with me?'

'Er, if it's all right with you,' mumbled Mhairi, 'I've invited Sandy Gillespie, the pathologist. I thought it would be more convincing that way,' she said, her red face causing the others to grin.

'Looks like DI Moore draws the short straw then,' said Farrell.

'Actually, the Super has already invited her as his guest. He's going to be making a speech, so she'll be with him at the top table, right beside Sheriff Granger,' said DC Thomson.

Mhairi shuddered. 'Rather her than me.'

'Looks like I'll be flying solo then,' said Farrell. 'Byers, are you still bringing Laura?'

Byers avoided his steady gaze and looked conflicted.

'You may as well,' said Farrell. 'She's been before a few times so will blend right in. That's settled then. We're not undercover as we're there as ourselves. You can have a few drinks but no getting legless. I want you all to be able to pick up on any tensions or arguments developing.'

He glanced at his watch.

'Barry McLeish?' he asked.

'Still in the wind. We found where he'd been staying. Basically, he's couch surfing. Not staying more than a couple of nights in each place. He's clearly still running scared.'

'He might have good reason,' said Farrell. 'I need him in custody as soon as possible, for his own protection as much as anything else.'

'You don't think he could have killed Aaron Sullivan, then?' asked DS Byers.

'No, I doubt he's got it in him. He's more loveable rogue than psycho killer. The fact that he's running, to me, means that he knows something and fears that knowledge might get him killed. He may even know the identity of Aaron's killer.'

'Maybe I could get him to come in?' said Mhairi.

'What do you mean?' asked Byers.

'Well, he still has no idea that I'm a copper. I allowed him to put his number in my phone in case it came in handy. What if I send him a text, asking him to meet up with me? It might be worth a punt.'

'Presumably, you're not meant to know he's on the run,' said Farrell. 'Where could you suggest meeting up?'

'I could text him all concerned and say I've heard the cops are looking for him and hope they're not fitting him up like they did my sister. Maybe offer to meet him for a drink to hear his side of the story?'

'Do you think he'd buy that?' said Farrell.

'Possibly,' said Mhairi.

Chapter 46

The following evening, Mhairi finished curling her hair and swept it up into as elegant an up-do as she could manage. It had been another full-on day and she was shattered. The last thing in the world she felt like doing was going out to socialize with a bunch of lawyers. The night would probably be one long yawn-fest and they'd learn sod all. She hadn't had anything suitable to wear. Fortunately, PC Joanne Burns was around the same build and had loaned her a gorgeous long red dress. The doorbell rang and Mhairi tried to convert her expression from tired and grumpy to vibrant and scintillating. It was difficult when her nose still hurt and her eyes were bruised.

'Think, zombie princess,' she muttered as she went to answer the front door.

Sandy Gillespie stood there in a tux. As soon as he saw her, he let out a low whistle.

'Looking hot to trot, DS McLeod.' He grinned.

She scowled at him.

'Left your glasses at home? Look at my face. You'd think I'd been ten rounds with Frank Bruno.'

'I'd a feeling you might say something like that.' He grinned. 'I've brought you a little something. Something we sometimes use in our line of work where concealment is required.'

She grabbed his hand and pulled him in.

'You're a star! Can you put it on for me?'

He stood with her at the window where the light was best and instructed her to close her eyes.

Again, she felt that strange but not unpleasant feeling of vulnerability as his delicate fingers gently moved over the planes of her face. In a weird way she felt she'd been more intimate with him already than any bloke she'd leapt into bed with during her wilder days. He was slowly getting under her skin and they hadn't even slept together yet.

To her relief, he successfully covered up the damage.

'You look stunning,' he pronounced.

'Thank you.' She smiled. 'You're not so bad yourself. Right, let's get this show on the road. Oh, and for the avoidance of doubt, if anything kicks off tonight and someone takes another pop at me, I want you to stay well back. I'm a police officer. Dealing with this shit is part of my job, so I need you to park the chivalry and hide under the table. Got it?'

'Feeling my man parts shrivel up and retreat inside my body,' he said.

'Good enough,' she replied with a satisfied smirk.

They joined the throng milling about in the reception area of the stylish hotel. Sandy grabbed them each a glass of champagne from a passing waiter and waited patiently as Mhairi located the whereabouts of the rest of her team. She felt on edge. For all they knew the killer could be walking about in their midst, stalking his next victim. She shivered. Farrell materialized at her elbow, looking distinguished in his rented tux.

He shook hands with Sandy before turning to her.

'Byers and Laura are over in that corner talking to Jack and Sarah Kerr. I'm at their table.'

Mhairi shot her boss a worried glance. That sounded like a recipe for disaster.

He nudged her.

'Look, over there. I didn't know that Sheriff Granger and the Super knew each other.'

True enough, they were sitting knocking back whisky at a small table with the relaxed demeanour of two old friends.

Mhairi spied a tight little group as the crowds parted. Were these guys glued at the hip or what? Fergus Campbell, Jack Kerr and Max Delaney were huddled to one side having what looked like an intense conversation while their respective partners stood together and made awkward small talk. Jane Pearson was wearing the silver gown that Mhairi had caught her trying on at the house. She'd lost weight and it now fitted her perfectly. Creepily her hairstyle too resembled pictures of his deceased wife. Mhairi felt her skin crawl but Fergus seemed clueless. He probably hadn't even noticed that she was morphing into Gina.

'DS McLeod,' said a voice in her ear. 'I'd like to say, once again, how truly sorry I am for hurting you.'

She turned away from Farrell to see Gabriel Ferrante, his eyes declaring the truth of his words.

'Is this the joker who assaulted you?' snapped Sandy. She should never have brought him. Civilians and police business didn't mix.

'Sandy, I've told you before, he didn't mean to.'

She turned to Ferrante and gestured to a couple of chairs nearby. Sandy shook his head and disappeared off to the bar.

'I didn't expect to see you here,' she said.

'I decided to come and brazen it out,' he said. 'I can't tell you what it took to get to where I am today. It seemed fitting that I should attend the Faculty dinner one last time.'

'I see you've brought your office manager with you,' she said, smiling across to where Joe Capaldi sat glowering in a seat near the bar, his tux looking like it was trying to strangle him.

'He's one of my dearest friends,' he said. 'I'd trust him with my life.'

'High praise, indeed,' she said. 'I feel the same about my partner, Frank Farrell. Even if he does drive me crazy sometimes,' she added with a laugh.

Mhairi heard Crawford Cunningham's loud laugh and looked round. He was still talking to Sheriff Granger. She glanced back at Gabriel Ferrante whose attention had also shifted towards the pair.

'The old boys' network lives and breathes,' he said.

'Really? Is that how they know each other?'

'Both went to Morrington Academy back in the day.'

'You went there too?' asked Mhairi.

'No, I knew someone who did. Granger is a cruel bastard.'

'What makes you say that?' asked Mhairi.

'You've seen him in action. He made a lot of enemies in Glasgow. Anyway, don't let me keep you, DS McLeod. I know you've got a job to do.'

He excused himself and Mhairi was left with the feeling he'd wanted to tell her something more about the sheriff but thought better of it.

The gong rang for dinner and everyone dispersed to their tables. She and Sandy were at Max Delaney's table.

As they stood for the top table to be seated, Chloe Delaney, who outshone every woman there in a midnight blue gown that would not have looked out of place at the BAFTAs, was busy snapping away. She pointed the camera at Mhairi who gasped in horror, not being a fan of having her picture taken.

'Don't worry,' Chloe whispered across the table, 'I have loads of filters.'

'Well, that's a relief,' Mhairi muttered sarcastically.

'Now, now, play nice,' murmured Sandy's warm breath in her ear.

Max Delaney was on her right and as the first course was brought he turned to her and said in a low voice, 'Do you think my wife and child are in actual danger?'

'Truthfully, I don't know,' she said.

'If anything happened to them ...' he said.

Time to take a punt, Mhairi decided.

'You need to tell us about what really happened in Jedburgh,' she whispered in his ear.

'I don't know what you mean,' he hissed, looking around to see if anyone else was listening.

'Someone knows what you did.'

Max Delaney went pale and said nothing for a couple of minutes, while Mhairi waited with bated breath for his response. His expression hardened.

'I didn't do anything. None of us did. Please, just drop it.' He turned away from her.

Reluctantly, Mhairi turned her attention back to the table. She noticed that despite photographing each course, Chloe Delaney barely picked at her food. Perhaps the strain was getting to her too underneath all the surface gloss.

Mhairi attacked her food with gusto.

'Is this a date?' asked Sandy in her ear.

Mhairi paused, her fork midway to her mouth.

'Not exactly.'

'You're a hard woman to pin down, DS McLeod.'

'I know,' said Mhairi, giving him a quick apologetic grin as she placed the fork in her mouth.

Chapter 47

Farrell knew he was drinking more than he should but it was incredibly galling to be at the same table as Byers and Laura playing Happy Families. He was uncomfortably aware of her sitting beside him, her perfume and the drape of her dress. Had Byers been right? Was he jealous? Feeling more and more tormented he took another deep swallow of red wine. They were clearing away the main course. Suddenly, one of the waiting staff, a young lad, knocked his glass over. As everyone paused in their conversation to look at the blossoming red stain spreading over the tablecloth, Fergus Campbell went grey and leapt to his feet, running out the room with his hand over his mouth.

Farrell excused himself, threw down his napkin and followed him. He looked in the gents but Campbell wasn't there. Going outside into the warmth of the summer night, his eyes penetrated the shadows. He couldn't have made it far.

Before long he located Fergus Campbell around the corner of the building, retching into a bin. He waited until he was done then walked over handing across a clean handkerchief.

Campbell took it to wipe his face and sagged back against

the building, his skin clammy as though alcohol was sweating out of the pores. Farrell offered him a cigarette and lit it for him. Campbell took it with shaking hands and dragged deeply on it. He was chalk white and his eyes were sunken pits in the darkness.

'Sorry,' he said. 'It was just seeing the wine stain spreading like that. It made me think of when I saw Gina ... all that blood.'

'I can't even imagine,' said Farrell.

'I still can't believe that Gina's murder can be linked to Jack's son Aaron in any way. I mean, I know that they were both stabbed but so are a lot of people.'

'We did catch someone watching Max Delaney's house,' said Farrell. 'If there's something that you're keeping back, then now's the time to tell me. If anything happens to that little girl ...'

'There's nothing more I can tell you.'

'What happened in Jedburgh, Fergus? You three are hiding something. Tell me what it is.'

'We're not.'

He drew deeply on the cigarette once more.

'You're barking up the wrong tree. It's got nothing to do with Jedburgh.'

'How can you be so sure?'

'I just know. Why can't you goddamn leave it alone?' he shouted. He turned and slammed his fist into the wall, yelling in pain.

Farrell was taken aback. Campbell was normally so controlled. This was a side of the man he hadn't seen before.

Perhaps a side that Gina saw the night she was killed if he'd twigged she was having an affair?

'You know I can't do that,' he said quietly. 'Why don't you just tell me?'

'I've never told another living soul. The others don't know.'

'Go on,' said Farrell, feeling his spine stiffen in anticipation.

'It's bad … really bad.'

'Did you kill her?' asked Farrell.

'No! Of course not!'

'Well, what then?' asked Farrell, confused.

'I'm the reason Colette Currie died in that fire.'

'What do you mean?'

'The day after the fire, I found the key to the front door of the cottage in my jacket pocket. I'd been drinking. We all had. I must have taken the key without thinking and locked the door.'

'You don't remember?'

'No, it's a complete blank. Like I say, we were young, playing drinking games and whatnot. I barely remember making it back to the guest house.'

'Wasn't there a key for the back door?'

'No, it was locked when we got there. The key had broken off in the lock and wouldn't budge. It needed fixed.'

'And you're sure you didn't tell the others?'

'No. What's going to happen to me now?'

'It was ruled to be an accidental death and nothing you've told me changes that. You did lie to the police, but if their conclusion would have been the same, then it's not in the public interest to pursue it.'

'I'd better get back inside,' mumbled Campbell, looking relieved. 'I've left Jane on her own at the table.' He staggered back round the corner heading for the steps into the venue, still much the worse for wear.

Farrell followed a distance behind him unsure what to make of his revelation. If he'd told nobody about the key then why were he and his friends being targeted? Maybe he wasn't the only one of the three with something to hide? Either that or the murders weren't connected at all.

Laura gave him a searching look as he returned. Her dessert was untouched. Byers was turning on the charm with Jane Pearson to see what he could get out of her.

It was now or never. Farrell sat back down beside Laura.

'Look, I'm sorry about the other day. It was a shock. I didn't see it coming.'

She sighed but her face relaxed.

'You weren't around to see it coming, Frank. But if it's any consolation neither did I.'

'He makes you happy?' he said.

Another sigh. She filled up her glass, took a long swallow.

'I thought so. I was adapting to the new normal.' She looked down. He suddenly knew there was something she wasn't telling him.

'Laura, what's going on?'

Her eyes filled with tears; her full lip trembling she turned to face him.

'Frank, it's John. He's been showing signs of awareness.'

Farrell felt electrified. He swallowed and strove to remain calm.

'For how long?'

'Only a few days. It's not much, he's squeezing the doctor's hand in response to pressure and his eyes are following the nurse about the room.'

'But that's wonderful, isn't it?'

'I'm not sure. The doctors say he has a way to go yet. It's early days but there's a possibility he might come up to full consciousness.'

'I need to see him,' said Farrell. 'What are you going to do about Byers?'

'I have no idea. It's such a bloody mess, Frank.'

'You sound as though you'd rather he never woke up,' said Farrell, his voice tinged with bitterness.

'You bastard,' she hissed. 'No wonder I didn't tell you before. You're such a fucking hypocrite.'

'Keep your voice down,' he muttered.

'Why the bloody hell, should I? I know how you feel about me. I've always known. Every time life gets messy or too real you run and hide in the skirts of the Church. It's moral cowardice.'

An awkward silence fell over the table. Byers gave Farrell a hard look and came around to Laura.

'Come on, time we were getting home,' he said, gently lifting her under the elbow.

'I'm sorry, Mike,' she said. 'I shouldn't have said anything.'

'Och, he had to find out sooner or later,' said Byers, his mouth compressed in a thin line. Arm in arm, they left.

Chapter 48

At the top table, DI Moore was sandwiched between the Super and Sheriff Granger. She'd never met Sheriff Granger before tonight and had no desire to ever clap eyes on him again. As his alcohol consumption increased so had his misogyny and, at times, crude comments. She had caught him squeezing the knee of that young solicitor, Beth Roberts, so hard she almost yelped. Had it not been for their over-arching purpose here tonight, she would have called him out over it. Peter Swift, sitting opposite his fiancée, was looking angrier by the minute. She decided to deflect him by engaging the sheriff in conversation herself.

'So, Sheriff Granger,' she said, leaning into his space so he had no option but to disengage from the young woman he was tormenting, 'how are you finding life in Dumfries after the hustle and bustle of Glasgow?'

He swivelled his massive jaw around to face her and impaled her with his cold blue eyes. Beth Roberts hurriedly rose from the table and headed for the toilets, followed by Peter Swift.

'Dull as ditch water,' he said, raking her with his eyes from head to toe in a way that was a calculated insult.

She wanted to slap him but instead smiled sweetly as she knew that would annoy him more. Bullies always wanted a reaction. DI Moore had dealt with worse than him in her time.

'A shame you were required to leave Glasgow then,' she said, curling her lip almost imperceptibly so that he would know she was aware he had been run out of the city by an enraged Bar. 'However, I suppose someone has got to draw the short straw,' she said, smiling sweetly.

He stared at her with his cold brutish eyes and she waited for his attack. It wasn't long in coming.

'Isn't your husband with you tonight?' he asked. 'Oh wait, that's right you don't have one. Any kids? No, of course, you don't. You career women don't want anything that could hold you back.'

He took a long swallow of whisky, some of it missing his mouth and dribbling down his chin. Then he leaned towards her ear.

'You're a skinny bitch who's going to end up dying alone and being eaten by your cat.'

Before she had time to react, he had lurched out of his seat and headed for the bar.

The Super saw her thunderstruck expression and leaned across.

'Kate? Are you all right?'

'That man!' she spluttered. 'He's a bloody nightmare. I've never met a more arrogant misogynistic bully. Sorry, I know that he's a friend of yours.'

Crawford Cunningham gave her a long look.

'He's no friend of mine, I can assure you. I hide my dislike

248

of him because it doesn't do to make an enemy of the sheriff in my type of work. If he's really stepped out of line, I have no qualms about telling him where to get off.'

'Nothing I can't handle.' She smiled. 'Didn't Frank say you and Sheriff Granger were at the same school together?'

'That's right, Morrington Academy. Bloody awful place. Granger was a vicious bully then and he's not much better now.'

'I can handle him but that young solicitor, Beth Roberts, was very upset.'

'Thankfully, not too long to go now. Here come the speeches.'

Just before the Dean of Faculty stood up and rang a bell, DI Moore excused herself.

As she left the room, the wave of sound behind her died down. Her body slackened and she realized how much strain she'd been under. The killer may well have been present but he'd done nothing to draw attention to himself.

Unsure whether to simply call it a night or go back in to mingle after the speeches she headed for the ladies. As she slipped through the heavy wood-panelled door, she heard muffled sobbing coming from a locked cubicle. She tapped lightly on the door. Immediately the sobbing stopped. There was silence.

'Beth, is that you? It's Kate here. Open the door. We can go somewhere quiet to talk.'

A bolt slid across and the tear-stained young solicitor stood there, her eyes red and puffy.

'I hate him,' she burst out. 'I wish that he was dead! Or, that I was. I can't go on like this. He's making my life a living Hell.'

As she turned away to get some more tissues, her wrap slipped down from her neck. DI Moore froze as she saw the livid red marks.

'Beth? Who did that to you?' she asked.

Beth spun around, pulling the wrap back up in place, her face flushed. She couldn't look DI Moore in the eye.

'It's nothing, really,' she protested. 'I've very sensitive skin. It gets blotchy sometimes.'

'If you tell me who it was, I can do something about it.'

DI Moore remembered Sheriff Granger squeezing her knee hard when he thought no one could see him.

'Nobody is above the law, Beth. No matter how powerful they might seem. Did Sheriff Granger do this to you?'

'Look, you don't understand,' she shouted. 'Just leave me alone. I've got nothing to say to you.'

Pushing past DI Moore, she ran out of the room. Her fiancé, Peter Swift, put out his hand to stop her but she pushed him away and sped off.

He spotted DI Moore and ran up to her, looking concerned.

'What's up with Beth? Did you say anything to upset her?'

'It wasn't me, I can assure you,' she said.

'Sorry,' he said. 'Of course it wasn't. I can guess who it was. Same person it always is.'

'If she decides to take things further, have her come and see me. I'll deal with it personally.'

'I'd best go after her. She won't get far in those heels. Thank you, DI Moore, you've been very kind. I won't forget it.'

She glanced at her watch. It was already after ten and she was exhausted. She slipped into a seat in the foyer and gratefully accepted a glass of champagne from a passing waiter.

Once the speeches were done, she slipped back in. Everyone was on the move now flitting from table to table, the formal part of the evening at an end. She spied Farrell sitting slumped at a table with a large whisky in front of him. There was no sign of Mhairi or Byers. She sank into the empty seat beside him before realizing that he was very drunk.

'Did you know too?' he said, his voice slurred.

'Know what?' she snapped, her patience at an end.

'That John is waking up and Laura decided to keep it from me,' he said.

Her heart sank.

'No, I didn't know,' she said. 'Is that why Byers and Laura have already left?'

Miserably, he nodded.

'I need to get up there and see him. He can't think we've all abandoned him. He doesn't deserve that.'

'Whatever you said, you need to apologize to both of them. I'm sure Laura will relent if you promise not to do anything foolish.'

'What? Like tell him she's shacked up with a junior colleague?'

She shook her head at him.

'Frank, this drinking has got to stop.'

Farrell felt a wave of irritation wash over him.

'At least I'm not trying to starve myself to death,' he snapped.

'What the hell?' she jumped to her feet. 'Where did that come from?'

As he looked at her hurt expression, he was tempted to backtrack, but he knew it was a conversation they needed to have, even if she hated him for it.

He reached up for her hand and pulled her gently back down on to the seat.

'Look, I'm sorry, I didn't mean to blurt it out like that, but I'm worried about you and so is Mhairi.'

'Frank, there's no need. I'm fine, honestly! In fact I've never felt better. I've been on a bit of a health kick, that's all. I may have dropped a few pounds but that wasn't my goal.'

'Kate, you can't weigh more than seven stones. It's as if you're disappearing in front of our eyes. Please, listen to me. It's turning into an eating disorder. Promise me you'll see a doctor this week.'

'Fine,' she said, her cheeks flushed. 'But only if you promise to speak to Father Murray at St Margaret's about the Lind situation and not drink any alcohol for the next two weeks.'

'Two for the price of one? You drive a hard bargain.'

Chapter 49

It was nearly 3 a.m. when Farrell arrived back at the house. He'd tried to redeem himself for becoming distracted earlier by circulating round the lawyers and their guests until the bitter end, trying to sniff out the slightest morsel of gossip or innuendo that might inform the investigation. To his frustration he learned nothing of value. Mhairi had left some time before him with Sandy's hand protectively placed in the small of her back. Part of him had wanted to charge up and smack it away for reasons he wasn't yet quite prepared to admit to himself. She had looked stunning tonight.

He collapsed onto the wooden bench in the front garden and inhaled the scent of the honeysuckle and moist earth. Dawn was already breaking in the sky and a few birds were starting to cheep and stir in their nests. He had always liked being there as a brand new day was unveiled, one that had yet to be stained with the taint of human interaction. He glanced at Mhairi's window and had an insane urge to throw stones at it in the hope she would come down and join him. The thought that she might be scooped up in Sandy's arms stopped him. He was getting maudlin. It was the drink talking, that's all, he told himself firmly, slipping inside. After downing a pint of water he was asleep in seconds.

The sound of his alarm clock jolted him from sleep with a groan. His tongue felt glued to the top of his mouth and his head pounded. DI Moore was right. The booze was doing him no favours. There was no sound of anyone else stirring yet. He showered and changed in record time and left the house twenty minutes later. It was still before seven. Almost despite himself, he found himself driving towards St Margaret's. It had been nearly two years since he had set foot inside a church. That connection he felt with the divine had helped him subdue his wilder side, his propensity to self-destruct. What happened to Lind had severed that ethereal link and he didn't like who he had become without it: smaller, meaner, more self-indulgent. Maybe it was time to dip a toe back in the water, to see if he could recapture that elusive feeling.

Mass was starting as he genuflected, made the sign of the cross, and slipped into an empty pew at the back of the church. He felt stilted, awkward, as though it had been so long since he last made his devotions that he'd lost the muscle memory. His friend, Jim Murray, was taking the Mass and his eyes reached out across the divide, as if trying to pull him back into the fold. Farrell gave him a small nod. It was a start. Awkwardly, he began to pray for forgiveness and that his friend John might in time make a full recovery.

Not being in a state of grace, he didn't go up for communion but felt an acute pang of loss as he watched the others shuffle forward one by one. As the Mass wound to a conclusion he realized that the words of the prayers were falling from his lips like well-worn pebbles. A sense of peace settled upon him, all the more precious because of the chaos and tension he knew was waiting for him back at the station.

He slipped out during the last hymn, feeling, if not fully restored, at least hopeful that it remained a possibility.

Chapter 50

Farrell walked in to the MCA room to find the investigative team already assembled and drinking mugs of freshly brewed coffee. He poured one for himself and joined Byers, Dave and Mhairi at the table. Stirling and DI Moore walked in just after him and did likewise.

'Right,' said Farrell, 'let's all share what we learned last night, if anything.'

'I'll go first,' said Mhairi. 'Max Delaney is hiding something about what happened to that young lawyer, Colette Currie. He became really agitated when I brought it up.'

'You didn't get anything out of him?' asked Farrell.

'He was a bit paranoid about being overheard at the time. Maybe that had something to do with it.'

'Interesting,' said Farrell. 'I took a shot at Fergus Campbell. He stated that he's the one with the secret, one he hasn't even shared with his closest friends.'

'Spit it out,' said Mhairi leaning forward in her seat.

'He maintains he's the reason Colette Currie burned to death.'

'He told you that?' said Byers, sounding sceptical. 'How much had he had to drink?'

'A bucketful. He claims he found the key to the cottage in his pocket, though he can't remember how it got there. Apparently, the door was locked and she couldn't get out. He blamed himself but kept quiet about it all these years.'

'We need to get all the original case work and try and have a meeting with the lead investigator,' said Mhairi. 'I'll run it past DCI Buchanan and, hopefully, she'll agree that this strand of investigation should be pushed up the agenda. Dave can you arrange to get access to the files?'

'Will do,' said DC Thomson.

'Any other information to share from last night?' asked Farrell, painfully aware that DS Byers hadn't yet been able to bring himself to look him squarely in the eye.

'Jane Pearson seems obsessed with Fergus Campbell,' said Byers. 'I sat beside her and piled on the charm.'

Mhairi snorted and he glared at her.

'Anyway, she acted like they're already a couple. She seemed very proprietary over him.'

'She's been darkening her hair,' said Mhairi, 'even adapting her make-up to reflect the style of his dead wife. It's a bit creepy. The weird thing is that I don't think he's even noticed.'

'Like a lamb to the slaughter,' said Byers.

'Unless he's the one who murdered his wife,' said Farrell. 'Stay sharp everyone, don't let any of this lot get under your skin.'

'I didn't make much headway last night,' said DI Moore. 'That vile sheriff was having a go at Beth Roberts. I thought Peter Swift was going to deck him. Apparently the Super and Granger went to the same boarding school. I thought they were friends at first but the Super said he was a bully back then too.'

'Gabriel Ferrante said the same thing,' said Mhairi. 'Granger bullied someone he was friends with who went to Morrington Academy.'

'Ferrante didn't take another pop at you then, Mhairi?' asked DC Thomson.

'No, he apologized again, actually,' said Mhairi. 'I get the feeling hitting a woman isn't his style.'

'Maybe so,' cautioned Farrell, 'but be careful, Mhairi. That man has a vicious temper and he's handy with his fists.'

Suddenly, the door crashed back on its hinges startling them. PC Joanne Burns rushed up to them.

'I've to tell you to get down to the Sheriff Court right away,' she said, her eyes wide with shock. 'There's been another murder.'

Chapter 51

It was nearly nine and the court wasn't open to the public yet. They parked round the back. Instructions had been given to those attending not to run sirens, so that it would simply look like business as normal. The SOCO van was the giveaway, but hopefully no one had noticed it turn in off Buccleuch Street. No sign of the ubiquitous Sophie Richardson, either, for which Farrell was grateful.

As they ran up the stairs from the basement they found a pale and trembling Bob waiting on a chair outside Court One on the ground floor. The sheriff clerk came along with a glass of water for him but he was shaking so much he could hardly hold it. The police surgeon, Rory McAllister, ran along the corridor towards them, breathless in his haste.

Farrell crouched beside the elderly man.

'Bob, can you tell us what's in there?'

He opened his mouth as though to speak but no words came out. His head dropped and his pallor increased. Farrell squeezed his shoulder and left him with the sheriff clerk.

He beckoned to the police surgeon and they quickly gloved up and entered the court. Standing in the entrance, they stared at the Bench, where there was a robed figure swaying eerily from a noose. It was Sheriff Robert Granger and there was no mistaking the fact that he was dead.

There was a black tricorn hat on the head of the deceased and the words 'Pronounced for doom' had been painted on the wall at the back of the court in red.

Farrell felt a chill deep within his soul. This murder was a cold-blooded premeditated execution. It had most likely been a long time in the planning.

He retreated back into the corridor where the rest of his team were waiting for instruction. Already he could hear members of the public banging on the door at the front of the building. There was no way they could open today. Peter Swift, the fiscal depute, came running along the corridor towards him.

'The procurator fiscal is out of the country. I'm the senior fiscal in his absence,' he said. 'What do you need me to do?'

'Get someone out front to tell everyone that today's court business will take place in the Municipal Chambers across the road instead, commencing, say, at 11.30 a.m. A temporary sheriff needs to be located as soon as possible to handle today's business.'

'Will do,' Swift replied, walking off to confer with the sheriff clerk on how to resume the business of the court. Farrell appreciated his level-headed approach in such trying circumstances.

'DS McLeod and DC Thomson, interview everyone who's had access to the court this morning. I want to know where every key to the building is housed specifically and who has access along with details of all key holders. Find out if there's a burglar alarm and if so whether it was set last night or subsequently disabled.'

'Mhairi, ask DI Moore to keep DCI Buchanan and the Super in the loop as well. DI Moore can coordinate all the intel flooding in from this point with Stirling's help. Get her to brief Andy Moran as soon as possible in relation to the inevitable press enquiries as well. We need to get ahead of this thing,' he said, aware that he was sounding tense and his pulse was racing.

'DC Thomson, get Stirling to gain access to all CCTV footage of the court and the whole street. Dispatch uniforms to interview staff from all the local businesses. This section of town needs to be flooded with as many bodies as possible. Pull in from the surrounding areas if you have to.'

'Byers, I need you as crime scene manager on this one,' he said. 'I'm going to be relying on your experience.'

Byers nodded and immediately gave instruction to secure the scene and delineated the inner and outer cordons.

'The preliminaries having been attended to, Farrell and Byers suited up and entered the court behind the two SOCOs, Phil and Janet. Inscrutable as ever, Janet immediately whipped out her camera and took photos of the bloated corpse from a variety of angles. Never had Farrell seen such a disturbing sight as the macabre gowned figure hanging before him. Sheriff Granger's face was mottled and swollen. It looked angry, even in death. The three men worked together. Farrell and Byers lifted the body up to relieve the strain on the rope while Phil Tait managed to cut the body down, taking care to preserve the knot. They lowered the body on to a plastic sheet on the raised area behind the Bench to avoid prying eyes. For a brief moment Farrell was tempted to examine the body to see whether it too had a Panopticon tattoo. It was unlikely but it would be good to know for sure. However, he couldn't take the risk of losing valuable trace evidence from disturbing the clothing. Farrell motioned to the police surgeon who was suited up in readiness and waiting behind the closed court doors for his signal.

Dr Rory McAllister walked forward looking rather unnerved, as well he might. Dropping behind the Bench he immediately felt for a pulse and pronounced life extinct. Once he was done with his observations, he left the way he had come, carefully retracing his steps.

It was going to take the SOCO team some time to process the scene. After a while, Farrell left DS Byers in the court and went to find the sheriff clerk, who had sent Bob home in a taxi after Mhairi had coaxed a brief statement from him.

'The press has arrived,' the clerk announced, jerking his head to the heavy wooden doors which remained locked. There was a concerted banging on the front door.

'They've been broadcasting live from outside the court for the last thirty minutes. A crowd is building up out front.'

'Sophie Richardson and her henchmen, I'll bet,' muttered Farrell. Dumfries was a small town and news spread like wildfire on social media. Someone from the court or the police station must have blabbed. They could now hear a news helicopter circling overhead.

'Can you escort me to the sheriff's chambers? I know they're somewhere behind Court One but it's a proper labyrinth back there.'

'This way,' he said, summoning one of his clerks to continue where he'd left off. Eventually after a disorienting number of twists and turns, Farrell found himself in Sheriff Granger's private chambers, which led directly, via a short corridor, onto the Bench in Court One. As he stood on the threshold and slowly looked around, he could see no signs of a struggle. He was sure that Sheriff Granger would not have gone willingly to his death. How had the attacker managed to overcome such a powerful man and string him up in that fashion? Of course, it was possible he'd been dead before he was hoisted, but it would still have taken considerable strength. He noticed that there was a jug of water on the table with a half-filled glass. Could he have been sedated or poisoned? Could the murders be linked? Farrell sighed and rubbed his gloved hand over bleary eyes. Where was it all going to end?

Chapter 52

It was some hours before the crime scene was processed and the sheriff was zipped unceremoniously into a black body bag and stretchered downstairs to the waiting vehicle from the morgue. Farrell followed behind and was disturbed to see that in the interval the crowd numbers had swelled, their faces distorted by anger. As the vehicle was obliged to stop on the slope at the side of the court before turning out into the traffic, it was surrounded by the angry mob, shouting 'Burn in Hell, you bastard' and other choice words as they thumped angrily on the vehicle. A number of women ran out of the crowd and spat on the van. Farrell was shocked to see Beth Roberts among them, her face contorted in hate as she too spat on and thumped the van with her fists. Their eyes met and the connection seemed to shock her back to her senses as she dropped her eyes and melted into the crowd.

The van was being rocked from side to side now and Farrell could see the eyes of the driver, white with terror, and the fear in PC Joanne Burns's face beside him in the passenger seat. Frantically, he radioed for backup and a number of constables came running to join him as he plunged into the fray. Eventually, after a tussle that felt like Glasgow on a Saturday night, the worst offenders were cuffed and led away still screaming obscenities at the now-departing van. Farrell stared after it, breathing heavily. His brow beaded with sweat. That was some last journey, he reflected. Sheriff Granger had been a cruel and miserable man who got his kicks from hurting others. You reap what you sow in life. An ignominious end to an oppressive rule. The town's criminals and a few criminal defence lawyers would sleep easier in their beds tonight.

He recalled the fury and pent-up emotion of Beth Roberts. She'd had more cause than most to loathe Sheriff Granger. Could she have snapped and murdered him? Probably not without help. Mind you, in her line of work she no doubt had connections that would have been happy to commit murder for a price.

Mhairi pulled up beside him and he slipped in to the passenger seat. As she was driving away, he noticed Gabriel Ferrante and Joe Capaldi watching events from the window of their first-floor office opposite. Ferrante raised his glass in an ironic salute and Farrell nodded at him. It was a bit early to be knocking back the amber liquid, but never say never. If events continued to spiral he might be breaking out a hip flask of his own soon.

'That was intense. Are you all right?' asked Mhairi scrutinizing her boss with her usual forensic glare. 'Do you really have to wade into every street fight going? Your suit's got a rip in it.'

Farrell squinted over his shoulder. Dammit she was right.

'So it has. Are you offering to mend it?' he said, with a wicked gleam.

'Bollocks to that, sir,' she laughed. 'I've been known to take a man down for suggesting less.'

'I never thought I'd be pining for Glasgow,' said Farrell. 'At this rate we're going to be stuck down here for months.'

'Tell me about it. Another court-related death. Do you think it's linked to the others?'

'At the moment I can't see how,' said Farrell. 'My gut is telling me there's some kind of bigger context here, but while we're bogged down in the detail, it's hard to get a feel for what is driving these murders.'

'Maybe the ten-year anniversary of the death of Colette Currie in Jedburgh is the trigger,' said Mhairi. 'You said that Fergus Campbell had been harbouring his own secret guilt about that night, thinking he had accidentally sealed her fate. Maybe they all have secrets from that night and someone found out about them?'

'There's another reason I need to get back to Glasgow. I need to visit Lind.'

'Frank, you can't! At least, not yet.'

'I'm not planning to. But what if he floats up to full awareness and nobody's even there, Mhairi?'

'It doesn't work like that. DCI Buchanan is being kept in the loop. She'll let us know the minute there's anything more concrete. Whatever happens, he's not just going to bounce back from this, Frank. It's going to take months of physical therapy. He may not be the same person. You have to prepare yourself ... for all eventualities.'

'He'll make it through,' said Farrell, his lips a tight line. 'I know he will.'

'I hope you're right,' Mhairi sighed, shooting an anxious look at him.

270

Chapter 53

Farrell and Mhairi slipped into the station at Loreburn Street via the back entrance as the front desk was under siege from reporters. She headed straight for the MCA room to post a briefing for 2 p.m., and Farrell made for his office. He wanted to get his thoughts in order in relation to the various cases, before the briefing. The investigative team was now stretched past breaking point. He had to focus on the most productive lines of enquiry. His phone beeped to remind him to take his daily dose of lithium. He felt his pockets before realizing he'd forgotten to put the packet back in to his suit. Oh well, a couple of days wasn't going to hurt him. He'd sort it tonight. Right now he had bigger fish to fry.

His phone rang, breaking his concentration and he snatched it up in annoyance.

'Moira Sharkey on the line, sir.'

'Put her through,' he said with gritted teeth.

'DI Farrell,' said the gravelly voice,' I have information that I might be persuaded to share with you,' she said. 'Meet me in The Globe Inn in ten minutes' time.'

'Ms Sharkey, can't you just tell me now? I really don't have time to—'

She hung up. Farrell slammed down the phone and picked up his jacket. Infuriating though Moira Sharkey might be, she'd never steered him wrong yet. She was a talented reporter, although there was something about her that made his skin crawl. He couldn't miss hearing what she had to say, but, as usual, she'd extract a high price for her cooperation.

Five minutes later, he was walking up a close to the historic pub. He nodded to the barman as he went in and found Sharkey inside a small wood-panelled alcove drinking whisky. She'd bought him one too, her malicious black-button eyes glittering with glee, as if she knew just how badly he wanted to down it.

'Thanks, but I can't on the job, as I'm sure you know,' he said with a tight smile.

'All the more for me then,' she smirked, considering him with one head to the side.

'I have to say, DI Farrell, you're looking a bit rough. Maybe you need to take better care of yourself. All that clean-living gone by the wayside?'

She was toying with him like she always did. He had no alternative but to play her twisted game. Quite why he held so much fascination for her, he had never been able to figure out.

'Ms Sharkey, Moira, I'm flat out busy today given recent events. Now, if you could just tell me the information you wish to impart, we can both be on our way.'

'I didn't say I wished to impart it,' she said. 'I said I *might* be willing to impart it. There's a difference.'

Farrell could feel his temper start to flare and bit down on the inside of his lip.

'What is this information in relation to?' he said, trying another tack. The temptation to down that whisky was building inside him. He was determined to resist at all costs.

'Sheriff Granger,' she said.

'Go on,' urged Farrell.

'I'd want my usual terms. A nice juicy exclusive before the rest of the press get a look in, especially that bitch, Sophie Richardson.'

'Agreed,' said Farrell. 'I've always kept my word.'

'Yes, you have. Quite the boy scout until recently.'

What the hell did she mean by that? What did she know?

'And I'd want something else too.'

'And what might that be?'

'I'm doing a feature for one of the Sunday supplements on modern policing. I'd like to follow you for twenty-four hours.'

Farrell stood up. It was too much; he couldn't agree to this. He valued his privacy more than most.

'It can wait until these cases are concluded. The timing is flexible,' Sharkey said, seeking to reel him in with her predatory black eyes.

Farrell sighed and sat back down.

'I take it you have information crucial to the case or cases?'

She nodded, licking her dry lips, sensing his capitulation.

'Fine,' he sighed. 'I'll do it, but not until after the cases are concluded. Now spill, I seriously do have to get back to the station.'

'I've been looking into Sheriff Robert Granger for some time,' she said. 'Some of my sources at the Glasgow Bar were very unhappy about his behaviour. That's how he fetched up down here. A young male solicitor hanged himself after months of constant bullying. They launched an investigation into his conduct and that's when I got wind of it.'

'I know all that already,' said Farrell.

'It wasn't just bullying, there was more of a stink to it than that. He was rumoured to be a sexual predator. A young lawyer claimed he had drugged and raped her. There were other rumours of groping and inappropriate behaviour.'

'He was never prosecuted?'

'Insufficient evidence and a lack of corroboration. Semen samples were taken from the complainant ... but the evidence went missing.'

'That's gross incompetence, if true,' said Farrell. 'I'm surprised I haven't heard about this.'

'It dates from well before your time,' said Sharkey. 'I had to dig deep and I mean real deep to find it.'

'Is the woman still alive?' asked Farrell.

'No, she died in a fire,' she said, watching his expression closely. 'According to those who knew her, she'd been going to try and mount a civil claim for damages.'

'And the fire?' asked Farrell.

'It was in a block of flats in Glasgow. She perished along with an elderly couple, and a middle-aged man. It was ruled accidental. The blaze started in her flat and spread. It's thought she'd left her hair tongs on.'

'You think it was him, don't you?'

'I do, but I doubt it can ever be proven now, unless he's left something behind in his papers.'

'I'll look into it, I promise,' said Farrell.

'He might have been an arsehole, but he had friends in high places,' she continued. 'He went to Morrington Academy and so did a lot of other powerful people in Scottish society.' She leaned in closer. 'There was rumoured to be a decadent and extravagant secret society there among the wealthier and most privileged boys. If there was such a thing, Sheriff Granger would have been right in the thick of it.'

She slumped back in her chair as though exhausted with the telling and sipped her whisky. A few sunbeams shone in through the small window, causing the dust motes to dance and illuminating Moira Sharkey's corpse-like pallor and the dark circles under her eyes. Underneath her trademark shaggy coat, which she had opened but not removed despite the warmth of the day, he could see that she had lost weight. Her collarbones jutted out and the collar of her blouse hung loosely.

'Moira, are you OK?' he asked gently.

He should have known better. She lurched to her feet and scowled down at him, black eyes fierce.

'Never you mind,' she muttered. 'Look to yourself. I've heard you're going to rack and ruin. You'll never find what you're looking for in the bottom of a glass.'

Startled, he stood up as well.

'I don't know what you mean ... I only ...'

'Save it for someone who cares,' she snapped. 'Now get the hell on and solve these cases. I can't do all the work for you. Oh, and don't forget, I'll be coming to extract my pound of flesh when you're done,' was her parting shot, as she lurched off in a toxic cloud of whisky and nicotine fumes.

Nothing like selling your soul to the devil, thought Farrell, as he slowly followed her out, giving the whisky on the table a last lingering glance.

Chapter 54

Farrell stood in the packed lecture theatre and held up his hand for silence. The ripple of voices died away. He could feel a twitch pulsing under his right eye and while his brain felt charged with adrenalin his body lagged behind. His team, together with the Super, DI Moore and Byers, were all seated in front of him looking as tense as he was.

'I've recently come across information in relation to Sheriff Granger that could suggest his murder was motivated by offences he committed in the past. These may go back as far as his schooldays at Morrington Academy. I need someone to speak to people who knew him there. See if they recall anything smacking of sexual harassment, severe bullying or the ilk.'

The Super raised his hand.

'I wouldn't normally involve myself directly in investigative work, but as I'm a former pupil there, people are perhaps more likely to open up to me. I'll dig around.'

'Thank you, sir,' said Farrell; though, truth be told, he worried about a possible conflict of loyalties. The ties to a school like that ran deep. 'Jack Kerr went there too,' he added, 'though they wouldn't have been there at the same time. I hate to say it but another valuable source of information might be Gina Campbell's father, Mario Lombardo. It might be an idea to look back into any prior criminal investigations against him that went to court and see whether any of them came in front of Sheriff Granger. It would be quite an asset to have a tame sheriff in your corner. DI Moore, given that you've had a previous connection with him, can I leave that with you?'

'Yes,' she said.

'The post-mortem for Sheriff Granger has been scheduled for 9 a.m. tomorrow morning. DS Byers, can you and DC Thomson cover that?'

Both men nodded.

'The way that the body was staged doesn't make a great deal of sense. Why not make it look like a suicide rather than signposting the way with the paint and the hanging judge hat? DC Thomson, have you looked into the quote? "Pronounced for Doom"?'

'Yes, sir. It dates back to the old days of hanging and was said by the judge to the accused on passing sentence.'

'The elaborate staging of this death suggests a revenge motive,' said Farrell. 'It's also a possibility, given the strength it would have taken to get the victim to the Bench and string him up, that this time there were two killers not just one.'

'Do you think that this death is the final killing?' asked DI Moore.

'Honestly? I have no idea,' he said.

'These murderers, whoever they are, have gone unchecked

too long,' said the Super. 'We're being crucified in the press for not having had the gumption to make a single arrest. It's time we called in an expert to give us some insights into what might be driving the killer or killers, so I've asked forensic psychiatrist, Clare Yates, to consult. Please ensure that she has your fullest cooperation.'

Farrell felt the inside of his mouth go dry, as Clare Yates rose to her feet. She'd been sitting off to one side and he hadn't even noticed her. The thought that she'd been observing him without his knowledge made him feel exposed. He forced a welcoming smile on his face just a beat too late.

'Excellent, I'll make sure that all the salient information is placed at your disposal, Dr Yates. I'm sure I speak for the whole team when I say we'll welcome your insights.'

Mhairi rolled the whites of her eyes at him. Fiercely loyal to her friends, Mhairi wasn't a fan of the psychiatrist after she'd burned him so badly in the past.

'Moving on to Gina Campbell's murder. Toxicology confirmed she'd ingested enough barbiturates to render her unconscious. It seems likely that she was unconscious when she was stabbed and then simply bled out from her wounds. However, the killer then appears to have applied a transfer of a Panopticon on to her body just above her heart under her left breast. This detail is what leads me to consider whether there is something seriously aberrant in the psyche of the killer? It could also function as a link between the killings, as Aaron Sullivan had a different version of the Panopticon tattoo.'

'His wasn't a transfer though, was it, sir?' said Mhairi.

'No. It looked to have been done fairly recently.'

'I don't suppose Sheriff Granger had one as well?' asked DI Moore.

'We'll find that out at the post-mortem,' replied Farrell.

'I've looked in to the nanny's background,' said DC Thomson. 'PC Green managed to get a copy of her CV from Fergus Campbell and I started with the references she gave. It turns out this isn't the first time she's formed an attachment to a child's father. In her last job, she had an affair with the husband. The wife caught them in bed together, but he begged her to take him back and she relented. Pearson didn't react well. She cut up their clothes and they believe she poisoned their dog.'

'I can't believe they gave her a reference,' said Farrell.

'Apparently, they didn't. She must have forged it. The time before that she was working for another family and again developed a crush on the child's father. This time it wasn't reciprocated. She was convinced that he was madly in love with her and kept bombarding him with letters and gifts. It got so bad that they moved house to get away from her.'

Clare Yates raised her hand. 'She sounds dangerously unstable. I think that you should warn anyone that she's currently working for. She could be close to a psychotic break, if she suffers any more rejection,' she said.

'Agreed. PC Green, can you pop over to see Fergus Campbell after the briefing? Make sure that you get him on his own and share our concerns. Find out if they phoned the referees to verify the references or just took them at face value.'

'Will do, sir.'

'Finally, the murder of Aaron Sullivan,' said Farrell. 'The pathologist has confirmed that the hair sample taken from the deceased tested negative for consumption of drugs. It appears that he wasn't a user himself but was moving the drugs around for someone else. It's becoming increasingly common to use schoolkids for this as it reduces the chance of the drugs being seized in transit, especially in a town the size of Dumfries.

'I suspect that the person who involved him in this is Barry McLeish, possibly out of some misplaced sense of loyalty to a friend of his deceased brother. It's imperative that we speak to McLeish.

'DS McLeod and I are going to Jedburgh first thing tomorrow,' said Farrell. 'I'm convinced that Colette Currie's death in that fire was no accident and that it might be the catalyst that sparked off this whole chain of events.'

Chapter 55

Clare waited behind as everyone else slowly filed out of the room. Farrell gathered up his papers and tried to look calmer than he felt as she approached him.

'I hear that congratulations are in order,' he said, striving for a jovial tone.

'Thank you, Frank, I'm very happy. How have you been?'

He felt like someone had peeled his skin off and she could see right through his bullshit to the miserable depressed loser he had become.

'Oh, loving life up in Glasgow,' he fibbed. 'Unfortunately, these cases are keeping us here longer than anticipated.'

'It must be difficult being back,' she said.

'Life moves on,' he said, desperately wanting to leave.

'I'm glad that I was called in. It sounds like I may be of some use. I'm surprised it didn't occur to you sooner,' she said, sounding faintly accusatory.

'I'll arrange for the witness statements and crime scene photos to be sent across to you,' he said. 'If you need anything else let us know. Once you've had a chance to consider matters it would be helpful if you could arrange to meet up with DS McLeod to share your insights about our culprit.'

Her eyes narrowed as she absorbed the snub.

Well, what did she expect? thought Farrell angrily. That she was going to waltz in here and have him dance to her tune once more. Not a chance.

At that point, Mhairi popped her head around the door.

'Sorry to interrupt, but they've just brought in Barry McLeish for questioning.'

'If you'll excuse me,' he said to Clare Yates and hurried towards the door.

As soon as they were out of earshot, he turned to Mhairi.

'Thanks for getting me out of there.'

'I have far more important things to do with my time than rescue you from women you don't want to talk to,' she said, her eyes flashing.

'What? You mean he's really here?'

'They picked him up attempting to hitchhike to Glasgow just outside Moffat. He's been sleeping rough and stinks to high heaven, apparently.'

'Has he asked for a lawyer?'

'No, he says there isn't one he can trust.'

The sorry specimen of manhood facing them as they walked into the interview room bore no resemblance to the cocky young man they had last clapped eyes on. Barry McLeish looked utterly terrified. He was hyper-vigilant and his eyes darted everywhere. His body was twitchy and restless.

As soon as he clocked Mhairi, he jumped to his feet and backed away from her, shaking.

'You!' he shouted. 'You're coppers! I should've known.'

Farrell and Mhairi glanced at each other. Now their lie had come back to bite them. They should have sent in someone else to conduct this interview. Farrell signalled to Mhairi to take the lead. She was better with people than he was.

'Barry, I know that was a shock but you can't blame us for trying to get some background before we headed inside. We'd just fetched down from Glasgow. It was nothing personal. You're clearly terrified of someone. Let us help you.' Mhairi's voice was low and soothing. It seemed to be working.

'Come on, Barry,' she continued. 'Sit back down with us. Let's see if we can figure this out. How about DI Farrell here organizes some hot tea and buttered toast? You must be starving.'

He slowly walked over and sat behind the table. Farrell nipped out and relayed the request for tea and a few rounds of buttered toast to the custody sergeant who looked like he was about to burst a blood vessel at the very idea.

'Right, Barry lad, that's being organized. Are you ready to make a start now?'

Barry nodded. They switched on the recording device and went through the preliminaries.

'Can you tell us how you and Aaron Sullivan got to know each other?'

'He was my kid brother's best pal. After school, Aaron would come round to ours to hang out with George. My brother didn't like going to his place. His foster mam was always poking her nose in. My mam was more relaxed, like.'

'So when your brother died, did you start hanging out with Aaron?' asked Farrell. 'To remind you of happier times?'

'I looked out for him. I knew what he was going through.'

'Was it you who got Aaron involved in supplying drugs?' asked Mhairi. 'Maybe you thought you were doing him a favour, giving him a chance to make a bit on the side?'

'Yes and no,' he said. 'Aaron's foster dad has always been a bit of a pothead but in the last five years or so he's hit the hard stuff.'

'Cocaine?' asked Mhairi.

'Bang on. He reckons he's got it under control, but he's full of shit. Aaron said his mum was raging at him cos he was messing with the adoption. If anyone found out, Aaron would have been shoved back in care.'

'So why did Aaron choose to get involved in drugs if it was causing his family so much grief?' asked Farrell.

'Don't you get it?' said Barry, shaking his head. 'His foster dad's got a major coke habit. He heard them arguing about money one night. Jack Kerr's run up thousands of pounds' worth of debt. The dealer's been coming on heavy. His foster dad was scared shitless. Saying they'd all be better off if he topped himself. He'd had threats delivered by the dealer's muscle man. He'd been told the next stage was broken bones. He couldn't go to the police cos of his job.'

'So what exactly are you saying?'

'Aaron's been trying to pay it off.'

'Did Aaron's foster parents know?'

'No, he said it would destroy them if they found out. He only wanted to help them out and it got him killed.'

Farrell looked at Mhairi, feeling sick to his stomach and seeing the same look reflected back at him. That poor kid.

'Who killed him?' asked Farrell.

'If I tell you, I'll be next. I'm not kidding around.'

'We can protect you, place you in protective custody,' urged Farrell.

'You've no idea who you're dealing with. They'd slit your throat soon as look at you.'

'Look, we get that you're scared,' said Mhairi. 'But don't you want whoever killed your friend behind bars?'

'Here's another way to look at it,' said Farrell, hardening his voice. 'For all we know you're the one who killed him and this whole "it wasnae me" number is just an attempt to pin the tail on another donkey.'

'Why would I kill him? The only thing I did was introduce him to—'

'To who?'

'I'm not saying. You pair have done nothing but lie to me from the minute I met you.'

Farrell and Mhairi looked at each other. He had a point.

'You were in the Pig and Whistle with Aaron that night,' said Mhairi. 'Walk us through what happened.'

'I'd arranged to meet Aaron outside at 5.30. He was in a bit of a state, said he wanted out. I told him it wasn't as easy as that. These guys don't mess around. You're only done when they say you're done.'

'Were you annoyed with him?' asked Mhairi.

'A bit. He couldn't get it into his head that there would be blowback on me.'

'Because you had made the introduction,' said Farrell.

'Only to help him out, cos he wouldn't stop banging on about his stupid foster dad and his shitty problems.'

'What happened then?'

'I told him to forget it. I told him he was in too deep and just to keep doing what he was doing. It was best for everyone.'

'What was his response?'

'He said he'd think about it. We had a few drinks and then we left. I thought he was going home. I headed to the Nith Arms to shoot pool with another mate. I was there until closing time. We went back to his place to play some X-Box. I switched on the telly in the morning and saw that minging bird banging on about it on the news.'

'We'll need your friend's name and address,' said Farrell.

'John Donnelly, 19 Smith Court, Lincluden.'

'Why did you go on the run if you had an alibi?' asked Mhairi.

'I wasn't running from you. I was running from him.'

'Who?'

'I don't want to say.'

This was going nowhere. Farrell changed tack.

'What can you tell me about Aaron's tattoo?'

'He didn't want to get it, but they made him. I've got one too. It's like a brand or something, means they fucking own you.'

'Where did you get it done?'

'In the town. That place near the car park. The guy is legit. Aaron just had to take in the art work and some ID.'

'Okay, Barry. It's decision time. We need to know who you and Aaron were working for. We can't help you if you don't give us a name.'

'If I do, I'm a dead man. Look what happened to Aaron.'

'If this guy is as well-connected as you say, wouldn't he already know you're here? If you can't give us a name, we'll have to let you go. Do you think he's going to believe you when you say you didn't give him up?'

Barry chewed on his lip, looking sick to the stomach.

They waited.

'Fine,' he said finally. 'I don't know whether or not he stabbed Aaron, but he was in the pub that night. That's why we didn't hang around there long. Maybe he heard us arguing. Aaron was saying he was going to go over and tell him he wanted out and I was telling him to forget it.'

He paused.

'Spit it out, Barry,' said Farrell.

McLeish slumped in his chair.

'It was Joe Capaldi.'

Chapter 56

Farrell and Mhairi left Barry McLeish devouring his tea and toast, courtesy of a disgruntled custody sergeant. They headed to the canteen and grabbed some coffee and a couple of sandwiches.

'I think he's on the level,' said Mhairi when they were sat down. 'Barry's not a killer. He seems genuinely terrified. I was surprised about Joe Capaldi, though. Thanks to Gabriel Ferrante, he's carved out a decent enough life for himself after prison. Why would he risk all that?'

'Maybe he didn't have a choice,' said Farrell. 'His former associates might have sought him out and leaned on him. Everyone has their breaking point. I don't see him being the brains behind the operation, though.'

'No, me neither,' said Mhairi. 'Do you reckon he might have murdered Aaron?'

'I don't know. We have to bring him in for questioning, but I doubt we'll get much out of him.'

'That poor kid, I can't believe he was murdered trying to save that piece of shit, Jack Kerr.'

'We're going to have to tell him and his wife,' said Farrell. 'That's one conversation I'm not looking forward to having.'

'The tabloids will be having a feeding frenzy over the murder of Sheriff Granger,' said Mhairi. 'I still feel that if we look hard enough there might be a connection to the other murders.'

'I agree but we have to keep an open mind. The list of potential suspects will be a mile long. There's all the people he's banged up for starters.'

'Not to mention all the lawyers he's bullied the crap out of or sexually harassed over the years,' said Mhairi. 'In fact, if I'd known him longer, I might have been tempted myself.'

'Right, let's go pick up Capaldi,' said Farrell, glancing at his watch. 'Hopefully, he'll still be at the office.

As they trudged up the stairs to the tiny first-floor office across from the court, Farrell felt a wave of exhaustion sweeping over him. He wasn't sure how long he could keep this pace up. Hopefully, Capaldi would provide some answers.

They arrived in reception to find Capaldi behind his desk.

'Can I help you?' he glowered.

'Joe Capaldi, we're detaining you on suspicion of being involved in the murder of Aaron Sullivan,' said Farrell. 'You do not require to say anything but anything you do say will be taken down and may be used in evidence against you. Do you understand?'

'Yes,' he replied, flashing them a look of loathing.

At that moment, Gabriel Ferrante stuck his head around the door.

'DI Farrell, what's going on? You're arresting Joe? On what grounds?'

'I'm not at liberty to say,' replied Farrell. 'Mr Capaldi, we have a car waiting downstairs.'

'Joe, I'll meet you at the station. Say nothing, and I mean nothing, until I get there,' said Gabriel Ferrante. 'I'll deal with this. It's obviously a misunderstanding,' he said, fixing Joe Capaldi with a penetrating gaze.

Capaldi slid his eyes out from underneath his boss's scrutiny. Ferrante looked worried.

'Whatever it is, we'll get this sorted,' he said. 'You know I've got your back.'

Capaldi broke his silence. 'Boss, I don't want you mixed up in this.'

'Nonsense! Makes life interesting,' Ferrante said with a twisted grin.

They trudged down the stairs and into the waiting police car. Ferrante locked up behind them then headed to the car park for his own car to follow them up to the station.

Chapter 57

Before questioning Joe Capaldi, Farrell and Mhairi checked back in to the MCA room where Byers, Thomson and Stirling were almost buried under paperwork from the various cases. Each investigation was located on a different wall.

'At this rate we're going to need a room shaped like a bloody hexagon,' said Byers as he attached an updated timeline to Gina Campbell's wall.

'We've got Joe Capaldi downstairs,' said Farrell. 'I'm hoping he might give us something to light the way forward,' he said. He and Byers had been tiptoeing around each other after the whole blow up over Lind.

Just being in the same room as the man at the moment made anger flare hot and heavy in his chest.

'Let's hope so,' replied Byers, equally circumspect. 'The Super was in looking for you a few minutes ago. I think he's been phoning round his old school chums.'

'Are you and Mhairi still going to Jedburgh tomorrow?' asked DC Thomson.

'Planning to,' said Mhairi. She glanced at her watch. 'I was going to pop in to the fiscal's office and ask Peter Swift a few questions about the house,' she said. 'It's too late now. The fiscal's office will be shut.'

'I still don't quite see what you hope to achieve by going up there tomorrow? It strikes me as a bit of a wild goose chase,' said Byers.

'Call it a hunch,' said Farrell. 'We're going to visit the police station and speak to the original investigating officer then once we've scooped up the files we'll take a look at what's left of the cottage.'

'Could someone have been blackmailing Colette's three friends over the years about what happened that night?' asked Mhairi.

'Didn't someone say that Mario Lombardo is rumoured to have been involved in extortion? Blackmail would be right up his alley,' said Byers.

'If that was the case then maybe one of his victims snapped and murdered his daughter as some twisted kind of payback,' said DC Thomson.

'I would've thought Sheriff Granger himself would be a likely candidate for extortion given his history?' said Mhairi.

'Dave, identify everyone who was involved in the case in Jedburgh. We're missing something. We must be,' said Farrell.

He arranged to meet Mhairi down in the custody suite in ten minutes then took himself to the Super's room.

Farrell tapped lightly on the door.

'Enter,' came the plummy tones of Crawford Cunningham. Farrell found the Super sitting behind his desk, nursing a glass of water and looking as if he wished it would turn into wine.

'You wanted to see me, sir.'

'Yes, sit down, Farrell. I don't mind admitting I've found Sheriff Granger's murder deeply upsetting. Not so much for the man himself but for what it represents. Total anarchy, the collapse of the old order. A strike at the heart of its institutions.'

'You think it might be political, sir?' asked Farrell, that angle not having occurred to him.

'I honestly have no idea. But an attack against a member of the judiciary could be ideologically motivated. The fact that he was such an unpleasant individual doesn't help.'

'Did you find out anything in relation to Sheriff Granger's schooldays?' asked Farrell.

'Yes, I did. Rather depressing, really. I got more than I bargained for there. The name of that secret society was "The Omniscient". It was very select.'

'I hope you understand, but I have to ask, sir ... were you?'

'A member?' Cunningham laughed. 'God no. I was rather dull by comparison. All about rugby and athletics in those days. Those that aspired to join were more your creative types with a penchant for Bacchanalian excess. Not my cup of tea. Anyway, I have it on good authority that Robert Granger rather blew their socks off with the audacity of his application. He sent in a video of him having sex with a girl who had a hood over her face and was tied to the bed, completely immobilized.'

'Bastard,' said Farrell, shaking his head. 'He raped her?'

'He claimed she had consented, but the identity of the girl in question was never established. No female ever came forward to make an allegation against him. They let him join their merry band.'

'That speaks volumes about the rest of them,' said Farrell.

'The other thing of significance I uncovered was that in Robert Granger's final year a girl was raped and murdered. Her name was Emily Drummond.'

'Could it have been Granger?'

'Well, that's not who was put away for it. My source claimed that Granger was obsessed with Emily, but she wouldn't give him the time of day. He wasn't used to people saying no to him.'

'I'll bet,' said Farrell.

'Anyway, Granger had a watertight alibi supplied by his high-powered parents and wasn't regarded as a suspect, and they fingered a local lad for the crime, Tony Marino, who claimed he'd been seeing Emily at the time. Marino was nineteen then, eking out a living by supplying a bit of weed. He had a duty solicitor who apparently couldn't be arsed and he was banged up for twenty years. He served every one of those years, as he maintained his innocence, so wasn't eligible for parole.'

'Where is he now?' asked Farrell, his interest quickening.

'Nobody knows. He did his time in Barlinnie and disappeared off the face of the earth.'

'A dead end,' sighed Farrell.

'It would appear so. I've made a note of his name, prison number and date of birth,' he said, handing over a slip of paper.

'Thank you, sir, I appreciate it.'

'There's one more snippet which might be of interest to you. Apparently, this club I mentioned adopted the Panopticon as their symbol. They were a fan of surveillance as a means of controlling information about their activities and keeping their members in line.'

'This source of yours, sir, am I permitted to know who it is?'

'I'm afraid I can't say. He only agreed to talk to me on the express condition that I not reveal his identity. If you have any further questions you'll need to go through me.'

Chapter 58

Mhairi popped in to the interview room and sat down opposite Gabriel Ferrante. Capaldi had been sent back to his cell until Farrell arrived.

'Sorry to keep you waiting,' she smiled. 'DI Farrell will be down in a minute. Can I get you a tea or a coffee?'

'No, thank you. How's your injury?' he asked, gesturing towards her nose.

'Oh, it's fine,' she said, making light of it, though truth be told, it was still bruised. 'I was rather hoping for a break so I could ask for it to be remodelled along the lines of Taylor Swift.'

'Who?' he asked.

'Where have you been?' She grinned.

'Sorry, I'm not terribly au fait with popular culture.'

'This must have come as rather a shock,' she said.

'There's very little left in life that would shock me, DS McLeod,' he said, with a weary smile.

'I get that, in your line of work, but even so ... the man works for you.'

'I try not to be a fair-weather friend, DS McLeod.'

301

'I'm impressed by your loyalty. I just hope that he deserves it.'

Ferrante looked exhausted. There were dark circles under his eyes.

'Why did you opt for criminal law? There must be a lot easier ways for a person with a law degree to earn a crust.'

'I felt I had no choice. The poor and oppressed need a voice. Justice in this country is becoming once more the sole preserve of the rich and entitled. Some of us must redress the balance.'

'That's very noble of you. I gather that more and more defence lawyers are being forced out of the court by cuts to legal aid?'

'Yes, it makes me worry about where society is headed. If justice cannot be seen to be done, then the citizens will eventually take matters in to their own hands.'

'It's already happening to some extent,' said Mhairi. 'You only have to look at what happens when someone suspects a paedophile is living in their street. A vengeful angry mob is conjured up by the click of a few buttons on social media.'

'That's true.'

The door opened and Joe Capaldi walked in with Farrell behind him.

'Sorry to keep you waiting, Mr Ferrante,' said Farrell. 'I had some urgent business to attend to.'

He switched on the recording device and they all identified themselves as present.

'So, Mr Capaldi, we've received some information that implicates you in the murder of Aaron Sullivan. Can you account for your whereabouts that evening from 5.30 p.m. onwards?'

Capaldi looked at his boss who nodded encouragingly.

'I locked up the office at the back of five and then went to the Pig and Whistle for a few beers.'

'Did you meet with anyone there?' asked Farrell.

'Not that I recall,' said Capaldi. 'I go there to relax and unwind a bit, so I usually have a few beers and a read of the paper or watch sport. I may well have passed the time of day with someone if they spoke to me but that's it.'

'Did you see Aaron Sullivan in the pub?'

'I didn't know the murdered boy so I wouldn't have noticed him if he was there.'

'How about Barry McLeish?'

'Who?'

'Are you telling me you don't know who Barry McLeish is either?' said Farrell.

'Correct.'

'Maybe this will jog your memory?' said Farrell sliding a photo of McLeish across the table.

Capaldi looked at it, his face immobile. 'Nope, no clue.'

Mhairi could tell Farrell was grinding his teeth.

'What time did you leave the pub?' asked Mhairi.

'Around eight thirty,' said Capaldi.

'Were you alone?'

'At that point, yes I was.'

'Where did you go then?' asked Mhairi.

'I went to Mr Ferrante's flat,' said Capaldi, looking shifty. 'He lives above the office.'

It was obvious that he was lying. Mhairi glanced across at Gabriel Ferrante, allowing her disappointment in him to show in her eyes. He dropped his gaze.

'And what were you doing there?' Farrell asked.

'We were working on some cases for court.'

'And what time did you leave?'

'I didn't. I stayed the night. It was so late when we finished all the buses had stopped running.'

'And can you corroborate Mr Capaldi's alibi, Mr Ferrante?' asked Farrell giving him a hard stare.

'Yes,' he answered, meeting it with an unflinching one of his own.

Farrell sat back in his chair and regarded them both.

'A young boy of fifteen was murdered. He'd had a shitty break in life and been knocking around the care system for years. The Kerr family were going to adopt him. Then, in the blink of an eye it was all snatched away. He was discarded in an alley like a pile of rubbish. Like the shit on someone's shoe. Don't you think someone should pay for that crime?' he said.

'Someone always pays, DI Farrell, you can be sure of that,' said Gabriel Ferrante.

'Aaron Sullivan was running around with drugs in his schoolbag,' said Mhairi, her lip curling with contempt as she looked at Joe Capaldi. 'Did you supply him with those drugs or introduce him to someone who did?'

'On the advice of my solicitor, I wish to make no comment.'

'Whether you stabbed him or not that kid died because of your actions, didn't he?' said Mhairi, her voice husky.

Farrell nudged her under the table with his foot. She was losing it.

'On the advice of my solicitor I wish to make no comment,' said Capaldi, his face closed off like he had already left the room.

This was getting them nowhere and in light of the alibi they had insufficient to charge him.

'Interview terminated,' said Farrell. 'You're free to leave after being discharged by the custody sergeant.' He opened the door and showed them out.

'Goodbye, DS McLeod,' said Ferrante. 'I hope we meet again under more pleasant circumstances.'

Mhairi turned her head away, refusing to acknowledge him. With a sigh and a shake of his head, he followed Capaldi out of the room.

Chapter 59

The next morning Mhairi was sitting in her dressing gown nursing a cup of coffee at the small round table in the tiny garden when Farrell joined her after his morning run, breathing heavily. It was still only the back of six and they wouldn't be leaving for another hour or so.

'The coffee's still warm,' she said, pushing the cafetière towards him as he loosened off his muscles with some stretches.

'Cheers,' he said coming over to sit with her and pouring a cup for himself.

He really had no idea how fit he was, she thought, staring at him through narrowed eyes.

'What?'

'Nothing, just thinking,' she replied.

'Should I be worried?' He grinned.

'That's for me to know and you to find out,' she said, waggling her eyebrows at him.

They lapsed into comfortable silence. It was going to be another scorcher. Mhairi turned her face up to the sun and closed her eyes, enjoying the scents of the summer morning

307

and the sounds of the birds squabbling in the trees. It was like an antidote to the stress of the last few days. If only she could just sit here all day ...

She awoke with a start as Farrell thumped down a plate of scrambled eggs and some orange juice in front of her.

'Eat,' he commanded. 'We need to get going in half an hour.'

She sat up at once, embarrassed to have been caught napping like an old lady. She sensed a trail of drool snaking down her chin and tried to casually wipe it away.

'Too late.' He grinned.

Feeling flustered she scowled at him.

'Your face will stay like that,' he remonstrated. 'Now eat your eggs.'

With a final glare for good measure she turned to her plate. Farrell was now dressed, his wet hair already starting to curl in the sun. He smelled good. She scowled at her thoughts. What the hell was wrong with her this morning?

Farrell laughed.

'Are you having some kind of argument in that head of yours?' he asked, looking amused.

'Something like that.'

She must be coming down with a type of brain fever, she decided. Being cooped up with Frank Farrell for days on end in this heat must be sending her nuts. It would pass. It had to. Even she wasn't that much of a masochist, surely?

It took them only one hour and forty minutes to reach Jedburgh. Once there, they headed for the local station down

Castlegate, where Farrell had arranged to meet DI Bill Coburn who had been the investigating officer at the time.

As they entered a young PC jumped to his feet knocking the file he had been reading to the floor. He glanced at Mhairi and blushed.

'Hello, can I help you?' he asked, trying to recover his composure.

It was true what they said, thought Farrell, the policemen really were getting younger. This one wouldn't look amiss in a school uniform.

'DI Farrell and DS McLeod to see DI Coburn,' he said.

'Third room on the left,' said the young officer and buzzed them through.

Farrell found the room and knocked lightly.

DI Coburn opened the door to them. He was a cadaverous man in his fifties with thinning hair and protruding sad brown eyes that looked like they'd seen a thing or two.

'Welcome, sit yourselves down,' he said. 'I was intrigued to get your call after all this time. What can I do for you? Why are you interested in an accidental death from ten years ago?'

'We suspect the ten-year anniversary of Colette Currie's death may have acted as a catalyst for two ongoing investigations – murders – in Dumfries,' said Farrell.

Bill Coburn whistled through his teeth.

'I'm aware of the murders, of course. Every time I turn on the news, that harridan Sophie Richardson has been banging on about it. She makes it sound as if you lot are sitting on your arses twiddling your thumbs, which I highly doubt.'

'I take it you're not a fan then,' said Mhairi with a smile.

'You could say that. I've been roasted over her hot coals before.'

'She's a total nightmare,' replied Mhairi. 'We're hoping that delving into this old case might give us some new leads to follow. If it gets Sophie Richardson off our backs for a while that would be a bonus.'

'What can you tell us about the circumstances around the fire? Anything occur to you looking back now with the benefit of hindsight?' asked Farrell.

'Honestly? Nothing at all. I was SIO at the time. All the evidence pointed to a tragic accident. Of course, forensic science wasn't as sophisticated then as it is now. There was no trace of an artificial accelerant. It looked like she'd taken her duvet downstairs to sit by the coal fire. In the absence of any indicators of foul play, it was surmised she'd fallen asleep and a spark had landed on the duvet, which caught alight.'

'Did you consider the possibility that the fire might have been set to cover up her murder?' asked Farrell.

'Of course,' said DI Coburn. 'The body was discovered by the door. It bothered me that she had got so close to getting out. What had stopped her? Had she simply been overcome by the smoke?'

'I gather no door keys were recovered at the scene,' said Farrell in light of what Fergus Campbell had told him.

'No, tragically there was a key right beside where she'd collapsed. The working theory at the time, in the absence of any foul play, was that she'd been fumbling in the dark, dropped it and not been able to find it again to unlock the door.'

Farrell glanced at Mhairi. Maybe there had been two keys? 'What about the back door key?' he asked.

'That was a nonstarter. It had broken off in the lock so the door couldn't be opened. The old lady hadn't bothered fixing it and her nephew hadn't had time to get around to it.'

'Did you interview her colleagues who were staying at the guest house?' asked Farrell.

'Yes, here are all the statements.' He handed over a bulging file. 'Take them.'

'Thank you, we appreciate that,' said Farrell. 'You were the one who questioned them. Did you notice anything odd about their demeanour at the time?'

'They were young and obviously in shock. All three of them looked like they'd had a good skinful the night before.'

'Did the results of the post-mortem throw up anything unusual?' asked Farrell.

'It was hard to draw much in the way of conclusions from any external examination because of the burns. However, the toxicology report indicated that she'd ingested a considerable amount of alcohol. There was also evidence of both cannabis and ecstasy consumption.'

'Was there anything else that stood out?'

'Obviously the body was badly burned. However, someone did drive by the road end, see the flames and call it in, so they got her out before the fire had completely consumed her. I do recall that two different semen samples were obtained from the body.'

'Did any of her friends admit to having had sex with her the night she died?' asked Mhairi.

'We did follow that up but they all denied it. Given that they swore they'd been together the whole night and that we had no grounds to suspect that a crime had been committed, we couldn't compel them to provide semen samples, and they declined to produce them voluntarily when asked.'

'That's a bit strange,' said Mhairi.

'She was young, perhaps blowing off steam,' he said with a shrug.

'But it was Jedburgh,' persisted Mhairi. 'She was here for work, had a fiancé at home. If it wasn't the guys she was up here with then where would she even have had the opportunity to meet anyone else?'

'What happened to the cottage? Has it been sold on?' she asked, following another train of thought.

'No, it's a charred ruin. The buildings insurance had lapsed. Peter Swift never did anything with it. Either he didn't have the money or he simply couldn't face it. One way or another that poor bloke lost everything that night.'

Chapter 60

DS Byers and DC Thomson arrived at the morgue. Reluctantly they exchanged the sounds and smells of the balmy May day for the squelches and odours of a decaying human body. The chemical smells of formaldehyde and disinfectant were trying but failing to gain the upper hand.

Byers had crossed swords with Sheriff Granger a few times in court while giving evidence. Now, as he nodded to Roland Bartle-White and his assistant, Sandy Gillespie, it felt somewhat surreal to be staring at his naked body without the trappings of power.

'DS Byers, observe the ligature marks around the neck,' said Bartle-White. 'The hyoid bone has fractured, which is consistent with hanging.' He then pointed out areas where the blood had pooled in the body causing a reddened appearance in the skin. 'If I had to make an informed guess, I would say that the lividity is consistent with him sitting for a time after death before he was hung up.'

'That would fit with the stained carpet beneath the table in his chamber and the rather unpleasant smell,' said Byers.

'I assume that you seized any liquids in the room to test for toxins?' said the pathologist.

'Yes,' said Byers. 'We haven't received the results back yet. Do you think that he was perhaps poisoned first?'

'I specialize in facts, not idle speculation,' said Bartle-White, looking at him over his half-moon glasses.

Pompous ass, thought Byers, striving to keep his expression neutral. He caught DC Thomson smirking out of the corner of his eye and glared at him.

'However,' droned the pathologist, 'he was a powerfully built man, so his resistance would have had to have been overcome somehow. The deceased seems to have suffered no blunt-force trauma. There are no puncture wounds or injection marks. However, he has a tattoo that might be of interest to you, if you care to approach.'

Byers and Thomson both approached the dead body and leaned over to look where the pathologist was pointing. There, on the far side of his ribcage, was a Panopticon tattoo.

'That one has been there for a good number of years,' said the pathologist. 'The ink has faded considerably.

'Would you like me to excise the tattoo to preserve'it before I excavate the organs?' Bartle-White asked, in the casual manner of one who was enquiring if they should pass the milk.

'Yes, that would be helpful,' replied Byers. His head was spinning and he saw the same confusion mirrored in the eyes of DC Thomson.

How on earth could such disparate murder victims be connected? It made no sense. The rest of the post-mortem passed uneventfully, although Thomson had to take a break once the saw got going to avoid contributing his own stomach contents to the proceedings.

After it was finished, Byers found him sitting outside on a bench, still looking a bit green around the gills.

'Sorry, Sarge,' he said. 'I'll eventually get used to them.'

'Don't worry, lad. They still make me want to heave even after all this time. I'm just better at hiding it.'

'These tattoos are freaking me out,' said DC Thomson, as they walked over to the car. 'The murders must be connected, right?'

'You would think so,' sighed Byers. 'But for the life of me I can't figure it out.

'Let's go take a look at his house,' he said. 'Sheriff Granger didn't have any immediate family but his niece has given us permission to search the premises. She drove down from the Borders last night to hand in a key he left with her for emergencies. It sounds like they didn't have much to do with each other. She said her mother couldn't stand him.'

Sheriff Granger's house was fairly isolated, but only five miles from Dumfries. Modern in design, it had a Japanese Zen garden to the front and a well-kept lawn wrapped around the other three sides. There were CCTV monitors at each corner, an electric gate and a good-quality alarm system.

'I've never seen security like that on a private house down here,' commented DC Thomson, as they let themselves in with the key and disabled the alarm by inputting the code.

The air hung heavy in the house which was furnished in the minimalist style. Each carefully chosen piece was clearly worth a fortune.

'Whatever you do, don't break anything,' cautioned Byers. 'The Police Scotland coffers aren't exactly equipped to handle breakages at this level.'

As they looked around the immaculate interior it was as if no one had lived there. The overall effect was one of sterility.

'Right then,' said Byers, 'let's split up to conduct the search. You do the lounge and the kitchen and I'll deal with the bedrooms and study. Shout if you need me.'

Byers soon located the master bedroom. It was dominated by a large bed with sumptuous red and black silk bedding. There were a number of disturbing mahogany wooden masks on the walls and a huge tapestry covered one wall depicting scenes of massacre. It looked vaguely familiar so was probably a replica of a famous museum piece.

'Bloody Nora,' muttered Byers. The sheriff must have been a right nutter to have his bedroom decked out like this. He rifled through the elaborately carved chest of drawers. Again, all the items of clothing were of the very best quality, if not to Byers's taste. He examined the inside of the wardrobe. There were a number of black tailored suits as well as expensive casual wear. The sheriff's oval wig box was sitting on a shelf along with a neat pile of folded cravats. To one side there was another wig box and he opened it expecting to find a spare wig but instead pulled out a coarse woollen balaclava. A shiver of unease danced up his spine as he placed it in an evidence bag. As he reached deeper into the recesses a tiny winking red light caught his attention. A spy camera? He delicately probed with his gloved fingers until he found it, disguised in a knot of wood and pointing directly at the bed. He carefully extricated himself hoping it hadn't caught him picking his nose or having an illicit scratch without realizing. There could be others as well, but that would be up to one of the Techs to determine.

'Sarge, come and look at this!' yelled DC Thomson.

Byers walked through to Granger's magnificent study. Thomson had his gloves on and was pointing to a large leather-bound book on an antique desk. Byers felt his interest quicken as he saw the Panopticon symbol on the cover. As he turned a few of the pages he was rendered speechless. This was bad. This was very bad indeed. The black-and-white photos of the young women leapt from the page capturing their vulnerability. He turned to the last page and felt a stab of recognition. Feeling sick to the stomach he contacted the station.

'Byers here. We need a full SOCO team down here right away with Tech Support.'

Chapter 61

Following DI Coburn's directions, Farrell and Mhairi drove to the outskirts of the pretty market town.

'Next on the left,' said Mhairi, as they left the houses behind in favour of hedgerows and rolling green fields.

Farrell braked sharply and turned onto a narrow road with the kind of potholes only a jeep could take in its stride. He winced as the Citroen lurched drunkenly from one side to the other. There were no houses. Both sides of the road were flanked by high hedges. Rounding a corner, they saw the ruined cottage at the end of the lane. Its brooding charred façade made Mhairi shudder as they drew closer.

'That poor girl,' she said. 'I can't even imagine the terror she must have felt.'

They parked and slowly walked towards the blackened remains which were set well back from the track. The garden was a riot of colour as it had been allowed to grow unchecked over the years.

The scorched wooden door swung back on its hinges when Farrell inserted the key he had been given, a gaping invitation to those brave enough to enter. Gingerly they crossed the threshold. The smell of smoke still lingered there, cloying and malodorous, even after all this time. The sky could be glimpsed through the roof in places.

Mhairi peered into the grate of the fire.

'I wonder why she brought her duvet in here?' she asked. 'It was summer time. Surely it wasn't that cold?'

'If she'd been drinking and doing drugs that could have caused her temperature to plummet,' said Farrell.

'I still don't buy that she had sex with two random guys,' said Mhairi.

'What do you mean?' asked Farrell.

'Well, she was engaged for starters. I could see her cheating with one man that night but two? She was here for work after all.'

'Where are you going with this, Mhairi?'

'I think it's far more likely she slept with one of the three men she'd been hanging around with all week. Is it possible that one of them raped her after that and set the fire to cover their tracks?'

'Her body would have been too badly burned to pick up any telltale signs of trauma,' said Farrell. 'Jack Kerr's clearly got a drug problem himself, so he might have been the one who supplied her with drugs.'

'We're going to have to ask them all to provide DNA samples,' said Mhairi. 'They've clearly been lying to us all along.'

'She didn't even have a family. She grew up in care as did Jack Kerr. That could explain why they felt drawn to each other,' said Farrell.

They picked their way through the remains of the cottage, startling a few pigeons who were nesting in the chimney.

'Look!' said Mhairi, pointing to a flight of wooden stairs with no banister at one end.

'I'm not sure how structurally sound those are,' cautioned Farrell, but Mhairi was already clambering up them. She disappeared from view at the top and there was complete silence.

'Frank!' she shouted. 'You'd better get up here.'

Lightly he ran up the stairs and joined her. The remaining floorboards creaked alarmingly under his weight and he could see the room below through the gaps.

However, all he could focus on was the bizarre scene in front of him.

'It's a shrine to Colette Currie,' he said.

There was a large framed photo of a young woman smiling at the camera. Surrounding the photo was a bank of tea candles, such as might be found in a church. However, that wasn't what caused Farrell's heart to pound like a drum. It was the carving knife lying alongside a dried red rose on the pristine white cloth. As if that wasn't chilling enough a crude Panopticon symbol had been painted on the wall behind the shrine. The eye appeared to be watching them.

'We've found our murder weapon,' said Mhairi, her eyes darting around.

'I don't fancy getting trapped up here in case whoever did this is on their way back. I'll get DCI Buchanan to send a SOCO team down to process everything here including the knife. In the meantime, we get officers from Jedburgh to keep

Jackie Baldwin

the cottage under covert surveillance until reinforcements arrive,' said Farrell.

Mhairi whipped out her phone and took photos of the shrine from different angles. Carefully, they made their way downstairs and had a brief poke around but there was nothing more to see.

As soon as a couple of officers arrived from Jedburgh to relieve them they pointed the car in the direction of Dumfries filled with a renewed sense of urgency.

Chapter 62

They arrived back at the station, quickly unloaded the boxes, and dumped them in Farrell's office until they had time to go through them. Byers had contacted them en route to advise them of what had been discovered at Sheriff Granger's house, and he'd been updated in turn about the recovery of the murder weapon and the shrine to Colette Currie.

The whole team was assembled in the MCA room looking grim. Even the Super was there, looking tight-lipped with anger. Clare Yates was present too.

'Farrell, I take it you've heard?' he said.

Farrell nodded. A copy had been made of the photos and the front cover of the book.

'What the hell?' muttered Mhairi, flicking through them, her face twisted in disgust.

There were several photos of partially clothed young women. They were all conscious and looked terrified but their eyes were unfocused as though they had been drugged. Mhairi was startled to see that one of them was Beth Roberts.

Byers put his hand over hers and removed the book from her hands.

'What is it?' she asked. The room had fallen silent. Everyone was staring at her.

'Frank, what's going on?' she asked.

'I don't know,' he replied, moving to stand beside her, his eyes on DS Byers.

'Take a seat, Mhairi,' said Dr Yates.

Mhairi sat down abruptly, her mouth dry.

Dr Yates took the book from Byers and pulled out three loose photos from the back of it. They were all of her. They'd been taken at the Faculty dinner, the hospital and outside her house. She suddenly felt dizzy and a glass of water was pressed into her hands.

'It looks like he was lining you up to be his next victim,' said Dr Yates, squeezing her shoulder.

'Just as well the bastard's dead or I might have killed him myself,' said Farrell.

Even the Super nodded in agreement.

'I knew the man was a vicious bully but I never thought for a minute he was capable of such depravity,' he said, looking sick to his stomach.

Mhairi sat up straight and squared her shoulders. The sheriff hadn't succeeded in intimidating her while he was alive and she certainly wasn't going to allow him to do so now he was dead.

'What do these photos tell us, Dr Yates?' she asked.

'I would say that it was all about power, dominance and control,' she replied. 'He was clearly a sadistic sociopath with delusions of grandeur. He also seemed to have a type. All of the women in this book are curvy brunettes.'

'One of his victims may have decided it was time for him to pay,' said Mhairi.

'How did anyone even find out what he had done?' said the Super, clearly still reeling from the discovery.

'One of his victims may have recovered some memories and told someone close to her,' said Farrell.

'Revenge is certainly a strong contender for motive. However, there's also a distinct possibility that Granger was being black-mailed,' said DI Moore. 'Maybe he stopped paying? The extravagant nature of the death could have been intended as a distraction to hide the fact it was a simple business transaction.'

'Rather a high-risk strategy,' said Farrell.

'Yes, but there's an element of ritual and symbolism that wasn't there in the murder of Gina Campbell or Aaron Sullivan,' said Clare Yates. 'It could be a red herring, as DI Moore has indicated, or it could be that the killer sees it as a righteous killing, as if he is judge, and executioner.'

'The first thing we need to do is get confirmation that one of the semen samples from Colette Currie matches Robert Granger's DNA samples from the post-mortem,' said Farrell. 'I'll contact DCI Buchanan to rush those through as top priority.'

'Wait, didn't we take DNA evidence from Colette Currie's colleagues when they were arrested for that brawl in court?' said Mhairi.

'Yes, we would have done,' replied Byers.

'We should send off all three samples for comparison against the semen samples as well,' said Farrell. 'We need to keep Barry McLeish in a safe house for now until things become clearer.'

'Is that really necessary?' asked the Super. 'We don't have the budget to maintain that arrangement indefinitely.'

'Yes it is, sir' said Farrell. 'Aaron Sullivan was murdered. Barry McLeish could well be next on the killer's list. Now that Joe Capaldi has been questioned, he's more at risk than ever. It won't take long for the person who's behind the drug-running and extortion to join up the dots. I think that person is Mario Lombardo.'

'Dave, can you arrange to get warrants to examine the financials for Robert Granger, Jack Kerr and Joe Capaldi?'

'Will do,' said DC Thomson. 'What about Mario Lombardo?'

'We've nothing tangible to offer up as justification yet. If money is seen flowing from one of the others into an account operated by him, however, that would give us enough to get one,' said Farrell.

'I understand from the fiscal, Peter Swift, that the court will re-open tomorrow. They've assigned another sheriff down here on a temporary basis,' said the Super.

'Didn't you mention previously that there was a girl raped and murdered in Robert Granger's year at Morrington Academy, sir?' said Farrell.

'Yes, I did. They put someone away for that.'

'I think that there's a distinct possibility it was the wrong man,' said Farrell.

'Joe Capaldi's been in prison by his own admission. Could they be one and the same?' asked Mhairi.

'That's what we need to find out,' replied Farrell.

PC Joanne Burns stuck her head round the door.

'They've brought that lawyer Beth Roberts in for questioning in relation to Sheriff Granger's murder. She's in Interview Room 4.'

'Right, Mhairi, you're with me,' said DI Moore, jumping to her feet. 'Let's see what she's got to say for herself.'

Chapter 63

Beth Roberts looked like she might bolt at any second. Her dark eyes were haunted and smudged purple with fatigue. A muscle twitched rhythmically at the side of her mouth. Her face was all sharp planes and angles and she had clearly lost a significant amount of weight.

'Miss Roberts, thank you for coming in,' smiled DI Moore, taking a seat across the table with Mhairi.

'I don't recall being given much choice,' she said.

As she took a sip of water, her hands started to shake and she quickly banged the glass back down.

'What's this all about? I've had to cancel some appointments to be here.'

'And we appreciate that,' said DI Moore, keeping her voice low and calm. She switched on the recording device and completed the preliminaries.

'Beth, we've brought you in to ask you some questions in relation to the murder of Sheriff Robert Granger.'

'I know nothing about it,' she said.

'You were seen spitting and banging on the vehicle that

329

was removing his body to the mortuary,' said DI Moore. 'It seems rather out of character.'

'I had my reasons,' she said, her face tight.

'You didn't like Sheriff Granger, did you, Beth?'

'I wasn't alone in that. He was a vile man. Nobody liked him.'

'You had more reason to dislike him than most,' said Mhairi. 'We've been in court and seen how he treated you. What he did to you was bullying, plain and simple.'

'I wish that's all it was.'

'Did he ever do anything to … make you feel uncomfortable?' Mhairi asked, probing delicately.

'That's one way to put it,' she said with a mirthless laugh.

Mhairi pushed a copy of the photograph across the table.

'You can tell us,' Mhairi went on. 'He can't hurt you anymore.'

'I couldn't have spoken up before. I had no proof. He would have buried me.'

'What happened?' asked Mhairi.

'Not long after he arrived down here, the court had a party as a bit of a send-off for someone. He handed me a drink and offered to show me around as I was new.'

'And then?' asked Mhairi, softly.

Beth bit her lip and looked away.

'The next thing I knew I was waking up in one of the interview rooms by myself. I felt drunk and woozy. I couldn't remember what had happened but my blouse was incorrectly buttoned up and I later discovered my underwear was a little torn. Although I couldn't remember him touching me, I had a really strong feeling it had been him. I think he left me those clues deliberately. The bastard wanted me to know.'

'Did you tell anyone?' asked Mhairi.

'No. How could I? He was a sheriff. Who would have believed me? I hardly believed it myself. I ... didn't want to believe it. My fiancé would have been so angry. He'd have confronted him and maybe lost his job. It was my word against his.'

'That must have been incredibly difficult to deal with,' said Mhairi, passing across a box of tissues.

'By the time I discovered his reputation for bullying and sexual harassment, it was already too late to say anything. By then he'd eroded my confidence to the extent I felt powerless to stand up to him. For the last year I've been in a really dark place. It has taken its toll on me both personally and professionally.'

Mhairi felt sick. Sheriff Granger had been a monster. His treatment of Beth Roberts had been criminal. Had she snapped and murdered him? She would have had every reason to do so.

The young solicitor had finally unburdened herself, but in doing so, she had made herself their number one suspect.

'Interview suspended,' said DI Moore. 'Beth, I'm stopping the interview to enable you to arrange representation. I'm sorry for what you've been through but unfortunately I'm going to have to formally detain you for questioning in relation to the murder of Sheriff Robert Granger.'

'You've got to be kidding.'

'You're a solicitor, you know how this works,' said DI Moore.

'I want you to have the opportunity to obtain legal advice before we proceed further. At this stage you are under caution, is that clear?'

'Yes,' she sniffed.

'I'll arrange for phone access,' continued DI Moore. 'Someone will also be in to see if you require any refreshments.'

Mhairi squeezed her shoulder as they left.

'If she did do it, I hope she bloody gets away with it,' she said in a low voice as they walked away together.

Chapter 64

DI Moore pulled into the kerb outside Mario Lombardo's modern bungalow. The luxury house was set in the middle of a large plot with high brick walls. There were coils of barbed wire around the top. Between the bars of the heavy electronic gates she could see the house was surrounded by a vast expanse of manicured lawns. There were no trees or shrubs. Nothing for any intruder to hide behind. She walked up to the gate and pressed the buzzer. Immediately she heard a low hum as the camera swivelled towards her. The gates swung open. She hoped she didn't have to leave in a hurry as it would no doubt be just as hard to get out as it had been to get in.

It had been a long tiring day and she hadn't manged to have lunch, which was probably why she was feeling a little lightheaded. The smell of something home-cooked wafted towards her from a window and her mouth began to water. She stepped up and rang the bell. Mario Lombardo came to the door with a dishtowel over his shoulder. She had clearly interrupted him in the preparation of his evening meal. Strains of opera drifted out into the garden.

'DI Moore. How may I help you?' he said with old-school courtesy.

'I'd like to talk to you about your daughter's investigation,' she said. 'But if you're busy, I can come back another time.'

'Please, come in. We can talk in the kitchen,' he ushered her through, 'but only if you join me for a bowl of pasta. Since my wife passed, I hate to eat alone.'

DI Moore hesitated for a second then smiled her assent.

'You've twisted my arm.'

They sat at a rustic pine table with two bowls of pasta and some freshly sliced bread and olive oil. She suddenly felt ravenous.

He poured himself a small glass of red wine and offered the bottle to her, but she declined and filled her glass from the water jug.

'We eat first and then we talk. Agreed?'

'Agreed,' she said, tucking in with unaccustomed gusto. She found this aspect of him hard to reconcile with the idea of him as an extortionist driving people to despair with his cruel manipulation of their frailties. However, if the last couple of years had taught her anything it was that appearances can be deceptive. She resolved to remain on her guard.

The simple but delicious meal was soon over and after she'd helped him clear away the dishes he brought two espressos and some biscotti to the table.

'Thank you for indulging the whim of an old man. Now, how do you say? Down to brass tacks.'

She chose her words carefully.

'Has it occurred to you that your daughter's murder might

have been directly linked to one of your ... er ... business assets.' She knew if she called them victims of blackmail he would snap shut like a clam.

He narrowed his eyes and tilted his chair back, staring at her.

'One of my ... assets ... rather than one of my competitors?'

'Yes. We know that your daughter was involved in your business dealings. She may have even interfaced directly with one of these ... assets.'

'You want to know who these assets are?'

She could feel the hair on the back of her neck prickle and a droplet of sweat head down her back. So far, she was groping about in the dark. Careful not to trigger him on the one hand but also trying to give the impression they perhaps knew more about his operation than he had realized.

'We're conducting a murder enquiry. If you're able to provide particulars of these ... assets ... then we would have the means to properly investigate and bring your daughter's killer to justice.'

'Do you have children, DI Moore?'

'No,' she said.

'They can hurt you in ways you can't even begin to imagine.'

'Were you and Gina close?'

'We used to be until she married that lily-livered toff. We stopped working together after that. She thought she was a cut above her old father. Looked at me like I was the dirt under her shoe at times.'

'I'm sorry,' said DI Moore. 'That must have been difficult.

Even so, I'm sure you want the person responsible for her death to be brought to justice?'

'Oh, I do,' he said darkly, 'one way or another, DI Moore. Bear with me a moment while I make my Christmas card list ...'

'But, it's only May,' she protested, wondering if he'd had more wine than she thought.

He pulled a pad of paper towards him, wrote a few names down, ripped off the sheet and carefully placed it before her. Immediately, she twigged and committed them to memory.

'These assets ... as you so diplomatically refer to them, DI Moore, do not deserve any consideration. If they were not shoddy ... or defective ... in some way, they would be of no use to me.'

'You heard that Sheriff Robert Granger was murdered?'

'I would like to take credit for that one. However, I was otherwise engaged. Father Jim Murray at St Margaret's will confirm that I stayed the night in Edinburgh along with members of St Margaret's social club.'

'Thank you, Mr Lombardo, I'll pay the good priest a visit.' Her face clouded. 'The next topic for discussion is rather more ... difficult.'

'Go on,' he gestured, his expression inscrutable.

'Aaron ... died trying to protect his soon-to-be adoptive father, Jack Kerr, as I'm sure that you're aware.'

'I've heard talk. His father is a weak apology for a man. He didn't deserve such a son.'

'So ...' DI Moore said, feeling her way delicately.

'You think I had something to do with that boy's death?' he exploded, leaping to his feet.

DI Moore leapt to her feet also and they stood staring at each other.

Mario Lombardo didn't flinch.

'I would NEVER hurt a child for the sins of its father. NEVER! Whatever you think you may have on me, you are absolutely wrong about this.'

'If that is indeed the case then do you have any other information you are prepared to share with me in relation to these deaths?'

Lombardo exhaled in frustration.

'I've been leaning on all of my contacts but I've heard nothing.'

'If anything else occurs to you, please get in touch. Your daughter was murdered. Her two children will grow up without their mother. That matters to me.'

He gave her a sad smile.

'I know it does. I can assure you that I will not rest until justice has been done, one way or another,' he said, the threat in his words underlined by an uncompromising stare.

DI Moore left the way she had come, feeling unmistakeably relieved as the gates opened on her approach. She drove away smoothly but pulled in to the side of the road once she was out of sight, her heart pounding. The forcefulness of Mario Lombardo's personality had reminded her of the man she had spent the last two years trying to forget. He was getting inside her head and she wasn't sure she could trust her judgement any more. Had she just broken bread with a cold-hearted killer or was he telling the truth?

Chapter 65

Mhairi knocked lightly on Farrell's door and popped her head round.

'Got a minute?'

'Sure, what's up?'

'Joe Capaldi isn't our fall guy for Emily Drummond, the girl in Granger's year who was murdered at Morrington Academy. He was remanded in custody at the time.'

'Another dead end,' said Farrell.

DI Moore entered. Normally impeccably attired, Mhairi noticed a small splash of tomato sauce on her pristine white blouse. At least she's had something to eat, she thought.

'Good, I hoped I'd catch the pair of you before you headed off for the night,' she said, taking a seat beside Mhairi.

'I've just come from Mario Lombardo's house.'

'You went on your own?' said Farrell, looking concerned.

'Yes, I made a judgement call,' she said, flushing in annoyance. 'I'm not a complete idiot.'

'No one would ever think that,' said Farrell.

But your judgement has been impaired before, thought Mhairi, striving to keep her expression neutral.

'I had developed some rapport with him after the murder of his daughter. I felt it was more likely he would open up to me if I went alone.'

'And did he?' asked Farrell.

'He's definitely in the extortion business, though we rather tiptoed around it. I formed the impression that he considers his targets are fair game.'

'A regular knight in shining armour,' muttered Mhairi earning herself a cold look from DI Moore.

Moore handed a hastily scrawled list of names over to Farrell.

'These are the people who he's been extorting money from,' she said.

'He told you this?' asked Farrell.

'Yes, but in a way that didn't constitute an admission. The one thing I'm fairly sure of, however, is that he didn't murder Aaron Sullivan or have him killed. He seemed genuinely outraged at the very idea.'

'He could be lying,' said Mhairi.

'I appreciate that, but I don't think that he is.'

'So,' said Farrell, hurriedly, 'there's a few names on this list: Sheriff Robert Granger, Jack Kerr, Jane Pearson, Joe Capaldi and Gabriel Ferrante. I imagine that there are many other people he hasn't mentioned, but broadly speaking, these are the most likely candidates.'

'Oh, and he did mention as far as the murder of Sheriff Granger is concerned, your friend, Father Jim Murray, can provide him with an alibi.'

'Did he now?' said Farrell.

'Gabriel Ferrante?' said Mhairi. 'What's he got on him?'

'Possibly extorting hush money for not putting it about that he's got a known felon running his law practice,' said Farrell.

'I gather that Gina used to work with him, but that tapered off when she got together with Fergus Campbell. Her father isn't his biggest fan. I think he blames him for turning Gina against him.'

'Do we think that Gabriel Ferrante could have killed Gina Campbell in cold blood, though?' asked Mhairi. 'The murder was definitely premeditated.'

'Honestly?' said Farrell. 'If someone had crossed the line by blackmailing him, I reckon he's got it in him to do just about anything. Gina may have let slip to him about being involved in her father's business and he might have felt betrayed. People have died for less.'

'I remember the look in his eyes that day when he was punching Fergus Campbell,' said Mhairi. 'It was like he didn't even know what he was doing.'

'Anyway, he's fetched up on that list so we need to do some digging around in his past, see what we can find out,' said Farrell.

'I'll do it,' Mhairi volunteered, secretly hoping there was nothing to find.

Chapter 66

It was already nearly seven by the time Farrell and Mhairi pulled up outside Jack and Sarah Kerr's house at Locharbriggs.

'I am so not wanting to have this conversation,' sighed Mhairi, getting out of the car. 'Jack Kerr was tortured enough before all this. What we have to say will most likely destroy him.'

As they walked up the path to the front door they could hear the sound of yelling.

'That doesn't bode well,' said Farrell.

He rang the doorbell. Angry footsteps approached and the door was flung back wide against its hinges. Sarah Kerr stood there, red-faced and with the glint of battle in her eyes.

'Yes?'

'We need to speak to you both about what happened to Aaron,' said Farrell.

'Of course,' she said, making an effort to calm down. 'Please, come in.'

She showed them through into the living room and invited them to sit on the sofa. Jack Kerr took a slug from the bottle of beer he was drinking as if to fortify himself and sat opposite them beside his wife.

'Aaron's toxicology screen came back negative. It appears that he wasn't using drugs himself,' said Farrell.

'Then how on earth did he get mixed up with all that stuff?' asked Sarah.

'I'm afraid that this is going to be hard to hear,' Farrell said, addressing his comment to Jack Kerr.

'Aaron discovered that you were in hock to the person feeding your drug addiction and got in touch to see if he could pay off some of your debt by working for him.'

Jack jumped to his feet, his eyes frantic.

'No! That can't possibly be right. I don't believe you!'

'Is this really what got Aaron killed?' asked Sarah.

'We can't say yet. We're working on a number of theories.'

She stood up and slapped her husband hard across the face.

'You bastard! she hissed. 'You DID this. You'd better go pack a bag because I want you the hell out of here in five minutes before I KILL you myself!'

Jack Kerr went as if to speak and then shook his head and looked at Farrell. It was too late. He left the room, his tread heavy on the stairs.

Sarah broke down in tears. Mhairi gestured to Farrell to go and make her a cup of tea.

'We were meant to be the ones who rescued him,' she sobbed. 'I can't believe he tried to take all of that on his shoulders. My poor boy. How could Jack do this to us?'

Farrell came back through and handed her a cup.

'I need to have a quick word with your husband before we go. Is it all right if I nip upstairs?'

'Knock yourself out,' she said. 'But tell him to get a move on. I want him gone.'

Farrell ran upstairs and knocked lightly on the open door.

Jack Kerr was throwing clothes into a leather holdall on the bed, tears running silently down his face.

'What? Haven't you done enough?'

'It's about Colette Currie,' he said.

Kerr froze.

'I need to know what you're hiding. We believe she may have been murdered.'

'But the fire ... it was an accident,' he said.

'We're looking at whether the ten-year anniversary of Colette Currie's death triggered her killer, who may hold the three of you responsible in some way for what happened to her.'

'And if that's the case it means that I won't be the one responsible for Aaron's death?'

'Yes,' said Farrell.

Kerr sighed heavily and sat down on the bed.

'Fine. I liked Colette. We were good friends. She was always up for a laugh but not when her fiancé was around. He was a bit strait-laced. I suppose she dampened herself down for him. Anyway, that night, we got absolutely smashed. You've got to remember we were only in our mid-twenties. We'd been cooped up in a tiny town in the Borders for two weeks. All we had to do the next day was go to court for the verdict.'

'We all went back to the cottage and had a smoke and did some Es to keep the party going. Colette let her hair down and we started playing these stupid drinking games. She was so happy that night. It's how I try and remember her.'

'I take it you scored the drugs?'

'Yes. The others were clueless.'

'Did you sleep with her?' asked Farrell.

'Yes. This was before I met Sarah. The reason I kept it quiet all these years was out of respect for her fiancé, Peter Swift. He was a decent enough bloke and I didn't want to pile on the agony after what had happened. She'd been having doubts about their relationship. He didn't need to know that.'

'Nothing else to tell me?'

'Isn't that enough? If we hadn't been drinking, if we hadn't done drugs, if I hadn't slept with her, would she still be alive today?'

'My advice, for what it's worth, get some counselling. Living with guilt eats you alive. Take it from one who knows.'

'I'll think about it,' Kerr said, getting to his feet and zipping his bag.

They walked out the house together.

Chapter 67

Farrell and Mhairi sat opposite each other at the kitchen table going through the case files for Colette Currie. It was stiflingly hot. Mhairi lifted her hair off the nape of her neck and pulled it into a makeshift bun using an elastic band from some papers.

'There's just no air in here,' she complained.

Farrell got up and padded across to the fridge in his bare feet and extracted an ice-cold beer.

'Want one?' he asked.

'Sure,' said Mhairi. 'Let's sit in the garden. It might be marginally cooler. I'm hoping the midges will be too knackered with the heat to bite me.'

They took their beers to the picnic table and sat in companionable silence. Oscar and Henry were sprawled on the grass side by side.

'Look at them,' said Mhairi. 'They're so much happier down here. They'll miss it when we go back.'

'You're not tempted to stay?' asked Farrell.

'No, not in the slightest. I want to keep working the big cases. My career matters to me. Why? Are you?'

'Maybe a little,' he replied.

'Your mother would like it.'

'Somehow I doubt that. These days she'd probably feel I was cramping her style,' he said with a laugh.

He reached into the box of papers he'd brought out and started sifting through some papers on the picnic table. Mhairi did likewise.

After a few minutes she came upon the crime scene photos of Colette Currie. They were horrendous and she closed her eyes briefly then peered closer.

'What the hell?'

'What is it?' asked Farrell.

She pointed out a bright blue patch of skin on the underside of the deceased just below her chest.

'Is that a Panopticon tattoo?' he asked.

'Yes. The upper layer of skin was removed by the fire, but the ink has been preserved,' said Mhairi. 'It could be a coincidence,' she said doubtfully. 'All law students probably come across that image in their studies.'

'I don't believe in coincidences,' said Farrell.

They returned to the boxes.

After half an hour or so, Farrell let out a low whistle. 'You'll never believe who the sheriff was on that case in Jedburgh ten years ago?'

'Not Robert Granger?'

'The very same,' said Farrell. 'He wasn't the sitting sheriff. That's why we never twigged before. He'd been sent down from Glasgow to cover for him when he was on holiday.'

'Given those disturbing photographs and what Beth

Roberts told us do you think it's possible he did the same to Colette Currie?' asked Mhairi.

'By all accounts she was quite a free spirit, not as timid as Beth Roberts. She might have put up a fight.'

'There was a balaclava recovered from Granger's house. What if he attacked her, there was a struggle and she managed to pull it off, so she discovered his identity?'

'He'd have had to kill her. There's no way he could let her live after that,' said Farrell.

'He left her for dead and set the place on fire,' said Mhairi.

'We can prove it,' said Farrell. 'His DNA wasn't in the system before so it didn't throw up a match against one of the two semen samples. Now we can have them run again, against his DNA from the post-mortem.'

'Remember what Fergus Campbell said about the key?' said Mhairi.

'Yes.'

'According to the papers, a key was found inside the cottage by the front door, though,' said Mhairi. 'Why wouldn't she have used it to unlock the door and get out?'

'Unless she didn't have a key. What if the killer had two keys: he hid one key under the doormat inside the front door before he set the fire? The mat would have been incinerated leaving the key exposed in the aftermath. It would look as if she'd been trying to open the door, seem much less like foul play than if the door had been locked and the key absent. The killer could've then locked the door behind him on the way out, and hidden the spare key in Fergus Campbell's coat pocket the next morning at court,' said Farrell. 'If it's anything like the agents' room in Dumfries, the lawyers dump their coats in there and put on their court gowns. The room is never locked but it's not uncommon for a sheriff or one of the fiscals to wander through in search of some case law from the library. Certainly, it wouldn't have raised any eyebrows if he'd been seen in there.'

Solemnly they clinked their bottles of beer together.

'To Colette Currie,' said Mhairi.

'May she rest in peace,' said Farrell.

'One case down, three to go,' said Mhairi.

By now it was nearly dark. Mhairi let out a huge yawn. She got to her feet stretching and promptly stumbled backwards over her flip flops landing in Farrell's lap as he reached out to grab her. Mortified she twisted around to face him, her arms still flailing. For an insane moment she had the urge to kiss him. His eyes were inscrutable in the darkness but she heard his sharp intake of breath. Before she had time to gather the shreds of her dignity around her his strong arms had righted her and propelled her to her feet. She could feel the heat of him despite the air cooling.

'Sorry,' she muttered. 'Night, Frank.'

She could tell he was struggling to keep a straight face. He must think I'm a total joke, she thought, stomping off to bed.

'Night, Mhairi,' he called after her. 'Sleep tight.'

Not a chance in Hell, she thought.

Chapter 68

Farrell had tossed and turned all night tormented by a slideshow of images from the three remaining unsolved cases. Mhairi had been acting a little weird last night too. For a moment he'd thought she was about to kiss him. He couldn't decide if he was glad or sorry that she'd refrained. What could she possibly see in a loser like him? She'd be taking self-sabotage to a whole new level. He didn't want to hurt her. She was too precious to him. Of course, he could have imagined it.

Maybe the stress of the cases was causing his mind to unravel and see things that weren't there. With a sigh, he flung back the covers and pulled on his running gear. He had to stay focused. The fear of losing his sanity again had never completely left him. It was a dull ache deep within his psyche that flared up like an abscess every now and again. A good run would sort him out.

It was still only 5.30 a.m. as he slipped from the house. The birds were making their usual din as he headed into Dock Park running along the tree-lined avenue beside the river. DI Moore had been convinced that Mario Lombardo was innocent of Aaron Sullivan's death, but could he trust her instincts to be right? After all, the last time he'd been in Dumfries she'd made a catastrophic error of judgement.

Joe Capaldi seemed to be involved somehow but he couldn't imagine either him or his boss, Gabriel Ferrante, colluding to cover up the murder of a child. Yet, Barry McLeish was clearly terrified of Joe Capaldi.

Gina Campbell's murder had also hit a wall. The nanny, Jane Pearson; Gina's husband, Fergus Campbell, and her lover, Gabriel Ferrante, potentially all had motive, means and opportunity.

Now that it appeared likely that Sheriff Granger had murdered Colette Currie in Jedburgh, it did make a connection between the other two murders less likely. Although the timing of the murders close to the tenth anniversary of Colette Currie's death was troubling. Also, how likely was it that two close friends would each have someone close to them murdered within two weeks of each other?

As he left the park and headed along the footpath to Kingholm Quay, breathing in the salty tang of the river banks, he felt a familiar pang of pain for the loss of his old friend, DCI Lind. He missed having him to bounce ideas off and keep him grounded. He hoped that Laura would relent soon.

Back at the cottage, Farrell ran into Mhairi in the hall. She already had her suit on. There were dark circles under her eyes and she seemed pale and tense. They sidestepped around each other in the narrow space, muttering apologies. Mhairi slid her eyes out from under his gaze. So, he hadn't imagined it then. He didn't like this new awkwardness that had crept into the spaces between them. It was up to him to fix this. Only he didn't know how.

'I'm just going to jump into the shower,' he said, attempting the faux heartiness of a double-glazing salesman.

'Whatever,' she muttered. 'I'll load up the car.'

They travelled the short journey to the station in silence, each lost in their own thoughts.

Farrell and McLeod entered the MCA room to find it a hive of activity.

Farrell walked to the front of the room and cleared his throat.

'Listen up, people. Mhairi and I were going over the files for the Colette Currie case last night. We think we may have made a breakthrough. I want Sheriff Robert Granger's DNA run against the two semen samples obtained from Colette's post-mortem. I've also obtained a DNA swab from Jack Kerr, which should prove to be a match for one of the two semen samples. He's admitted they slept together the night she died.'

'You reckon Granger murdered her?' asked Byers.

'Yes, subject to the samples matching up from the Scottish DNA database.'

'Where does that leave us in relation to the three active murder cases?' asked Byers.

'Beth Roberts had motive and opportunity to have killed Sheriff Granger. If she was responsible, though, I doubt she acted alone. She doesn't have the strength that would have been required to drag him through from chambers and hoist him up in that fashion,' said Farrell.

'Maybe she had help?' suggested DC Thomson. 'What about her fiancé, Peter Swift?'

'The fiscal? That's all we need. I suppose that we can't rule him out. Let's bring him in for questioning. He'll either be behind Beth Roberts one hundred per cent or already beginning to distance himself for the sake of his career.'

DC Thomson looked up from his computer terminal.

'You asked me to trace Tony Marino, the man who was put away for the murder of that girl, Emily Drummond, at Sheriff Granger's school.'

'And?'

'Well, the weird thing is that he walked out of jail after his sentence and disappeared into thin air. Nobody's seen or heard anything from him since. There's a long-standing warrant for his arrest as he was released on life licence.'

'So if he does turn up he'll be hauled back to jail?' said Farrell.

'No one's that good at keeping hidden in this digital world,' said DC Thomson. 'He should've been seen somewhere by now.'

'That could mean one of two things,' said Byers. 'Either he's dead or he had a new identity waiting, ready to slip into.'

'But if he really didn't kill that girl then his sentence should be quashed,' said Mhairi.

'Unless, he decided to exact his own retribution and murdered the real killer,' said Farrell. 'Sitting in prison for twenty years for a crime you didn't commit? That's a lot of time to plan your revenge.'

'I still think it's suspicious that Joe Capaldi turned up in Dumfries a matter of weeks after Sheriff Granger arrived down here. How many ex jailbirds work in a solicitor's office?' said DS Byers.

'It was probably good PR for Gabriel Ferrante to employ a former criminal,' said Farrell. 'Must have given him a bit of street cred with his clientele.'

Farrell turned to DC Thomson.

'Do a bit more digging into Capaldi. I want the man's whole life history. Ascertain who visited him in jail. Check out his cellmates, known associates, that kind of thing. Go through his previous convictions. Did he ever appear in front of Sheriff Granger for anything, no matter how minor? He's connected somehow to these murders. I just don't know how.'

'So far we've uncovered two of the secrets Colette Currie's three friends were hiding,' said DI Moore. 'Max Delaney may have been hiding something too.'

'Dave, have you heard back from Tech Support in relation to Aaron's social media accounts, emails etc?' asked Farrell. 'They should have cracked the passwords by now.'

'They have, there was an email waiting for me this morning,' DC Thomson replied. 'His phone and laptop have been opened and have been placed in the evidence room meantime. I'll sign them out and take a look.'

He bent over his computer once more. 'I've just received an email from DCI Buchanan. There were no prints on the knife and no recoverable DNA either as it appears to have been wiped down with bleach.'

There was a collective sigh of disappointment.

'That's unfortunate,' said Farrell, 'but we knew it was a possibility. As Mario Lombardo has indicated Father Jim Murray can alibi him for the night of Aaron Sullivan's murder, I'll pop to St Margaret's now, nail that down.'

'It doesn't mean he didn't instruct Joe Capaldi to kill him on his behalf,' said Mhairi, eyeballing DI Moore, who met her stare with detached coolness.

'No, it doesn't,' said Farrell. 'I wasn't terribly convinced by Joe Capaldi's alibi, either. I got the impression that Gabriel Ferrante was covering for him out of some misplaced sense of loyalty.'

'I still don't think that Gabriel Ferrante would protect a child killer,' said Mhairi. 'I'd be prepared to stake my reputation on it.'

'Really?' said DI Moore.

Mhairi flushed with anger.

Farrell exchanged a glance with Byers. Things between the two women were becoming tense.

'The alibi may be bogus because he's genuinely convinced that Joe Capaldi is innocent,' said Farrell. 'Whether or not that belief is misplaced has yet to be determined.'

Chapter 69

Farrell exhaled in relief as he exited the station car park. It felt good to be on his own, albeit briefly. The frustrations and pressures were getting to his team now. The media were hounding them, using their failure to apprehend anyone to further their political agenda. His boss, DCI Buchanan, in turn was coming under fire from those above her. She had cut him far more slack than he deserved within the last couple of years. He didn't want to let her down.

Glancing at his watch, he realized that morning Mass would now be over so Father Murray would likely be at home. Parking at the side of St Margaret's he walked round the back of the church to the well-worn sandstone house and rang the bell.

A cheerful middle-aged woman in an apron answered the door and showed him into the parlour. It was stuffed with an eclectic mix of furniture that looked like it had come from a charity shop. The overall effect was one of comfort and welcome. Farrell sank onto a well-stuffed sofa and leaned his head back, closing his eyes.

With a start, he woke up as his friend came and sat opposite him.

'Sorry, I must have dosed off,' he said, rubbing his neck and blinking.

'I was tempted to leave you there, you looked so peaceful. How are you, Frank?'

'Surviving, just about,' he said. With the sun streaming in through the bay windows, he noticed that Father Murray himself was looking tired and a bit worn. He'd put on weight since the last time they'd met and his face was puffy and tired.

'You?'

'It's been a difficult few weeks,' the priest sighed. 'You'll know about the death of one of my parishioners, Aaron Sullivan. A tragic business.'

'I didn't realize the family were Catholic,' said Farrell.

'Yes, they've been coming here with the lad since they fostered him years ago. A terrible tragedy, for sure.'

'I'm afraid Jack and Sarah have split up. They might need even more of your support now.'

'I'll bear that in mind.'

The housekeeper brought them in a tray of tea and buttered scones. Farrell thanked her and gladly helped himself, thinking that Mhairi should have been here. She would generally sell her soul for a bit of home baking. He felt a twinge of guilt as he thought about that moment between them. He forced his mind back to the subject in hand.

'What do you think of Mario Lombardo?' he asked.

His friend's eyes clouded and he looked away.

'He's a regular attender here,' he said.

'That's not what I asked,' said Farrell.

'I know, but it's all I'm prepared to say.'

358

'He's unburdened himself in the confessional, hasn't he?'

'You know better than to ask me that,' the priest snapped.

Farrell knew he would get nowhere if he pressed further. The sanctity of the confessional was absolute. His friend's reaction spoke volumes, however. He changed tack.

'Mario Lombardo sent me here, actually. He said you can alibi him for the night Aaron was murdered. Apparently he went on a church trip to Edinburgh with you all?'

Father Murray reached for a well-worn leather diary and thumbed through it.

'Yes, he's quite correct. I remember he was there. I heard about Aaron the morning we got back. Mario's popular with the ladies. They make a fuss of him since he lost his late wife, Maria. They attended church together. A lovely lady, no idea of the full extent of her husband's ... activities. After her death he kept coming on his own.'

'What about his daughter, Gina Campbell?'

She came here regularly too but not with her father.

'With her husband?'

'No, he's not Catholic. She always sat beside another man. They arrived and left separately but I formed the impression it was a close attachment, nevertheless.'

'Who?'

'Frank, I'm not in the habit of gossiping about my parishioners.'

'I know that but Gina was murdered, her children left without a mother.'

'Fine. It was Gabriel Ferrante. Satisfied?'

'Yes, for now.'

'How's your friend John Lind? Any progress?'

'I haven't seen him since I got here because Laura has banned me from visiting,' Farrell said, aware that he sounded bitter. 'My boss has been quietly feeding me progress reports. He's aware but not communicating yet. He seems very withdrawn and passive. They've removed his feeding tube and he'll swallow pureed food but makes no effort to eat.'

'That's really encouraging,' said Father Murray. 'It'll take time. Laura will relent, I'm sure.'

'I hope you're right. It's killing me. I hope he doesn't hear about her and Byers before he's strong enough to withstand it. I fear that knowledge could snap his mind forever.'

'And what about you, Farrell? Still having a time out from God?'

'The anger is fading, I suppose. I don't have the energy for it. My faith has taken a battering.'

'Take your time,' said Father Murray, leaning over to clasp his hand. 'You'll find your way back to us. I'm sure of it.'

Chapter 70

Peter Swift sat across the table from Farrell and Mhairi in the small interview room. He looked tired but hadn't bitched about having to come in and talk to them, for which Farrell was grateful. After all, they were nominally at least on the same side here. Nonetheless it was going to be a tricky interview. It was his fiancée they were here to discuss after all.

After they'd identified themselves for the purposes of the tape, Farrell took the lead.

'Thank you for coming in to help us with our enquiries, Peter. We appreciate that this is difficult for you.'

'I'm always happy to help the police in any way that I can.'

'We appreciate that,' said Mhairi, smiling to put him at ease.

'Has your fiancée, Beth Roberts, shared with you what allegedly happened to her at the hand of Sheriff Robert Granger?'

Peter Swift's mouth tightened into a thin line.

'Yes, she told me what that bastard did ... I couldn't believe it.'

'When exactly did she tell you?' asked Farrell.

'Not until after he'd been murdered. I think if I'd found out before, I might have been tempted to take him out myself. I'd heard the rumours, of course, we all had. I never imagined he'd go as far as that, though.'

'How did it make you feel?' asked Mhairi, keeping a close eye on his reactions.

'Honestly? Absolutely fucking furious. You have no idea,' he added quietly but with an unmistakable note of sincerity.

'Were you angry that she hadn't let on to you before?' asked Mhairi.

'No, of course not! She was terrified. He bullied her till it was all she could do to force herself into work each morning. It was painful to watch. But she was determined not to let him get the better of her.'

'Did you ever try and have a word with him? Ask him to stop tormenting her?' asked Farrell.

'I would have done but I knew it would have only made him worse.'

'I've watched you in court,' said Farrell. 'He didn't seem to rattle you or the other guys so much?'

Swift gave a mirthless laugh.

'We're the last ones standing. He regarded himself as something of an equal opportunities bully. There's a couple of young male lawyers he's seen off in the course of the year. One of them has left law altogether.'

'You know that we detained Beth Roberts for questioning in relation to the sheriff's murder?'

'You're barking up the wrong tree. Beth isn't a killer.'

'She has a motive,' said Farrell.

'But she wasn't the only one to have had issues with him. That's the reason he was punted down here in the first place.'

'You could have helped her,' said Farrell.

Swift stiffened. 'What? You surely don't think *I* had anything to do with it, do you?'

'Well, like Beth, you had means, motive and opportunity,' said Mhairi.

Swift sighed.

'Look, I'm a procurator fiscal for God's sake. Don't you think you might be clutching at straws here? I get that you have to do your job but ... still!'

'Humour us,' said Farrell. 'Where were you between the hours of midnight and 9 a.m. when the body was discovered?'

'Home with Beth. Neither of us left the house. My fiancée is innocent of any crime here, DI Farrell. She's a victim. You need to realize that.'

'That's all for now. Thank you for your time,' said Farrell, showing him to the door to be escorted out by PC Joanne Burns.

'What did you think?' asked Mhairi as they trailed back upstairs.

'He's clearly devoted to his fiancée,' said Farrell. 'Whether he'd kill for her? I really can't say. If she did murder Sheriff Granger, I reckon he would cover up for her.'

'In the circumstances, I could understand that,' said Mhairi.

'Unless we can disprove the alibi by finding one or othe

of them on CCTV or a witness placing them in the vicinity of the court that night, we're on a hiding to nothing.'

'God, these cases are doing my head in,' said Mhairi.

'Have a lithium,' said Farrell offering her the packet.

'Are you crazy? Sorry, don't answer that,' snapped Mhairi.

'I was attempting to lighten the mood,' said Farrell mildly, returning the packet to his pocket.

'Epic fail,' she muttered, hurrying away.

He stared after her. She'd never been this cranky before. It was giving him a headache.

Chapter 71

Mhairi poured herself another coffee. It had been so hot and humid that she'd tossed and turned all night. The black clouds were swollen with unshed rain and the birds were agitated. There was an unnatural hush as though nature was holding its breath waiting for the storm to break. A flash of lightning lit up the sky and she moved away from the window and back to her desk as the first fat drops pelted the window. A crack of thunder ripped the sky above and lights in the MCA room blinked on and off.

She'd been scrolling through Aaron Sullivan's social media accounts and come up with a big fat zero. There were no messages from Joe Capaldi or Mario Lombardo. He really had very little social media activity for a boy his age. Even with the deleted posts and messages for the past six months that had been retrieved by Tech Support there was nothing helpful at all.

'Anything?' asked DC Thomson, looking up.

'Zilch,' she sighed.

'Given his age, he's more likely to communicate with his mates while playing computer games anyway. Pass his laptop over and I'll look at what games he was into. Some of them will have message boards. There might be some traffic between him and Barry McLeish.'

'Thanks, Dave, knock yourself out.' She passed across the sticker-covered computer, reminding her just how young Aaron had been. She swallowed hard. Getting emotional wouldn't solve anything.

'I reckon we're not going to be able to bring down Mario Lombardo unless we get Joe Capaldi to roll on him,' she said. 'He's the only direct conduit we've discovered so far.'

'Hang on. I've just received an email about Joe Capaldi from the Prison Service. Guess who his cellmate was when he did his last stretch?'

'Spit it out or I'll come over there and make you.'

'The mysterious Tony Marino,' he said.

'What the hell?' said Mhairi. 'Capaldi shared a cell with Tony Marino who was wrongly accused of raping and murdering that girl at Morrington Academy, and then did a disappearing act on his release?'

'So it would appear.'

'Have we got a mug shot of Tony Marino?'

'They sent one across, but it's old and grainy.'

Mhairi leaned over his shoulder to look at it and felt a jolt of recognition. She peered closer. Surely, it couldn't be?

'What? What is it?' asked DC Thomson.

DS Byers burst through the door, startling them. His eyes alighted on Mhairi.

'Max Delaney's kid has been abducted. Drop what you're doing and come with me. Farrell's meeting us at the scene.

Dave, stay here and man the fort. DI Moore's on her way to join you.'

Mhairi picked up her jacket and ran out of the room, her heart in her mouth. This was too much. If anything happened to that little girl ...

'Where are we headed?' asked Mhairi as Byers roared out of the car park ahead of the SOCO van and a couple of patrol cars.

'Some beauty parlour on the edge of town, called The Pink Flamingo,' replied Byers.

The storm raged unabated as they fought their way through the town traffic, sirens drowning out the thunder and blue lights vying with the lightning flashes to illuminate the slick roads.

They pulled into the business park and skidded to a halt beside Farrell's Citroen, which had arrived just ahead of them. The Pink Flamingo was as garish as its name suggested. Running inside behind Farrell, they found a distraught Chloe sobbing in reception with make-up sliding down her face. Seeing them she lurched to her feet.

'Oh thank God, you need to find her!'

The young girls who worked there, clad in their flamingo pink tunics, were clearly out of their depth. A woman introduced herself as the salon owner. DS Byers and PC Joanne Burns quickly noted down their details.

'Tell us what happened,' said Farrell, sitting Chloe down and taking charge.

'Mia was getting the Princess Sparkle makeover. I was

having my facial. It was taking a while and Mia was getting restless. One of the therapists came in and offered to take her through to select her princess dress. She seemed so nice and friendly. She worked here. I thought Mia was safe with her. Once I was finished I went to find her but she'd gone. The girl ran off with her,' she sobbed.

'Is this true?' Farrell demanded of the tall, elegant owner.

'Yes,' she said quietly, white as a sheet now. 'The girl's name is Sharon Clements. Today was her first day in the salon. She came as maternity cover. Here's her address and references.'

Farrell cast an eye over them. He was certain they were bogus.

'Did you take these up?' he asked.

She lowered her eyes.

'Not yet. We were busy and she was the only applicant. I'm so sorry,' she whispered, her voice wobbling.

Mhairi gave her a withering look. Sorry didn't cut it. Not today.

'What did she look like?' asked Mhairi.

'I only saw her briefly,' said the woman. 'She would be in her late twenties, I think. Shorter than me, maybe about her height,' she nodded towards Mhairi. 'Green eyes, black rimmed glasses and long auburn hair. Very slim. She did seem nervous, but I put that down to it being her first day.'

Farrell turned back to Chloe Delaney who was still weeping into a hankie. 'Did you come here often?' he asked. 'Was it part of your routine?'

'Every fortnight.'

'On the same day and at the same time?' asked Farrell.

'Yes, it was a standing booking. Mother and Daughter time.'
Mhairi abruptly stood up. She looked about to blow.

'Take five,' said Farrell in a tone that brooked no argument.
She nodded and walked over to Byers.

Farrell had a sinking feeling. Whoever took Mia had obviously planned this meticulously and been watching her for a while. Now that Max Delaney's child had been snatched, he knew without a shadow of a doubt that the murders of Gina Campbell and Aaron Sullivan were connected. Little Mia Delaney was clearly in terrible danger. It might already be too late. The killer's diabolical agenda had been set in motion ten years ago and was heading towards a shattering conclusion. He had to find a way to defeat the killer before it was too late.

Chapter 72

Max Delaney burst through the door.

He saw his wife sitting weeping, but instead of attempting to comfort her, he grabbed her roughly by the arm.

'You did this. It's all down to you,' he shouted. 'All that painting Mia in make-up and pimping her around on Instagram. Some nutter has her and it's all your fault!'

His wife became hysterical, clawing at her arms in distress.

Mhairi came running back across to try and defuse the situation.

'Max, easy there. This isn't helping. Leave that for later and focus on getting your daughter back,' she said, looking directly into his eyes.

'Sorry, you're right,' he said, after a moment. 'What do you need from us?'

Farrell spoke to Chloe Delaney. 'Have you ever met Beth Roberts before?'

'Beth? What's she got to do with this?' asked Max, confused.

'Just answer the question.'

'A few times.'

371

'She doesn't come out with us,' said Max, 'bit of a home bird.'

'How about Jane Pearson? Mrs Delaney. Have you ever met her before?'

'No, of course not, she's Fergus's nanny. She'd be minding the boys.'

Farrell slipped into another room and phoned DC Thomson.

'I need you to ascertain the present whereabouts of Beth Roberts and Jane Pearson,' he said. 'The description given by the witnesses could apply to either woman if they wore glasses, coloured contacts and a wig. Find them and bring them in. I'm not taking any chances.'

'There's something else,' said Thomson.

'About this abduction?'

'No.'

'Then, save it for later. I want every resource looking for this child. All leave is cancelled until further notice.'

'Got it, boss.'

He stuck his head back inside.

'Max? Mhairi? a word?'

Once they had joined him he eyeballed Max Delaney.

'Right, let's hear it. I know you've been hiding something about Jedburgh. You have to tell me right now.'

Max Delaney froze and looked away.

'I can't.'

'You have to,' snapped Farrell. 'Your daughter's life could depend on it.'

'Fine,' said Max Delaney in a quiet voice. 'I'll tell you.'

'Go on,' said Mhairi.

'I was in love with Colette Currie. I fancied her from the first moment I met her, but she was superglued to Peter Swift. I was driven half mad with jealousy.'

'When I found out we were all going to be in Jedburgh for a couple of weeks, I thought that was my chance. I sensed she'd been cooling towards Peter.'

'And?' prompted Farrell, resisting the urge to hurry him in case he retreated.

'That last night, I was poised to make my move. We all got bladdered. I went to the toilet and when I came back there she was snogging with Jack Kerr right in front of me.

'I felt betrayed, as though she'd been mine already. Later, I crept up to the bedroom and could hear them getting down to business. I snuck the door open a crack and then slid my phone round and videoed them.' He paused and ran a hand through his hair. 'I sent it to Peter Swift anonymously. I was too ashamed to tell the others. When she died I was devastated that I had sullied her memory for Peter in that way.'

Farrell and Mhairi looked at each other in horror as the pieces clicked in to place.

It was clear to them now that Peter Swift was hell-bent upon the most terrible vengeance and he had persuaded Beth Roberts along for the ride.

Chapter 73

More police cars arrived to deal with witness statements. Farrell, Mhairi and Byers stood to one side. The pressure was on. They had to act fast. There was little doubt that Swift intended to kill this little girl, the culmination of his thirst for revenge.

'I say we go to their home first,' said Byers. 'Even if they're not there we might find out their intentions.'

'Agreed,' said Farrell. 'Let's go. 'We'll take your car, Byers. I'll brief DI Moore on the way.'

The three of them ran back to the police car Mhairi and Byers had arrived in. Byers sped off to the address he'd obtained from the fiscal's office. Peter Swift lived in a cottage out at Amisfield, a small village just a couple of miles from Dumfries.

Farrell contacted DI Moore by radio.

'We're on our way to the suspect's house at Dove Cottage, Amisfield. I need the Firearms Team mobilized to meet us there.'

'Already standing by,' she replied. 'A child rescue alert has been issued throughout the UK and a photo of Mia has been circulated to all social media outlets. We've put out alerts for cars belonging to both Peter Swift and Beth Roberts. The Air Support Team is on standby and I'm reporting back to DCI Buchanan in Glasgow.'

'What about the airports, trains, buses and ferries?' asked Farrell.

'All notified and on high alert. I was able to get a good clear shot of Mia off Instagram. Both Swift and Roberts have closed down all their social media accounts. Their phones are switched off too, so we can't ping them for now.'

'I think that Swift has been planning this for some time,' said Farrell. 'Locating them in time isn't going to be easy.'

Ten minutes later, they arrived outside the cottage, the rain an unrelenting drumbeat against the windscreen. The Firearms Team had beaten them to it and were standing in loose formation behind the highly capable Sergeant Forsyth. There were already a number of uniforms surrounding the property, undeterred by the rain penetrating their defences. Despite the time of day the curtains were drawn on all the windows meaning it was impossible to see what was going on inside.

Farrell leapt from the car with Mhairi and Byers. He pressed the button on his radio.

'Listen up everyone. We've no reason to expect that the suspects are armed but we do know that they are highly dangerous. Proceed with extreme caution. The life of a child is at stake.'

Farrell and Mhairi approached the front door, once the property was surrounded. Farrell rang the bell. Nothing.

'Police, open up!' he yelled.

Still no response.

He motioned to the tactical support team to move into position.

'On my mark,' he said. 'Advance.'

There was a loud crash as the front and back doors burst open simultaneously and the officers moved in, with Farrell and Mhairi bringing up the rear.

The cottage was empty.

'Dammit,' hissed Farrell in frustration, thumping the kitchen table with his fist.

Together with Mhairi he swiftly searched the property looking for any indication of where they might have gone.

'Look! They've definitely been here,' said Mhairi producing a half-finished drawing and a packet of wax crayons.

'This too,' said Farrell holding up a pink sparkly ribbon.

'No sign of any passports,' said Byers, striding through from the master bedroom. 'Their cases are gone too. There's a number of empty hangers in the wardrobe suggesting they're going on the run.'

Farrell's eyes widened as he looked at a framed photo on the kitchen dresser.

'Beth has the Panopticon tattoo,' he said. Mhairi and Byers turned and saw a framed photo of Beth Roberts in denim shorts and a bikini top. The tattoo was under her left breast, exactly where Colette's had been. She was smiling in the photo, but the smile didn't reach her eyes.

'Do you think Beth Roberts is a willing participant?' asked Mhairi. 'My money's on her being coerced.'

'I agree it's a possibility,' said Farrell. 'He might exert such strong psychological control over her that she feels she has no ability to act on her own.'

'She walked in there this morning, bold as brass,' said Byers. 'I reckon she's all in.'

'Time will tell,' said Farrell. 'We need to figure out where they've gone. And fast. There's no laptop or computer here.'

'What about his work computer at the fiscal's office?' said Mhairi. 'He could have planned something on there, bought tickets, done some prep?'

'Good idea,' said Farrell. 'Ask DI Moore to call them and get one of our Tech team down there? I imagine that they'll cooperate.'

Mhairi, walked away speaking into her radio.

Farrell paced up and down. Where in hell's name had they gone? What twisted thought processes were going on in Peter Swift's mind? What was his end game and where was it going to take place? Pulling out his phone, he brought up Mia's photo, all gap-toothed innocence, staring fearlessly at the camera. He had to save that little girl. Failure wasn't an option.

Chapter 74

Farrell and Mhairi ran up the stairs to the MCA room to find DI Moore and DC Thomson hard at work. To Farrell's surprise, Clare Yates was also there, sitting quietly to one side. He was pleased to see her.

'Clare, what do you think Swift's next move is likely to be?' he asked, sitting down beside her. 'I'm sure you've been brought up to speed. Talk to me.'

'The ten-year anniversary has clearly triggered him. Sheriff Granger moving down here a year ago may also have been a catalyst given that he was the presiding sheriff in Jedburgh.'

'What do you think his end game is?' asked Farrell. He knew the answer. He just so desperately wanted to be wrong.

Her eyes sought his, confirming his fears.

'I'm as sure as I can be he intends to murder that little girl. Thereafter, I think he'll either murder Beth Roberts and commit suicide or attempt to flee with her. Either way we don't have much time. I hate to say it, but Mia may already be dead.'

Farrell jumped to his feet, his pulse racing. He saw Clare looking at him with concern.

'Peter Swift could have killed her at his place, dumped the body there and fled. He must know we're already on to him. Why wait? Why not complete his revenge and kill her straight away then flee unencumbered by a child?' said Farrell, raising his voice in frustration.

Mhairi appeared at his elbow.

'Frank! You have to keep your shit together,' she hissed.

His face tightened, then consciously relaxed.

'I'm fine,' he said.

Suddenly, Clare stood up.

'Is it possible he's gone to Jedburgh?' she asked. 'Think about it. That's where all this began. He may need to deal the final blow there symbolically to complete his revenge.'

'The ruined house,' said Farrell. 'The shrine.'

He ran over to DC Thomson.

'I take it no one's spotted either Peter Swift's or Beth Roberts's car?'

'Not a glimpse. Neither of them has any other cars registered in their names. No cars have gone missing in Dumfries during the last week,' said DC Thomson.

Farrell made a snap decision.

'Right everyone, listen up. In the absence of any compelling evidence to the contrary, I'm surmising they're en route to Jedburgh, possibly to the ruined house where Colette Currie died.'

He could see a few sceptical faces. The Super had arrived and was watching him closely. 'What's the plan then, DI Farrell?' he said.

'DI Moore can liaise with Jedburgh police. They can

advance on foot into the site as there's a lot of cover around to avoid detection. We need a couple of ambulances parked up nearby and an air ambulance on standby. Absolutely no sirens or lights once within range.'

'They've had quite a jump on us,' said the Super. 'Jedburgh is fifty miles away.'

'Perhaps not all that much, depending on how long they spent at Swift's house,' said Farrell. 'And they won't want to draw attention to themselves by speeding. Mhairi and I will take one car. DS Byers and DC Thomson can take the second, if DI Moore is content to coordinate things from here?'

DI Moore nodded.

'We also need the Firearms Team. Sir?' said Farrell, turning to the Super.

'In the absence of any other firm leads, I think it's worth a shot,' he said. 'I'll liaise with DCI Buchanan in Glasgow in case we need further support and resources. If anything occurs meantime we can pull you back.'

Less than ten minutes later, equipped with vests and Tasers, the two police cars and the tactical support van pulled out of the car park with a screech of tyres, sirens wailing. Farrell glanced at Mhairi's face as he turned the car towards the A701. She was white as a sheet, her mouth set in determined lines. The stakes couldn't get higher than the life of a child. His team was the only thing standing between that child and certain death.

Chapter 75

The white-knuckle blue-lighted ride meant that they reached Jedburgh not long after they received police reports that the couple had arrived at the cottage with their precious cargo. They abandoned their cars to the side of the track and raced towards the cottage in a crouching run using the wild hedge on one side to hide their approach. The rain clouds hung low in the sky and thunder rumbled punctuated by occasional flashes of lightning. The only sign of occupation was the black Ford Fiesta that had no doubt been stored at the lock-up garage with Peter Swift's old car.

DI Bill Coburn sidled over to greet Farrell as he and his team fanned out through the undergrowth. The unrelenting rain soaked into their very bones.

'There's another three officers around the perimeter,' he said tersely. 'All awaiting your command.'

The thin wail of a child rose like smoke from the burned house. The sound was abruptly choked off and all those present tensed, ready to spring into action the moment Farrell said the word.

His phone vibrated, startling him. An unknown number.

Some sixth sense told him to answer. He could hear a young child quietly sobbing in the background.

'Hurry! He's going to kill her,' whispered the voice.

'Stay tight, we're coming for you,' he said. 'Keep the line open if you can.'

He pressed the button on his radio.

'Advance all units,' he commanded. He moved forward in a running crouch, alongside Mhairi, Tasers at the ready. Byers and DC Thomson advanced from the rear of the house. The Jedburgh officers fanned out, at the sides, keeping low to the ground. The Firearms Team took up positions near all points of entry, weapons cocked. This was it. It was now or never. The wooden front door was still hanging off its hinges. Mhairi and Farrell paused at either side. Their eyes met. Then Farrell slowly crept into the charred remains of the lounge with Mhairi following at his heels. Through a hole in the back wall he could see Byers and DC Thomson enter via the back door into the kitchen.

There was no sign of Swift or the child.

Suddenly, they froze as they heard a female voice arguing. Beth Roberts was trying to let them know their location. Her voice drifted down from upstairs. It was hard to see in the gloom. Farrell gestured to Mhairi and the two of them hugged the wall to the stairs at the other end of the house. The voices were louder now as they crept up the stairs hoping the shouting voices would mask the creak of the rotting floorboards.

As Farrell's head reached the level of the first floor he saw Peter Swift standing with his back to him. Farrell could see that his arm was raised but whether he was pointing a finger or a gun was impossible to determine. Beth Roberts was pressed against the opposite wall holding the child. She looked terrified. Mia's eyes were facing the stairs and Farrell saw them widen in surprise. Her thumb slid out of her mouth.

Peter Swift stiffened and started to turn around. He did have a gun and it was heading his way. Farrell ran at him discharging the Taser. Swift jolted backwards, getting a shot off as he fell, screaming in agony as the electricity raced through his body. Total chaos ensued as the Firearms Team erupted up the stairwell, positioning themselves around the large room. Sergeant Forsyth removed the gun from Swift, and Farrell pulled him to his feet and cuffed him, trembling with suppressed rage. He read Swift his rights with gritted teeth, determined to do nothing to compromise a conviction. DC Thomson led a sobbing Beth Roberts away in handcuffs. The terrified little girl was picked up and soothed by DS Byers.

Time suddenly seemed to slow down. Where the bloody hell was Mhairi? he wondered, his eyes searching anxiously for her amidst the throng. It wasn't like her to be away from the centre of the action and he could swear she'd been right behind him. His heart missed a beat as he saw a smear of blood on the wall beside the stairs. Please God, no! He swayed as the room faded at the edges. He could see peoples' mouths moving but couldn't hear the words, his ears still ringing. Byers approached, holding the little girl who was sobbing into his shoulder. The sounds of the room slowly floated back.

'Mhairi's been shot. Don't panic, she's all right.'

Farrell stood rooted to the spot, his eyes fixed on the wet stain.

Byers turned to follow his stare.

'The blood's not hers. Swift headbutted one of the men and bust his nose. They're taking her back to Dumfries in the ambulance. She's going to be fine.'

Farrell nodded at Byers, unable to speak for a minute, struggling to compose himself.

'How's Mia?' he asked.

'Unharmed. I think we got here in the nick of time,' said Byers. 'Once the paramedics have checked her over we can take the poor wee mite home.'

'You're good with her,' said Farrell.

'I've had plenty of practise,' said Byers.

With John's kids, thought Farrell, though he managed a brief smile.

He stumbled out from the gloom into the sunlight. The ambulance had made it halfway up the drive until thwarted by the potholes. A paramedic was attending to a very grumpy Mhairi McLeod.

She scowled on seeing him approach, masking her relief. He wasn't fooled.

'What's the damage?' he said to the paramedic.

'Excuse me! Sitting right here,' she muttered, grimacing in pain.

'No sign of a penetrating injury,' replied the paramedic. 'The vest absorbed the impact of the bullet.'

'Like I say, I'm fine. Stop fussing,' Mhairi murmured.

The paramedics exchanged concerned glances. Mhairi's eyes

were becoming unfocused. She looked sleepy, her breathing increasingly shallow.

'My chest hurts,' she whispered, as her face twisted in pain.

Farrell stood to one side looking on helplessly as they inflated a blood-pressure cuff.

'Hypotensive,' said the paramedic. 'We could be looking at a tension pneumothorax if she suffered a rib fracture?'

Mhairi's eyes rolled back in her head.

'She's stopped breathing,' said the paramedic.

'She's in cardiac arrest,' said the other, after feeling her neck for a pulse. 'Get the defibrillator! Starting compressions.'

This can't be happening, thought Farrell, watching in horror as the paramedics switched the defibrillator on, attaching sticky pads to Mhairi's chest. A small crowd of officers had silently gathered round.

'Clear!' They stood back.

'Shocking.'

Mhairi's body jerked upwards and there was a hushed silence.

'Back in sinus rhythm,' pronounced the paramedic.

They hurriedly secured her and loaded her into the back of the ambulance, slamming the doors.

'Where are you taking her?' demanded Farrell, frantic with worry.

'Borders General Hospital, in Melrose. It's quicker.'

'I'll escort you there,' said Farrell, leaving Byers to organize the removal of the prisoners and the return of Mia to her parents. He sprinted to the police car and threw it into gear, wheels spinning in the dirt as he drove past the ambulance which was reversing now to follow him.

His face grim, he switched on the siren and lights. Mhairi would survive this, he told himself saying it over and over as if that might make it true.

The alternative was too awful to contemplate.

Chapter 76

DC Thomson pulled up outside Max Delaney's house. DS Byers got out of the back seat and went around to open the car door for Mia. Her parents came running from the house, her father scooping her up in his arms.

'How will I ever be able to thank you?' he said, turning to them both.

'You just did,' said Byers. 'Both Peter Swift and Beth Roberts are now in custody. We're not sure yet to what extent Roberts was a willing participant in Swift's plan, but I can tell you that she did try and help us rescue her in the end.'

They got back in the car to drive to the station.

'Moments like that make all the crap we have to put up with worthwhile,' said DC Thomson.

'They do, lad. Let's hope that on this occasion, the price we have to pay isn't too high.' They both fell silent, lost in their own thoughts.

'Have you heard anything from the hospital?' asked Byers as they entered the MCA room.

'Not yet,' said DI Moore, her forehead creased in worry. 'How's little Mia?'

'A bit withdrawn but she'll bounce back,' said Byers.

'I can maybe give them a phone later and offer to pop round?' said Clare Yates.

'That would be helpful,' said DI Moore.

'Good job all round,' said the Super. 'I still can't believe that Peter Swift was behind it all. It beggars belief that someone from the fiscal's office could have so lost their way.'

'I suspect that he's always been a dangerous and narcissistic sociopath,' said Clare Yates. 'Where else better to hide? It'll be interesting to see what Beth Roberts has to say for herself.'

'I understand his plan for revenge on the three lawyers,' said the Super. 'He clearly received a serious affront to what is no doubt a monstrous ego. But killing a sheriff? And in the manner he did?'

'About that, sir,' said DC Thomson. 'I'm not convinced that he did.'

'What? How so?' asked the Super. 'Spit it out, lad.'

'Well, sir, just before Mia was abducted, I discovered something. Joe Capaldi shared a cell with Tony Marino, the person accused of the rape and murder of that young girl, Emily Drummond, at Morrington Academy, thirty years ago. I managed to get a hold of his mug shot.' His hands flew over the keys of the computer and everyone crowded round to look.

The image was taken many years ago but the likeness was unmistakable.

'Gabriel Ferrante,' breathed the Super. 'As I live and breathe ...'

'The DNA swab for Sheriff Robert Granger has come back as a match for the semen recovered from Colette Currie,' said Byers. 'It was also tested against the sample obtained from the dead girl from Morrington Academy all those years ago. It seems that Granger raped and murdered them both.'

'But how was Gabriel Ferrante, sorry Tony Marino, convicted of murdering the first girl if he was innocent?' asked DI Moore.

'I looked back over the trial transcript and witness statements,' said DC Thomson. 'He maintained he was her boyfriend at the time. Her father was a powerful figure in the local community. He rubbished that idea. He said Ferrante was a two-bit drug dealer who was obsessed with his daughter and followed her around. He said she was terrified of him and that he was delusional if he thought they were together.'

'And was he?' asked DI Moore. 'A two-bit drug dealer?'

'Yes, so it would seem. He said he did a bit of dealing to put food on the table for his alcoholic mother,' said DC Thomson.

'He claimed he'd met the girl at a party. She and her friends bought some dope off him. They got on and started to see each other. She knew her father wouldn't approve, so kept it from him and her friends. She seems to have told one friend but that friend never made it on to the witness list.'

'Changed times,' said Byers. 'Hopefully, wouldn't happen now.'

'Ferrante claimed that she was terrified of one of her class-mates, not him. His name was Robert Granger.'

Byers let out a low whistle.

'I can guess the rest. The boy's sent to prison maintaining his innocence so not eligible for parole. He serves every single day of his sentence burning with a desire for revenge. Then he's released, sheds his identity like an old skin, and turns up on our patch with his old cellmate in tow.'

Clare Yates looked up from her phone.

'The name "Gabriel" means Avenger,' she said. 'I looked it up as I thought it was likely chosen with great care.'

'If he's the one who murdered Sheriff Robert Granger then that bastard is going to be responsible for him serving yet another life sentence,' said DS Byers.

'Is he even a real lawyer?' asked DI Moore.

'Apparently, he hit the books and sat his Bar exams inside,' said Thomson. 'No wonder he chose to specialize in criminal law.'

'But what I don't understand is how he was admitted to the roll of solicitors?' said the Super. 'He must have set up an elaborate false identity.'

'I wonder how much Joe Capaldi knows?' said DI Moore.

'I should think he knows everything,' said Byers. 'I'll order up the various warrants then we'd better bring them in. For once, this is an arrest I'm not going to relish. Bastard had it coming,' he muttered under his breath, turning away.

'What was that, DS Byers?' asked the Super.

'Nothing, sir,' said Byers. He'd only said what they were all thinking.

Chapter 77

Farrell sat beside the bed as the monitors beeped, his eyes fixed on Mhairi's white face and trying to ignore the terrible sense of déjà vu sweeping over him. Although he'd been told the procedure had gone well, he was almost demented with anxiety.

What if she didn't wake up? He tried and failed to imagine a world without her in it and could feel emotion swell in his chest. She looked so small and vulnerable asleep. When she was awake she was loud, opinionated and could drive him to distraction with her mess and chaos. He'd give anything for her to be nipping his ear about something right now.

'It's rude to stare,' she mumbled.

He squeezed her hand in relief.

'Ow.'

Her eyes fluttered open and she managed a small smile. Then the tension returned to her face as she remembered.

'Mia?'

'Safe at home with her parents. Peter Swift and Beth Roberts are both in custody.'

'What happened?'

'The impact of the bullet on your vest fractured a rib, causing a tension pneumothorax. It's been fixed but you'll need to stay put until tomorrow at least.'

He decided not to let on about the cardiac arrest for now. She rolled her eyes and he laughed.

'I see that normal service has been resumed.'

'You're blethering, Frank Farrell.' She glared but she gave his hand a quick squeeze, looking away from him as her eyes teared up.

'Is there anyone you want me to call? Sandy, maybe?' he asked, realizing he was holding his breath.

'I'm not bloody dead yet, thank you,' she said.

'You and him aren't ...?'

'No,' she said, avoiding his gaze. 'I ended it. Nice bloke but not for me.'

Farrell felt unaccountably relieved.

'Now that I know you're all right, I'll have to go. There's stuff to sort out.'

'Sure, bugger off,' she said, snippy as ever.

He hesitated then leaned down and gently kissed her on the cheek.

'Keep yourself out of trouble till I'm back, DS McLeod.'

He looked back as he left, but she'd already closed her eyes.

Arriving at the station, he felt a wave of fatigue wash over him as the adrenalin finally left his system. Entering the MCA room he found everyone gathered with the exception of the Super. Pouring himself a mug of coffee, he joined them.

'Mhairi's op went well,' he said. 'She'll be transferred to

Dumfries tomorrow and out a couple of days after that, hope-fully.'

'Thank God,' said Stirling. 'It's a lot quieter round here without her.'

'You can say that again,' said Byers.

'I phoned DCI Buchanan on the way down. She brought me up to speed on the Gabriel Ferrante situation. Have we managed to apprehend him and Joe Capaldi yet?'

'They're both downstairs waiting to be interviewed,' said Byers. 'I thought you'd want to take a crack at Ferrante your-self?'

'No time like the present,' said Farrell. 'Care to join me?'

It was an olive branch and Byers took it.

'Sure.'

They headed to Interview Room 4.

Farrell and Byers sat down opposite Ferrante.

Farrell switched on the recording device.

'I'd like to remind you that you're still under caution,' he said.

'Those present are DI Frank Farrell.'

'DS Mike Byers.'

'Gabriel Ferrante.'

'Also known as ...' said Farrell. He eyeballed Ferrante. The game was up and he knew it.

'Tony Marino,' Ferrante sighed.

'We know who you are,' said Farrell. 'We're also aware that you served a life sentence for the rape and murder of Emily Drummond.'

Ferrante's eyes hardened.

'I was innocent. I served twenty years for a crime I didn't commit.'

'We believe you,' said Farrell.

'What?' said Ferrante, unable to hide his surprise.

'We believe that the crime was carried out by one of her then classmates, Robert Granger. After his death we ran his DNA against the sample obtained at the time. It was a match.'

Ferrante shook his head as though he couldn't process what he was hearing.

'I can't believe it,' he said. 'After all this time ...'

'If you'd only left Sheriff Robert Granger alive, he'd have received his comeuppance and you yourself could have reclaimed your identity and lived as a free man,' Byers said.

'What do you mean?' asked Ferrante.

'You murdered Robert Granger in cold blood,' said Byers. 'You'll most likely spend the rest of your life behind bars.'

'No, no!' Ferrante said, his voice rising in horror. 'It's happening again! I didn't kill him! For God's sake, I didn't kill him!'

Farrell and Byers looked at each other in consternation. Either Ferrante was an even better liar than they'd thought or he was telling the truth.

'I admit I *wanted* to kill him. I followed him down here from Glasgow. But the bottom line is I'm not a killer. I wasn't a killer before and I'm not one now.'

'What about Joe Capaldi? He's far from squeaky clean,' said Byers. 'He's stuck by you through thick and thin. Maybe he was willing to kill to protect you?'

'Joe? No way. He's loyal to me, yes. We went through Hell together in that place. But he's no more a killer than I am.'

'Someone found out about your secret, didn't they?' said Farrell.

Ferrante sighed and nodded.

'Mario Lombardo started blackmailing Joe. He's got a file on half the town. A real nasty piece of work. He'd worked out who I was and was threatening to expose us. We'd have lost everything.'

'What did Joe do?'

'I didn't find out about this until after Aaron Sullivan had been murdered, but Lombardo made Joe handle some local drug distribution. He was horrified when he found out he was dealing with a kid but he was in too deep by then. It was gnawing away at him. He felt responsible after the murder and told me what had been going on. He thought that Lombardo had murdered the kid. I wasn't so sure.'

'Interview terminated,' said Farrell.

'Are you going to charge me?' asked Ferrante.

'Not at the moment,' said Farrell. 'We need to keep you in custody for the time being, though. Are you sure you don't want a lawyer notified?'

'The only lawyer I trust is myself,' said Ferrante.

They left the room and walked along the corridor, leaving Ferrante with his head in his hands.

'What do you reckon?' asked Byers.

'I think he's telling the truth.'

Chapter 78

Farrell marched into the MCA room.

'I'm as sure as I can be that Ferrante didn't kill Sheriff Granger,' he announced.

'Well, who did then?' asked DI Moore.

'Peter Swift and Beth Roberts.'

'But how does that fit into his revenge fantasy and the house in Jedburgh?' she asked. 'I know Robert Granger was responsible for Colette Currie's death, but Peter Swift couldn't possibly know that. We've only just discovered it ourselves.'

'Think about it,' urged Farrell. 'All his crazy Panopticon stuff. That image is based on the all-seeing eye. What if he was such a control freak he had set up micro cameras in the cottage to spy on Colette Currie? We've heard she was starting to cool off. Maybe she was finding him too controlling? Maybe he decided to spy on her? It was his late aunt's cottage. He had access to it. He could have seen the rape by Robert Granger. That would give him motive.'

'I remember at the dinner she was covering up bruising to her throat with a scarf. I thought Granger had done it, but maybe it was Swift? Also, if he'd got away with spying on Colette

399

Currie and had his fears vindicated by catching her cheating on him with Jack Kerr, it might have fuelled his paranoia to the extent he monitored Beth Roberts too. He could have witnessed Granger attacking her in the agents' room, which would explain why he came upon her so soon after,' Moore said.

'We need proof,' said Farrell. 'Peter Swift's house was only given a cursory search this morning. Dave and I can head there now.'

The sun was low in the sky as they drew up outside the modest house where Peter Swift and Beth Roberts had seemed to lead such unremarkable lives. He thought of the times he had passed the time of day with the young fiscal with no notion that he was in the presence of such evil.

He entered the house with DC Thomson, who had brought along a gadget to detect micro cameras. They started in the master bedroom. As DC Thomson opened the wardrobe door, the gadget beeped and he jumped. Thomson carefully ran it over the nearest jacket until he found the source of the signal. It was a brooch on the lapel. He moved the device around the whole room and it kept beeping as more and more cameras were identified. There were cameras on jackets, on the ceiling above the bed, on her briefcase. They found more in every room of the house. Eventually, they discovered a laptop inside a ventilation duct in the bathroom together with a separate hard drive. Beth Roberts's every move had been recorded.

'What's the betting we'll find footage from the night of the fire stored on here too?' said Farrell. 'We've got the bastard. Once we tell Beth about this, I'm betting she's going to sing her heart out.'

Chapter 79

Peter Swift had been remanded in custody to await trial in the High Court for the murders of Gina Campbell and Aaron Sullivan. The short formal hearing in chambers was over in seconds and completely blindsided the press. Farrell had held good on his promise to Moira Sharkey, so she had scooped her rivals.

Before he was taken up the road to Barlinnie, Farrell had arranged to interview him at Dumfries in relation to the murder of Sheriff Robert Granger. Beth Roberts had been granted bail, pending psychiatric reports.

Swift entered the interview room still wearing his suit but accessorized with handcuffs. His demeanour was arrogant, almost as though he was enjoying being the centre of attention. The mask had finally slipped to reveal the heartless psychopath beneath.

Farrell nodded to DC Thomson to switch on the tape and asked all those present to identify themselves.

'I'd like to remind you that you remain under caution in relation to the murder of Sheriff Robert Granger,' he said. 'Is it still the case that you wish to decline legal representation?'

'What would be the point, DI Farrell? If I can't have my liberty I might as well enjoy a degree of notoriety. It seems only fair. I should cast around for someone to write my memoir.'

Farrell felt his skin prickle. 'I assume you were a member of the Omniscient Society at Morrington Academy?'

'Not just any old member. Such was my inventiveness I rose to be the President. During my reign we took our surveillance and methods of subjugation to a whole new level.'

'Really?' said Farrell, pretending to stifle a yawn and glancing at his watch.

The anger was quick to flare as he'd hoped.

'Colette betrayed me. I trusted her. She was all mine and they took her away from me in the cruellest of ways. Each of them played a part.'

Farrell laughed in his face.

'You trusted her? The hell you did!'

'What do you mean? She was my everything.'

'Then why did you have cameras rigged up all over the cottage that night?'

Swift's face went white.

'Yes, we found the saved recordings. It shows everything that happened until the cameras themselves melted in the flames. I'm guessing you watched the live footage unfolding and it sent you nearly mad with rage.'

'You tried to control Colette with your sick version of love, but you failed, didn't you? She was about to leave you.'

'No! She would never have left me. That druggie bastard

Jack Kerr took advantage of her when she was drunk. She loved me not him. They were all complicit in stealing her away from me. Max Delaney filmed them together and sent it to me, but the worst treachery of all came from Fergus Campbell. That's why I killed Gina Campbell first.'

'What did he do that was so bad?' asked Farrell. 'He thought he'd accidentally locked her in the cottage, but the last to leave was Granger.'

Swift laughed. The sound was chilling.

'Is that all he told you, Inspector? That wasn't the half of it. He was there when Granger arrived. He could have saved her. I could see her desperation as she begged him to intervene. But all he could think about was saving himself. He fled and sealed Colette's fate.

'Don't you see? I had to avenge her. I had to make them suffer. All of them. Justice had to prevail.'

'Robert Granger raped Colette, but she fought back, didn't she? She clawed off his mask and he killed her for it. And you had to sit there in front of your screen and watch.'

'I thought he'd killed her,' Swift said, his face twisted in remembered pain, as he relived the events of that night. 'She was lying there not moving after he hit her. I saw him start the fire.'

'Why didn't you call the fire brigade?'

'I thought she was already dead. I couldn't face everyone finding the cameras, seeing what I'd done. I was in shock.'

'Then what happened?' said Farrell, gentler now, as he heard the raw emotion.

'The flames were starting to take hold. I was just staring

at the screen, numb, I felt as if I couldn't move, could scarcely breathe.'

He raised his eyes to meet Farrell's and he saw the ruin of a man buried within them.

'I saw her start to move. I screamed at her to get out of there but the flames had taken hold. She went to the front door but it was locked. That bastard had locked her in. I could hear her screams. I can still hear them,' he whispered.

'You killed Robert Granger, didn't you?' said Farrell. 'You did it for her.'

'Yes, I killed him. And nothing would give me greater pleasure than being able to do it over and over again for all eternity.'

'Peter Swift, I'm charging you with the murder of Robert Granger. You do not need to say anything but anything you do say will be noted down and may be used against you in a court of law. Do you understand?' said Farrell.

Peter Swift laughed.

'I bloody should do after all these years.'

'The only thing I don't understand is why wait ten years to take your revenge?'

'Because I didn't know who he was until he came down here a year ago. It was obvious from the tape that Colette knew her killer. If it had been one of the other men she would most likely have shouted out their name. She didn't. All I had was a partial shot of his face but I knew I would recognize those ice blue eyes if ever I came across them again.'

'When did you realize?'

'The first day he came on the Bench in Dumfries, I thought

he looked familiar but I couldn't place him. It never even crossed my mind that it could be him.'

'We know how closely you watched Beth. All those tiny hidden cameras,' said Farrell.

'You can hardly blame me for having trust issues.'

'That's how you realized it was Granger who had raped Colette. You saw it happen in the agents' room, didn't you?'

Peter Swift's face hardened at the memory.

'It was a few months after he'd come down here. He'd been giving her a hard time in court, making her life Hell. Still, I didn't guess. It's hardly likely to be the bloke in the wig. We were at some function at the court. Beth had been getting pally with those three bastards and I didn't like it. I thought I'd walk off and leave her to mingle, watch her on my phone with live streaming from the camera on her brooch and see if any of them were trying to move in on her.'

'I was sitting downstairs in Court One just watching what was going on upstairs when I saw Sheriff Granger hand her a drink and walk off to the agents' room with her. At first I was pleased, thought he'd decided to bury the hatchet, be a bit nicer to her. The camera was in her brooch on the lapel of her jacket. She sat down, slumped as though she was sleeping. I saw him unbuttoning her shirt, pushing up her skirt. Then I saw his eyes. And I knew. I knew it was happening again. I raced up the stairs but by the time I got there he'd left. Beth was groggy and seemed to have no notion of what had just happened. I knew from that moment I was going to kill him. They were all going to suffer, as they had made me suffer. Every single one of those bastards. They had it coming.'

'Interview terminated at 12.06,' said Farrell.

He stared at Swift who met his gaze unflinchingly across the divide that now separated them.

Farrell nodded to the guards.

'Take him away.'

Chapter 80

Farrell placed his key in the lock and entered his cheerless flat in Glasgow. Although he'd only been away eight months it felt like a lifetime. It had taken forever to clear up the tangled web of cases in Dumfries. Gabriel Ferrante had been disbarred but was expected to have his original conviction overturned. He wouldn't need to work again after the sizable payment for wrongful conviction headed his way. Joe Capaldi and Barry McLeish had rolled over on Mario Lombardo and were giving evidence against him in exchange for immunity. They hadn't been able to get Lombardo for extortion, so he would probably not be inside for long.

The air felt stale and heavy. He switched on the lights and drew the curtains. The place was freezing. It looked institutional, he thought, like a cheap motel on a nameless motorway.

He released Henry from the cat carrier and set about filling the litter tray and opened a can of cat food. His cat stretched and looked around him lazily, as if unimpressed with his surroundings after the freedoms of the cottage. He seemed disappointed that his buddy Oscar wasn't there too. With a pang he realized that he was already missing Mhairi.

He'd visited Lind every week since Laura had relented. He knew that Byers had been instrumental in changing her mind and he was grateful. It would take time but his friend was making steady progress now. Even though he had lost Laura, he could still recover enough to have a meaningful relationship with his kids. He knew that Laura and Byers would do everything they could to facilitate that. They would become a blended family of sorts. Kate Moore visited Lind every week too. His eyes would spark with pleasure when she entered his room. Supporting him had given her a renewed sense of purpose.

He was still no clearer to figuring out his own path through life. He had made his peace with God but felt no great pull to serve the Church. In truth he felt emptied of everything. All his angst and torment had ebbed away to be replaced by a new kind of peace. For now, he was living in the moment.

There was a knock at the door and Mhairi McLeod bowled in wearing a colourful dress, her eyes flashing. The flat suddenly felt like home with her in it.

'I thought you'd got lost!'

'You do know, I've got two left feet,' he warned her, as she grasped his hand and pulled him out the door.

Acknowledgements

I'd like to say a big thank you to my brilliant editor Finn Cotton for his helpful suggestions and attention to detail. Thanks also to my copy editor, Janette Currie. I've made some wonderful writing friends along the way who have been unstinting in their support and kindness including my Twisted Sisters, Moffat Crime Writers and the Crime and Publishment gang. I'd also like to give a big shout out to my Ohana Twitter family for all the hilarity and encouragement. A debt of gratitude is owed to the bloggers who have unselfishly supported my work and give so much to the book world in general. I've been fortunate to meet so many of you now in the real world. I'd also like to thank my local Waterstones in Dumfries for stocking my books and supporting me in any way that they can. Huge thanks to my lovely family for putting up with all the chaos my writing inflicts ranging from late meals to digging me out of the trenches of self-doubt. They ensure that I never completely lose the plot. Finally, I'd like to thank my wonderful readers for accompanying me into my fictional world. I couldn't do this without you!